SEA AND SAND

TIDES BOOK 3

ALEX LIDELL

DANGER BEARING PRESS

SEA AND SAND

Copyright © 2018 by Alex Lidell.

For information contact :

www.alexlidell.com

Sign up for news from Alex Lidell: www.subscribepage.com/TIDES

First Edition: January 2018

ALSO BY ALEX LIDELL

TIDES

FIRST COMMAND (Prequel Novella)

AIR AND ASH (TIDES Book I)

WAR AND WIND (TIDES Book II)

SEA AND SAND (TIDES Book III)

TIDES Book IV - Coming 2018

SCOUT

TRACING SHADOWS - coming April 8, 2018

UNRAVELING DARKNESS - coming 2018

THE CADET OF TILDOR

SIGN UP FOR NEW RELEASE NOTIFICATIONS at
www.subscribepage.com/TIDES

Reviews are an author's lifeblood. Please consider saying a few
words about this book on Amazon.

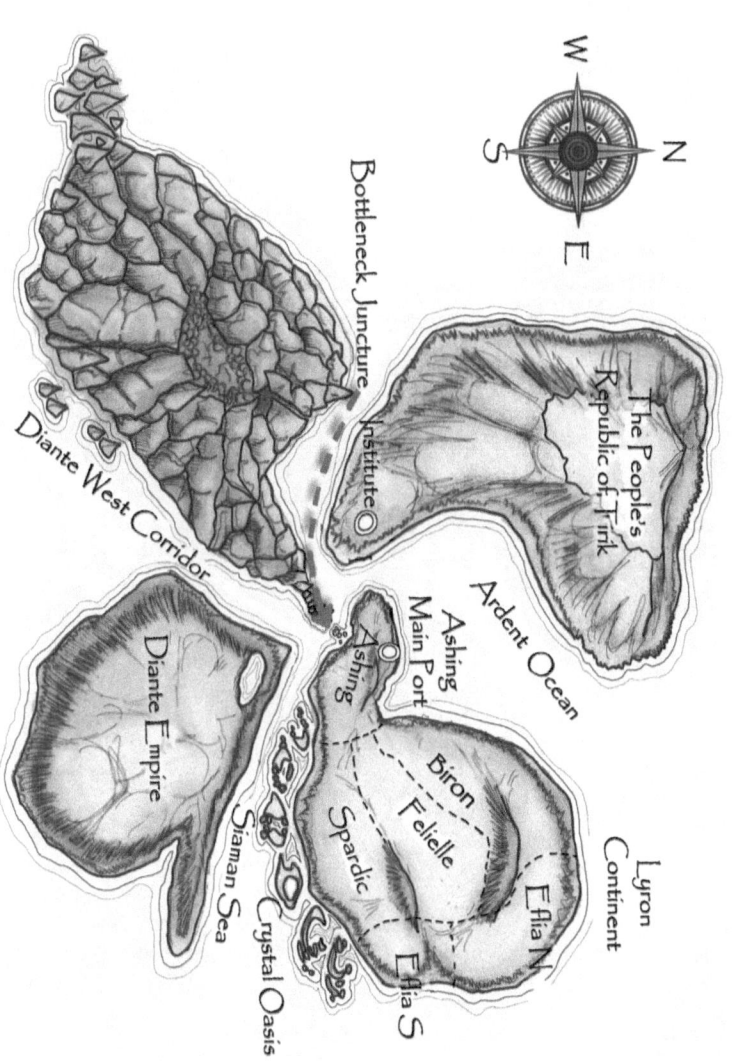

Bottleneck Juncture Institute

The People's Republic of Tink

Diante West Corridor

Ardent Ocean

Ashing Main Port

Ashing

Diante Empire

Biron

Felielle

Spardic

Eflia N

Eflia S

Lyron Continent

Siaman Sea

Crystal Oasis

N

W

E

S

CHAPTER 1

KYRA

"That price is ten times what I paid for passage here to Biron," Kyra told the merchant skipper. The sympathy she'd tasted emanating from him minutes ago now oozed with irritation, but she pressed on regardless. She needed to go home. "Has the eastern archipelago *moved* in the last three months?"

The chubby man took a long drag of his pipe, the embers glowing red in the well. He blew a smoky breath out one side of his mouth, disturbing the hanging corner of his mustache. "Three months ago, girl, the People's Republic of Tirik had its tail tucked between its legs. Three months ago, the Tirik were too busy piecing their supply chains together to hunt Lyron merchantmen. That is no longer the case. Something evil sails the high seas under a Tirik flag now, and no merchant skipper with half a brain will venture into open ocean without a naval escort. And most won't go even with one."

It was an effort to avoid staring at the tiny flame. The magic in her blood longed to call the heat as desperately as her heart longed to leave this shore, where neither Kyra nor her magic were welcome. Home. Yes, for all its traps, home was better than here.

Kyra clutched her threadbare cloak tighter around her slender frame, warding against the merciless wind tangling her long black hair. She should never have left the only family she had—no matter how isolated their island, how vile her brother's tastes, how dull the people. Home was far from war and accepting of all those born to it—be they normal or Gifted. Here, Kyra was different, like a stray cat wandering unfamiliar streets. Even her skin, olive like a deep tan, didn't fit, not in a place full of cold fog and little sun. With each day, Kyra's mistake seemed more impossible to correct. She had been bored, curious about life on the main continent, drunk on stories of markets and libraries, of scholars meeting in coffee shops and science men gathering to create the future. Instead, she found hate and loneliness and death and war. Kyra's fingers toyed with the cloak's metal clasp.

The skipper's face softened, and he puffed his pipe once more before taking it out of his mouth to speak. "Don't fret, lass. There is nothing worthwhile in the archipelago. Scattered villages in the midst of a wet jungle. You are better off here in Biron. If—storms take me!" He jumped, staring at his pipe. The flame, gently dancing atop the glowing embers moments ago, was suddenly hand high.

Hand high and stretching toward Kyra like a snake.

Kyra jumped back, her heart pounding against her ribs.

Yesssss, the magic in her blood whispered to the heat. *Come. Come.*

Kyra's pulse quickened, the blood coursing with increasing speed even as she struggled to snuff out the magic's call. Not fast enough. Not well enough. "The wind—" she started to say, her mouth dry.

The merchant skipper backed away, his face a storm. Bitterness coated Kyra's tongue. Bitterness mixed with the coppery tang of fear. The man was furious and afraid. A bad combination.

Stars. Kyra knew better than to let the hold on her magic slip around here, she did. But she was cold and upset and tired. And...

"You're a flame caller." The captain spat on the ground.

Kyra raised her palm in a placating gesture. "It's not what you think," she said quickly, truthfully. "I'm not like other Gifted. My magic is weak. Very weak. Just think—I'd have incinerated myself in infancy if it were stronger."

"Stay away from my ship." The captain's voice was hard, his shoulders thrown back as if protecting his ship with his body. Behind him, a deckhand pushed a clanking wheelbarrow along the docks, and a pair of fishing men secured their boats, the ropes complex and alive in their weathered hands. A man called for a hammer. A woman giggled. The day was moving on, uncaring of Kyra's plight.

Kyra bit her lip and swallowed a lump in her throat.

A small trace of pity slithered into the bouquet of the captain's emotions, intertwining with the fear. Kyra held her breath and her hope.

The man shook his head. "Stay away from *all* ships here, girl. Before you have an accident and burn us to cinders." The taste of pity disappeared. "You've some nerve coming to the docks, knowing we carry timber and gunpowder, putting our lives at risk for your selfish whims. Mark my words, by day's end, every merchant in Port Mead will know who you are, so don't think you can trick some other poor sod into letting you near a ship."

"Please," Kyra whispered, the words fading away as the merchant skipper turned on his heel and strode to a cluster of other captains. Within a minute, Kyra tasted jolts of bitter anger. The villagers in Kyra's home had despised her empathic ability, but at least no one feared her weak affinity for flame. Not in a wet jungle. Here in Biron, the Gifted were pitied as cripples at best, feared as sparks beside gunpowder at worst. At least she'd been smart enough to keep her empathic sense hidden.

She walked away from the pier. There'd be no hope of finding passage today. Or tomorrow. Not with the merchants.

Fear. Desire. Fury. The pulsing emotions of passersby melded on Kyra's tongue. The approaching evening herded people away from Port Mead's docks, where crowds gathered by day to read posted newsleafs or wait for loved ones who would never return. Nine months ago, when the great earthquake rewrote the coastline, Kyra thought that things had changed. The People's Republic of Tirik had eased off its aggression, the resources of the archipelago became valuable, the traffic between the islands and mainland had increased. Kyra had thought peace had come.

The reprieve lasted six months. Six glorious months after a decade of war. And then, just after Kyra arrived on the mainland, something had changed, as if the reprieve had injected new life into the Tirik Republic, made them more ruthless and resolved than ever. Each day's postings carried new accounts of the dead and lost and captured. Kyra understood little of warfare, but surely such a massive enterprise should have winds both fair and harsh. Yet there were no Lyron victories, no accounts of heroes who faced down the Republic and came home to glory. Not in months.

Something—someone—pushed Kyra from behind. She stumbled, barely keeping herself from falling into the cobbled path. That wasn't new either. She was small to begin with, and her large brown eyes, tan skin, and unusually patterned skirts gave her the appearance of an exotic pet that men found amusing to prod.

"No need to run like that," a soldier called, slurring his words while one of his companions pinched Kyra's behind. "I can give you all the exercise you want."

Soldiers—that was another new challenge for Kyra. Men far from family, unburdened by concerns of reputation, rewarded for violence, living each day as if it were their last. Port Mead swarmed with them: soldiers, sailors, marines of every kingdom —as if Biron didn't have enough of its own troublemakers. For a heartbeat, she considered setting the men's britches smoldering, but that would require touching them.

Kyra kept her pace brisk until she cleared the docks, which gave way first to the fish market, then to rows of indoor shops and inns. The town of Mead sprawled just beyond that, extending south along the ocean shore. Northward along the same shore lay untamed wilderness edged by a brown, fifty-foot-high limestone ridge that stood like a natural fence between the ocean's rocky beach and the forest.

Until two weeks ago, Kyra had a warm room in one of the southside inns. Then half the bloody Felielle Kingdom's navy arrived for war games at Port Mead, and Kyra's rent tripled overnight.

So, instead of turning south at the end of the fish market, Kyra headed north into the woods. The limestone was sheer, neck-breaking cliff on its ocean side, but sloped more gently on the forest side, creating paths and nooks and caverns. One of the latter, Kyra had called home for the past two weeks.

Snatching up dry branches as she walked, Kyra let the magic in her blood rouse and seek the heat inside the wood, coaxing it to the surface. Night came more quickly in the woods, under the cover of light-blocking trees, and it was best to prepare early. Kyra stopped once before a large blueberry bush to fill her pockets for dinner, and once more to collect mushrooms peeking from beneath brush. The mushrooms she would sell tomorrow. The people at Port Mead were fishermen and knew little of edible plants. So long as Kyra demonstrated the mushrooms' safety by taking a bite in front of a customer, they were willing to hand over coin.

By the time Kyra slipped into her cavern, a small fire bloomed on the tip of the smaller stick. She fed the flame carefully while surveying the space.

The cavern looked exactly as it had when she'd left it this morning: a bedroll tossed into the corner, a few scattered clothes, a pot turned on its side and getting underfoot. The far wall sloped gracefully toward a dirt floor, beautiful ridges patterning the stone. All looked well.

But it didn't *feel* well.

At first, Kyra thought the salty anguish she tasted was echoing her own soul. The day's failures crashed atop her like waves, awash with loneliness and despair. A quarter hour later, however, when her own feelings had calmed but the taste did not, Kyra acknowledged the shiver racing up her spine. She examined the cavern again, assuring herself that she was, in fact, alone. She was.

Except...she wasn't. Someone was nearby. And in agony. The feeling was so raw and intense that it gave Kyra a headache. Banking the fire, Kyra slipped outside.

The pain was louder outside, its salty tang heavy on Kyra's tongue. Still, she saw no one but a large stray dog, a muscular, shorthaired beast with a square muzzle and angry eyes, lying at the base of a path up the ridge. Kyra stepped closer to the cliff face, and the dog growled.

"Hello?" Kyra called up the stone. "Is someone here?"

Silence. She walked farther, but the pain's taste weakened as she did, and soon she'd returned to the original spot. And the dog.

Kyra sighed. If no one was to the left or right, the only way remaining to go was up. And if she was going to climb, better to do it now before darkness set in. Giving the dog as wide a berth as she could, Kyra grabbed on to the jutting holds in the stone face and began to haul herself to the top. She took the easiest route she could, but her muscles still burned by the time she'd cleared the top of the ridge, its rough edges scraping her knees. The ridge top was miles long but only ten paces wide, an uneven plateau of limestone spanning the space between Kyra and the drop-off on the ocean side. Bracing her hands on her thighs, Kyra panted as she took in the view.

The sky glowed orange, the sun bleeding as it slid toward the abyss of the horizon. Silhouettes of ships, large and small, swayed on the dark, gentle waves. And, at the edge of the cliff, kneeling on the hard stone, was a man.

Seemingly in his early twenties, just a few years older than Kyra, the man was as still as the stone beneath him, only the mist curling off his breath and a fine shiver racking his lean body providing proof of life. His dirty blond hair hung loose to his shoulders, brushing a wet shirt that clung to sculpted muscle. He looked like a hunter caught in the jaws of his own invisible snare.

"Are you all right?" Kyra stepped forward slowly so as not to startle Hunter. She didn't expect a response, not from someone half-frozen and kneeling on stone. But she needed to say *something*. "Are you cold?"

"Yes." The answer came immediately, calmly. At utter odds with the salty pain flowing from him. "On both counts."

Kyra jumped, her foot sliding on wet stone.

Hunter's arm shot out, steadying Kyra's shin before she could fall. His green eyes met hers, each movement feline smooth. Calm. Steady. Betraying nothing of the truth lurking inside him. "If you insist on climbing stones you cannot safely navigate, could you do so elsewhere, please?"

Releasing Kyra's shin, the man returned to his vigil as if Kyra no longer existed.

Kyra rubbed her arms. She had been born an empath, just as she had been born Gifted to attract heat and flame. It was a miracle she'd survived childhood, and she'd certainly never met anyone else like herself. Was it possible her empathic sense malfunctioned with certain people? Spardic people, perhaps? Hunter's accent placed him in the Spardic Kingdom, and, on closer inspection, his black clothes proved to be the uniform of a Spade, one of the Spardic's elite warriors. Kyra had met a few Spardics before and might have overlooked the discrepancy in a crowd. Perhaps the man was training. From the glimpses Kyra saw of the Spades' nearby camp, they were a sadistic bunch with an absurd habit of inflicting as much suffering on themselves as on the enemy.

Now that she stood beside him, Kyra felt nothing more from

the man. Not relief from pain—if it had ever even been so—but rather a shield blocking her reading of him. She'd felt shields from people before, a by-product of a tight rein on emotion they'd developed for reasons of their own. Hunter's shield was unusual, though, woven tightly enough that it blocked Kyra's empathic sense completely. When it was up. She thought it was likely up whenever other people were around.

A new gust of punishing wind hit the stone platform, and the man flinched as the freezing draft cut into his flesh. This was ridiculous.

"Why are you out here?" Kyra asked.

Hunter slowly turned his head toward her. Just his head. Nothing else. His gaze gripped hers, never straying to her breasts or hips or anywhere men's eyes usually enjoyed journeying to. "Because it is cold here." His voice was low and dangerous, as if the limit of his patience had finally been breached. "And, until very recently, private. I would very much like to reacquire the second condition."

Kyra only caught the split-second slip of the man's guard because she was curious and had been looking for it. A fleeting, accidental drop of his shields when a bird's call sounded overhead. Salt, harsh and potent as the sea, washed over her mouth. Yes, she'd been right. Hunter was in pain, and as alone as she.

Taking off her cloak, Kyra laid it down on the stone and backed away, taking her intrusion with her. On the beach below, the rolling waves cascaded onto the shore in a steady *lub dub woosh, lub dub woosh, lub dub woosh.*

Returning to her cavern, Kyra hunkered down by a warming fire and wondered whether, now that he knew Kyra was here, Hunter might come calling. Whether it might be safer to gather her things and meld into the night. She was still considering it when the soft patter of paws sounded outside the cavern entrance, a sad whimpering following in its wake.

Dogs, like men, were dangerous. So Kyra couldn't quite explain why she found herself spreading a sweater before the fire and coaxing the stray to come in from the cold. Or why she was more worried for Hunter than for herself.

CHAPTER 2

NILE

Standing on the *Eclipse*'s tiny quarterdeck, I watch my opponent—*Raptor*, a frigate of twenty-four guns—make a smart turn around a buoy and take aim at the empty wine casks our lords in the Felielle Kingdom's admiralty sacrificed for target practice. The casks bob on the choppy seas, occasionally ducking beneath foamy waves only to resurface again moments later. The cold wind whips rain and salty ocean spray into my face, but my heart pounds too quickly to feel the chill. This war game is a competition, and not only am I about to lose, but I'm about to lose to Domenic.

Again.

The last time I lost was three months ago, when Domenic and I went before the Felielle Admiralty board to compete for command of that very frigate whose quarterdeck Domenic now holds.

The red and orange of the frigate's belching guns color the drab morning, and a cask explodes in a fountain of shards. A second. Two more together.

"That's four more for Captain Dana," Quinn, my first officer, announces as the last of the spraying wooden splinters flops to the water. "Plus the three he struck at the beginning of the run. A handsome job he did of it too, ma'am."

Domenic *did* do well, but the match is inherently uneven. Domenic's *Raptor* has twenty-four guns, while my little *Eclipse* carries fourteen, making my ship more akin to an armed royal yacht than a man-of-war. It's not just Domenic, of course—all seven ships in this game outgun me, exactly as the admiralty intended. If it had a choice in the matter, the Felielle navy would never have allowed a girl to wear an officer's uniform at all, much less command a ship—even one as small as *Eclipse*.

Unfortunately for the admiralty, the Diante Empire—which we desperately need to woo into an alliance against the People's Republic of Tirik—invited one *Captain* Nile Greysik for a diplomatic visit. And for a Captain Nile Greysik to exist, the admiralty has to acknowledge her—me—at least as an officer in its navy. Not that they are being graceful about it. The six months since the original invitation passed in a flurry of coordination details, and we are now two weeks from setting sail, with no movement in my rank or assignment. I am a captain in the sense of my position in the *Eclipse*'s charge. My true rank in the naval hierarchy is that of a junior lieutenant.

My hands clench tightly around my spyglass as I focus on keeping my face coolly unconcerned—the way the naval officer I've trained my whole life to be is expected to behave. Focusing the spyglass on Domenic's ship, I find his rain-soaked face smiling as he shakes his first officer's hand. With his height and broad shoulders, Domenic is easily the largest man aboard and would be simple to spot even if he weren't on the quarterdeck. *His* quarterdeck. The one he beat me out to win.

Domenic deserves the *Raptor*, of course, both for his seamanship and hard work. I told him so when the admiralty announced its decision to award him the post, and Domenic's blue eyes lit with cautious, shocked triumph. I tell myself that too.

"This is ludicrously unjust," says Lord Vikon, the seventeen-year-old midshipman I had no choice but to add to the ship's company on account of him being Prince Tamiath's distant nephew. This technically makes Vikon my nephew—since, as far as the Felielle Kingdom is concerned, Prince Tamiath and I are married. "That daft commoner's ship has twelve guns on a side, and our *Eclipse* only has seven. We'd have to hit over half our shots just to match the brute's scores."

I twist toward Vikon, my eyes flashing with more fury than a dignified officer should allow herself. "You will refer to Captain Dana with respect, Lord Vikon," I say, my dog Bear growling his support as rainwater drips from his shaggy black coat. The pup has grown as big as his mother—my twin Clay's bitch—and his slobbery head easily reaches my hip. Resting my hand on Bear's warm coat, I draw a calming breath before continuing with more restrained tones. "Now, thank you for that arithmetic, and be quiet."

Everyone aboard has done the math already, but the last thing the *Eclipse*'s crew needs is words of discouragement from the quarterdeck. In theory, the admiralty will count the percentages relative to our armament when calculating the scores, but in reality, it is the total number of hits—not relative arithmetic—that counts in battle.

Wiping the rain from my eyes, I study the other Felielle vessels participating in the exercise before turning to Port

Mead's wounded shoreline. The water is murky, the waves breaking at odd points in deference to chaotic currents and treacherous ocean floor, both courtesy of an earthquake nine months past.

Vikon knocks the toe of his boot against the wet deck. "We shall be the laughingstock of the fleet when we lose. As if it isn't enough that we've a skirt on the quarterdeck instead of a real officer, we're—"

"Vikon," Quinn growls. Any other middie would have been bent over a gun and thrashed thoroughly for such words, but we are under stern recommendation to treat Vikon gently.

I'd love to gently throw the boy overboard.

"Look! Zolan's *Lily* is heading out!" Vikon leans over the rail, training his spyglass on the next frigate coming to the line of trials. The largest of the ships in the war games, the fifty-four-gun *Lily* is just shy of a ship-of-the-line designation reserved for the strongest ships in the fleet. "Did you know Zolan turned down an admiralty position to keep *Lily* for himself?"

"Enough," I snap at the boy as the report of a judge's gun starts *Lily*'s time. Zolan now has ten minutes to fire his starboard gun battery at the target casks, swing around a buoy, and make a return run to fire the port gun battery at any targets still afloat. My heart quickens as Captain Zolan's sails fill with a loud *pop* and his ship moves majestically from her starting line. The silence that I know rules *Lily*'s deck now echoes through me.

Two minutes later, twenty-four guns fire in perfect harmony, and the Ardent Ocean explodes in spray and splinters.

"Eighteen hits." Quinn's voice is calm, the opposite of my racing thoughts. I'm not just going to lose, I am going to lose spectacularly.

My stomach sinks as I realize why the admiralty finally invited my ship to partake in the war games. Not to evaluate my skill, but to paint a clear picture of my inability to hold my own, even at the cost of sullying my crew's reputation as so much collateral damage. It's a last-ditch attempt to change the king's mind about allowing me to sail for the Diante Empire. Lord Vikon's words, for all their spoiled, undisciplined entitlement, are simply repetitions of other officers' thoughts, voiced behind closed doors.

The Felielle navy would truly prefer to forgo the chance at meeting the Diante rather than be represented by an eighteen-year-old Ashing-born girl.

The *Lily* makes a tight turn around the buoy, her sailors scampering from guns to the sails and back again. Zolan's careful aiming on the first battery had cost precious minutes, a luxury he no longer has. The *Lily*'s guns fire as they bear, iron balls spitting into the ocean as the gun captains hurry to work their beasts before time is called.

"Ten hits," Quinn announces as if we aren't all counting. Water soaking his hair runs in a near stream down his angled jaw. "Twenty-eight altogether. And Admiral Pyre's ship is hoisting our number, ma'am."

Of course she is. Where better to place me than in the wake of the best captain in the Felielle fleet? The gazes of my crew pierce me, some doing better than others to hide their dread. Their careers and reputations are as much on the line as mine. Despite my pounding heart, I raise my chin high and survey the wind and water while an admiralty cutter rows out to reset the course, laying out new targets. Absent a miracle, we *will* be humiliated. A miracle or something else.

I swallow, my mouth dry as recklessness tingles in my blood. We have fewer guns than the others, but if we could fire the guns we do have several times, we could send as much shot downrange as our opponents. It all comes down to time.

I can count on my fingers the number of people in the world who know I'm a Gifted wind caller. My family, Tam's, Domenic, Catsper, and Quinn. My wonderful Gifted twin, Clay, whose mind is locked away from the world just as he is hidden away in the Ashing palace. Should the secret of my Gift leak out, not even an edict from the Felielle king himself would keep me at sea. My life's purpose is to lead ships in battle. If I am to stay the course, no one must learn what I am.

A Gifted is an abomination. A pitiful cripple. A weapon that turns on its wielder as readily as the enemy. Elemental attraction is a ghastly condition with no cure, one that can no more be allowed on a naval ship than can an open flame. One whose sufferer can never, *ever* be permitted to command others.

Fortunately, I'm very good at keeping secrets. And I'm not about to let my whole crew suffer for the admiralty's dislike of me.

"Don't do it," Quinn murmurs, coming up behind me. Like my dog, Bear, who can sense my convulsions before I can, one of Quinn's secret duties aboard is to protect me from my own treacherous body. "I see it in your eyes."

"You are staring at the back of my head, Quinn." I spread my shoulders, as if a bit of puffing can make my slender frame match Domenic's towering height and broad back. "Did the rules specify that guns on both sides of the ship had to be discharged?"

Quinn makes a warning sound in the back of his throat. "No. But as much was *implied*."

"Implied," I agree, "but not specifically required, correct?"

"Yes," he concedes with a sigh. "The requirement is to

complete one turn about the buoy and destroy as many targets as possible within a ten-minute period."

A touch of a smile tugs the corner of my lips. And, because I'm certain Domenic's glass is trained on me right now, I allow my grin to fill my face. "Mr. Quinn," I say loudly enough for all on the *Eclipse* to hear, "redistribute the crew. We will not be firing the starboard battery."

"You're giving up?" Vikon hollers, his face turning an alarming shade of red. The boy's perfectly tailored uniform is soaked with rain, and he holds his hands in his armpits to warm them. "I knew it. You're nothing but—"

Quinn backhands the middie, sending the boy sprawling across the deck before he finishes the sentence. "You are dismissed to your berth, Mr. Vikon." Quinn's usually calm voice booms as loud as any gun. He looms over Vikon until the boy grudgingly picks himself up and trudges down the ladder.

I wonder what the other watching captains make of the display on my deck. No matter. I'm about to give them something else to be outraged about.

With Vikon gone, Quinn turns to me and touches his hat, disapproval glinting in his eyes. If Catsper were here, he'd grin along with me, but Quinn shares Domenic's dogged worship of rules and regulations. "Aye aye, ma'am," Quinn answers, repeating the order as is the navy's tradition. "No starboard battery."

I nod. No turning back now. "Signal Admiral Pyre that we are ready," I say, and, as the report of a flagship gun starts our time, I let the magic in my blood awaken to the wind.

CHAPTER 3

NILE

The magic in my blood smells the coming freedom and sings out to the wind, calling it to come and play and blow blow blow. My lungs open, my blood accelerating in my veins. I feel alive, as if each fiber that makes me up is waking. It's all I can do to keep the gathering force in check until... "*Now, Mr. Quinn.*"

I let my magic loose to answer the wind's call just as our sails open. The sudden gale descending upon us is strong enough to lift the *Eclipse*'s bow from the water. The canvas fills and strains, the crew first cursing, then cheering our sudden fortune. All except Quinn, who knows exactly from whence the convenient gale came and just how easily it can twist away from me. How rapidly I might collapse into convulsions at just the wrong moment.

Bear hops to his feet, his large brown eyes watching me warily, his tail swishing like a pendulum.

My magic howls its pleasure, fighting me for more. More air. More wind. More power. More play. The whistling gale quickens with each heartbeat, turning the raindrops into needles that strike chilled skin. The pricks sting my eyes, cheeks, and lips, the pain glorious in its proof of our speed. I'd throw my arms wide if I didn't know that every spyglass on every ship is trained on me just now, all the captains wondering how the hell I am going to back sail, stop, and aim in the middle of the storm.

The answer is that I *won't*. Instead of firing only twice—once from port and once from starboard—I will get the *Eclipse* around the buoy so quickly that we'll have time to fire *three* port batteries. Maybe four.

Quinn hollers orders, tweaking the sails and reinforcing the helm as we fly toward the buoy, ignoring the targets set up before us. The men sprint to keep up, holding on to lines and stays to avoid falling as the *Eclipse* turns so tightly that the whole ocean seems to rise up toward our tilting hull.

Quinn sends a third man to support helm. Dangerous as this is, at least we have a fighting chance to keep us on course now—six months ago, my wind would have tossed the ship on its side as likely as propel it forward. Then again, six months ago, my magic was one third of what burns in my veins today, as if joining magics with my twin, Clay, had destroyed some dam inside me. If wind calling is my curse, it's my power too.

"Steady," Quinn says into my ear. To an onlooker, the action appears a simple adjustment of a busy officer on a crowded deck, but in reality, Quinn is giving me the support of his body should I become unable to stand. "Steady."

The *Eclipse* straightens as it clears its turn. It is a struggle to find my voice, the words drawing on every ounce of willpower. "Back... Sails..."

Entrusting the racing sailors to their duty, I pour my strength into clamping down on the wind. The air chokes me at once, the magic protesting its tether. Pain explodes in my chest, my lungs stretching, threatening to tear. Quinn has me by an elbow before I can double over in plain sight. The world swims and shimmers in my vision.

I force myself to straighten. To draw a breath. Another. To survey the ship and targets and ocean. With her sails backed, the *Eclipse* is in line with the targets now. Excellent. "How much time, Mr. Quinn?" My voice has a rasp, and I swallow to wet my throat.

"Eight minutes, ma'am," he answers, trying and nearly succeeding in hiding the concerned once-over gaze he sweeps across me.

I let myself grin. Let them all see me grin. Eight minutes. I'd not dared hope for more than six. "And how many times can you fire our port battery in eight minutes?"

Quinn presses his lips together, still unhappy at my creative interpretation of rules, but ready to make the most of our advantage. All hands on the *Eclipse* are. Seven gun crews are already busy loading and aiming their beasts. "Five, ma'am," Quinn says after a moment's thought. "We can fire the guns of our port battery five times."

The seamen cheer. Five batteries of seven guns each, thirty-five rounds of shot. Those are better odds than Domenic's twenty-four gun *Raptor* had. Better than anyone's, bar Zolan's *Lily*.

Putting my hands behind my back, I wait as one after the

other, the gun captains raise their fists into the air. "On the up roll," I call, my breath stilling as the ship dips and rises on the coming wave. "Fire."

CHAPTER 4

KYRA

Kyra awoke to rain beating the ground outside her cavern. The dog was gone. The man she named Hunter had left the ridge as well. Or at least Kyra thought he had left, as she tasted none of the acute emotions that coated her mouth last night. She supposed Hunter could simply be asleep. Or relaxed. Or blocking her again.

Either way, Kyra was alone.

Ducking out of her cavern, Kyra climbed up the steep path leading to the top of the ridge. The wet rock was slippery and cold, but having grown up in wet Milan, Kyra was used to rain. The ridge was empty except for her cloak, which lay untouched under a small overhang that protected the cloth from the worst of the rain. Wrapping it around herself, Kyra walked across the stone until she stood on the edge of the cliff, the wind and rain whipping her black hair back from her face as she stared into the great expanse of land and sea beneath. The Ardent Ocean, the rocky shoreline, Port Mead's pier and inns, Felielle men-of-war rocking at their distant mooring, the camp of Spardic soldiers set up on a rocky beach well away from the pier.

Perhaps Hunter had gone there. He certainly moved like a man trained and honed for violence.

It was good that he'd left before Kyra came up.

Kyra was turning to leave when the bit of sunlight that survived the clouds caught the edge of something gold and shiny wedged into the cracks of the stone. Stepping closer, Kyra pulled out the dropped object, rubbing it against her cloak to clean off the specks of dirt. It was a pin, the kind soldiers wore to signify things Kyra little understood beyond knowing they were important. This one was simple, a gold-plated metal square stamped with an outline of a ship, a dagger, and some angled lines. The clasp was loose, which was how the pin likely fell free from Hunter's uniform the night before.

The metal felt cold beneath Kyra's fingers. The lost insignia would likely get Hunter punished, and Kyra little wished to see anyone endure what passed for discipline among the soldiers. If Hunter was a Spade as she thought, it would be simple enough to return the thing. She could see their camp from here, could hear the muskets of morning practice firing. If the Felielle navy occupied the best inns, bought the best food, and walked the best repaired paths, the Spardic Spades lived on the cold and rocky beach and hunted their own meals.

The Felielle navy. That was the rub. Kyra's mind snagged on the thought, her stomach clenching. Since none of the merchantmen were willing to take Kyra to the archipelago, the Felielle navy was now her last hope of returning home. If the rumors that had Princess Nile sailing for the Diante empire within weeks were true. If Kyra could get herself hired into the princess's crew. If she could get to Nile before the merchantmen spilled Kyra's secrets.

Stars. Kyra sat, pulling her knees up to her chin. A naval ship. With guns and orders and battles. Were any of the seamen even literate?

A thin prick of pain lanced Kyra's hand, and she opened her palm to find she'd squeezed the pin hard enough that its sharp corners pierced her skin. Rain diluted the drop of blood, the pink liquid running down the groove of her hand. Just like soldiers to turn even a decoration into a weapon. She really should give the pin back to Hunter. It was the right thing to do, especially after Hunter had protected her cloak from the rain and kept her company last night. Even if he hadn't known he was doing the latter.

All she had to do was go to the Spardic camp and hand it over. Kyra's shoulders tightened but she made herself rise. If she couldn't summon the courage to walk into a training camp to return a lost pin, how in the name of stars would she survive on a naval ship? Perhaps the fates had left the pin here on purpose to guide her way. To challenge her into finding a home.

Kyra walked along the top of the ridge toward the sounds of the Spardic Spades. The camp lay on the ocean side of the ridge, and finding a safe path down on that side might take some time, but Kyra little minded. The view was good, and it would be nice to see what she'd be walking into, to check whether Hunter was even there, before strolling into a nest of trained killers. Around Kyra, the wind and rain danced along with her steps, marrying the salt of the sea with the sweet scent of sap and pine of the forest. On her right, seagulls squawked and circled the waves, landing on the occasional piece of floating wood. On her left, an eagle rose above the treetops, silently seeking a kill.

By the time Kyra reached the Spades a half an hour later, her hopes of a safe descent down the limestone had all but vanished. There was no safe descent here. Not even if the stone wasn't weeping in rainy streams. Maybe she could call to Hunter, toss the pin down, and leave.

Sitting down on the ridge, Kyra studied the camp sprawled on the narrow rocky beach sandwiched between the Ardent Ocean and the cliffs. Except for a pair of tents that must belong to the unit's commanders, whatever shelter the Spades had used to sleep was now put away. The soldiers were training, teams of men carrying logs over their heads as they ran in and out of the bubbly turf, while a smaller contingent of women fired muskets at distant targets.

Kyra studied their faces, trying and failing to pick Hunter out from the crowd. Perhaps he wasn't here. Perhaps Hunter wasn't a Spade at all.

Kyra saw him a moment after the soldiers did, strolling along the beach toward the training camp, which had gone still at the sentry's call. The men bearing logs set their burdens down in neat piles, sand clinging to their wet clothing. Women shouldered their muskets. Although the wind and distance swallowed the noise, Kyra knew that silence ruled the beach.

Kyra's gaze focused on Hunter, whose blond hair trailed behind him in the chill wind. His face was high to welcome the downpour, his hands casually in his pockets. The distance and presence of the dozens of others masked the taste of whatever Hunter was feeling, but she didn't need to be an empath to sense the crackling tension filling the air. Unlike the wet, sand-caked clothes of his companions, Hunter's ink-black uniform was pristine, the gold epaulettes and pins on his collar shining in the scant sun. If the pin Kyra clutched in her hand left a hole in

Hunter's set of decorations, it was one a casual onlooker would easily miss.

Hunter stopped in the middle of the camp. Shoulders spread, chest out, hands out of his pockets now, with fingers stretched down along the seam of his pants. A statue. The watching soldiers exchanged glances.

A minute passed with no motion but a shift of weight in the watching crowd, and the smallest of the Spades darting into the commander's tent. Another minute. Five. Ten. Kyra's legs fell asleep, and she shifted, tucking her cloak beneath herself. Fifteen minutes and Hunter still hadn't moved, the water running off him now a puddle around his feet. The others too held their places, their heads turning toward each other and the command tent with increasing frequency.

"What did you do, Hunter?" Kyra whispered into the wind, her chest tight.

Twenty minutes. Twenty-five. A full half hour, when the Spade commander finally ducked out of his tent and stalked to Hunter. Twice Hunter's age, with a peppering of gray in his black hair and a musket slung over his large shoulders, the commander had the aura of a man who Kyra hoped never to be alone with. Power clung to him like fog. No, like a great gray storm cloud ready to explode at any moment.

One by one, every Spade pressed a fist to his heart as the commander passed. Every Spade but Hunter, who still stood statue still, only his hair whipped in the wind like a flag of defiance to the soldiers' perfect order.

Kyra's heart quickened. In Hunter's place, she'd have melted into the sand by now. She was melting into the rock just watching.

The Commander stopped before Hunter, crossing muscular arms over his chest. The words exchanged didn't reach Kyra's ears, but with each passing sentence, the commander's chest puffed out a bit more, his fists clenching and unclenching until he finally spat on the ground.

For the first time since walking onto the beach, Hunter moved. Slowly. Precisely. As if careful to give no sign of aggression as he raised his hands up to his lapel and undid the pins clipped there. One by one, he tossed the gold bits to the soggy sand at the commander's boots. The golden epaulettes received the same treatment a moment later. Hunter dropped his hands to his sides again, and stared into the commander's face. Perfectly erect. Perfectly still. And waiting.

The camp stilled with Hunter, holding a collective breath.

The commander unslung his musket, and Kyra stuffed a fist into her mouth. It wouldn't help to scream. Wouldn't save Hunter's life. She squeezed the pin in her hand, letting its edges dig into her skin. *The dog.* The thought came unbidden into Kyra's head. Hunter had left his dog somewhere, awaiting a master who would never return.

"I'll take care of your dog," Kyra whispered, the limestone digging into her knees.

On the sand below, the commander raised his musket.

Hunter raised his chin.

The commander's face pulled back in a snarl as he twisted his weapon and slammed the musket's stock into Hunter's abdomen. For an absurd moment, relief washed over Kyra, a ludicrous, disgusting relief that a man was getting a beating. That he'd return to his dog.

Hunter dropped to his knees, gasping for breath. The moment he could move, he rose to one knee, braced his hands against his bent leg to push himself upright, straightening slowly to his full height. His arms dropped to his sides.

The commander's second blow was as vicious as the first.

When the third one landed, Kyra scrambled away from the ledge to empty her stomach into the lone bush peeking out through a crack in the stones. She wasn't going back to see how it ended, and she doubted Hunter would want his pin back now anyway.

CHAPTER 5

NILE

"What the *hell* were you thinking, Nile?" Domenic demands, bursting into the room Prince Tamiath and I share at Port Mead's best dockside inn. Domenic's uniform is still soaked from the rain beating the windows, and water drips from him onto the wooden floor. The war games ended hours ago, but Domenic had kept his *Raptor* at sea, running and rerunning the course long after the admiralty hauled the exercise flags down. Getting control of himself, Domenic draws breath and repeats in a more measured tone, "What were you thinking?"

Before I can reply, Aaron looks up from the chessboard he and I are hunched over and twists toward the door. "I imagine Nile was thinking that she won," he drawls, his curly golden hair catching glints of the firelight beside us. "And you...lost."

I kick Aaron's shin. My blood brother means well, but his

dislike of Domenic only feeds the tension that's been simmering between Domenic and me for months, ever since the Felielle Admiralty chose Domenic to command *Raptor*, and I chose to remain in command of my little *Eclipse* instead of following as his subordinate to the larger frigate.

Aaron raises his palms, his light green eyes proclaiming innocence. "Did I not hear the events correctly? I was certain the word on the docks is that a little fourteen-gun ship came in second only to Zolan's *Lily*, leaving Captain Dana behind to polish his pride with a toothbrush."

Domenic opens his mouth but Tam—sitting a few paces away at the breakfast table—clears his throat before anyone can say more. "Captain Dana." Tam's calm melodic voice chimes like a bell between us, the prince's manicured brows and perfect face contorting into resigned wariness. "Please come inside and close the door. Might I get you a drink?"

Coloring, Domenic bows quickly to the prince and murmurs an apology while I swallow a sigh. That Domenic failed to note Tamiath's presence until now bodes poorly for the rest of the evening's conversation.

Domenic closes the door and removes his dripping hat and boots before advancing into the room. His back is straight as always, but the cold dusts his lips with a blue tinge, and his muscles shiver beneath his soggy shirt. Seeing the fire, Domenic removes his wet coat as well.

"Anything else you wish to take off?" Aaron slides a lazy gaze over Domenic's sculpted chest. "Please, don't stop on our account."

Storms and hail. Domenic's color shifts from pink to white to a deep burgundy that clashes with his sea-blue eyes.

"Ignore him," I tell Domenic. Hooking a chair with my boot, I slide it toward him, coaxing the man to come closer to the warm flames before speaking again. Despite my light tone, my chest is tight with the knowledge that the conversation Aaron tried so hard to shield me from now hangs poised to strike.

Domenic's hands grip the wooden back of the chair, but he remains standing. "You risked yourself over a game, Nile," he says finally, his voice quiet and controlled as he looks down at me. "Made a mockery of the admiralty's rules. You think cheating is going to ingratiate you with anyone in the navy?"

I think it's easy to follow the rules when they are skewed in your favor. "I didn't cheat," I say, keeping my voice even in a mirror of his. "I used the rules to creative advantage when the whole power of the Felielle Admiralty was stacked against me for the sin of being born female. The war games exercise had an objective. I met it. If losing to a girl from Ashing makes the Felielle navy uncomfortable, then they need to wipe their noses and rethink their views."

Clearing his throat, Tam rises to his feet and pulls Aaron out the back door, which swings closed silently on well-oiled hinges. I wish it creaked, for the sudden silence is stifling.

A heartbeat passes. Two. The crackling of the fire marks the time and casts dancing shadows along Domenic's angular jaw. We've had little time together since separating to serve on different ships. *Eclipse*'s and *Raptor*'s business keep us occupied but for an occasional evening stolen between exercises and orders and repairs. Something I can't put my finger on has changed in the past three months of the Tirik war, blanketing all the sailors and soldiers with unease.

A log in the fire breaks in two, and my heart cracks with it. I don't want this fight. I long for Domenic to draw me into his arms with raw, unchecked need. I want him to celebrate my small victory, the rules and dangers be damned to a bloody hell. "Please just say 'congratulations,'" I whisper. "The admiralty might have my hide tomorrow, but you, tonight, please just say 'good work,' and leave it at that."

Domenic's jaw tightens as if he's tasting his own words before they come. "I can't congratulate you for risking your life, Nile." He covers the space between us in two large steps and crouches before my chair. His hand rises to my face, pushing a lock of hair behind my ear. His fingers, calloused and still cold, cup my chin. Worry and concern spill from his gaze into mine. "Never mind that you could have capsized your whole ship," he whispers. "I damn well know that your body pays dearly for these outbursts. You think *congratulations* is what's coming to my mind when I see you choking or writhing on the floor? When you bite your tongue so hard, it's a miracle you don't drown on your own blood, and I can do nothing but watch?"

"It's *my* body," I say softly, leaning toward him until my mouth is close enough to seal his lips into silence at a moment's notice. "I'll decide what it can bear. I think we can both agree that the last time you tried to decide that for me, it ended poorly."

"Nile—" Domenic breathes, but that is as far as I let him get before covering his mouth with mine.

"And where is our favorite Captain Dana?" Aaron asks, returning with Tam and Bear in tow. Outside, the rain has stopped, but the darkening sky shows few stars thanks to lingering clouds. "You two were getting along so well when we left."

Wiggling past Aaron, Bear jumps on me with both paws and sniffs. "I'm fine, you beast," I tell him, defending myself from the dog's wet nose. "I've only been alone a few hours."

Pushing Bear away, I cringe at the room's new wet-dog scent. "Domenic wanted to run the *Raptor* through another sail drill and search the ship's spirits the sailors no doubt smuggled aboard in barrels by now," I tell Aaron with a non-challenge I've perfected in the past months. As if talking about the *Raptor* costs me nothing.

Tam takes Aaron's coat from him and hangs it alongside his own on a hook beside the back door. "Did you two come to an understanding about this morning's exercise?" the prince asks. "Are you a resourceful young officer or a cheating scoundrel?"

"The question remains open." I cross my arms and glance out the window at the scurrying foot traffic. Port Mead's central location makes it a favorable meeting point, and between the Spardic Spades, Felielle navy, and Biron's own land and sea forces, the streets are filled to bursting with people. "We'll let the admiralty decide when they announce the results tomorrow morning." I hope they'll have decided how I'm getting to the Diante Empire as well. We are due to set sail in two weeks.

Aaron strides over to the table, where a servant left a tray with fresh bread, butter, and jam to tide Prince Tamiath and Princess Nile over until dinner. "My offer to find a courtesan still stands, you know," Aaron says over his shoulder as he pulls a heel of fluffy bread apart. "Someone knowledgeable. Good. Someone who can make your first time enjoyable, take the mystery out of it."

My face heats.

"Aaron." A low warning from Tam.

"How is she supposed to bed a man if she can't even talk about it?" Aaron demands, spreading his hands. "As her brother, it's my duty to help with such things. I'm certain I can find her something better than that righteous prat."

"His name is Domenic Dana," Tam says with exaggerated patience.

I glower at Aaron. "And I'm not interested in bedding *a* man."

"Why, in the Goddess's name, *him?*" Aaron throws up his hands. "You both want to be captains. Of ships. On an ocean. Sailing for a long time in different directions. And might I remind you that the prat had you flogged?"

I cock a brow at him. Aaron's meeting with Tam had been no less bloody. "Pot. Kettle. Black." Grabbing the bread in Aaron's hand for myself, I turn to Tamiath. "Have you heard back from Spardic Command about Catsper?"

I know the news isn't good when Tam puts a hand on my shoulder before speaking. "Between the odd uptick in the Tirik Republic's aggression and the Spades' recent losses, Spardic Command isn't releasing anyone just now. Catsper will be unable to come with you. I'm sorry, Nile."

"Are we expecting someone?" Aaron interrupts. His head is turned to the main door instead of the back entrance we usually use, and there's a growing sound of footsteps approaching the suite. With a sigh, he strides off to kiss Tam's lips and slips out the back just as a loud knocking echoes through the room.

I reach for the handle only to jump back as the door flies open and a thin, red-faced man with gray-peppered hair bursts inside.

"Did you hear what your little pet pulled, Tamiath?" the man sputters, his face turning from red to an alarming shade of purple. "She—"

"If you are referring to Lieutenant Greysik, she is standing right beside you," says Tam, arching a manicured brow. He shifts his weight and somehow, without moving from his spot, seems to blade his body between me and the newcomer. "Lord

Darius," Tam continues, his voice the perfect cool of royalty, "allow me to present my wife, Her Highness, Princess Nile Greysik of Felielle. Nile, this is my cousin Darius. Lord Vikon's father."

Well, that explains Vikon's delightful personality.

I incline my head to the newcomer. "My lord."

"I don't care a damn where she's standing." Darius spits the words, advancing on Tam. "Have you heard what happened during the war games today?"

Tam turns gracefully and retrieves a bottle of wine and three glasses from his chest. "The Goddess blessed me with exceptional hearing and attention, so yes." Pouring the amber liquid into the goblets, Tam hands one to me and the second to Darius, who appears too bewildered to do anything but grab the stem. Tam inhales the aroma of his own drink before speaking. "In fact, Princess Nile and I were just discussing the exercise. To best frigates with trice the armament and crew is quite an accomplishment for a young captain, would you not say?"

Darius's face contorts into a frown at Tam's rude deviation from the conversation script Darius had previously worked out for himself. "Pah," he proclaims finally. "A sloop maneuvers more easily than a frigate, that's all."

I smile sweetly. "Thank you for the kind words about my ship. She does handle smartly."

A vein pulses at Darius's temple, and I wager he is thinking of a way to clarify that no compliment was intended. "No matter," he says finally, clearing his throat. "I'm not here to talk about the silly games of a bored admiralty. This is a personal matter, Tam, and I would appreciate it if you give it the gravity it deserves." He pauses, straightening himself to his full height. "Your wife mutilated and tortured my son!"

Wine sputters from my mouth, the drops peppering my coat and the floor. "What?"

Beside me, Tam's expression gives nothing away.

Darius finds a chair and sits, shaking his head. "I just left the poor lad. Face bloodied, teeth missing. His body broken. It's all he could do to rescue himself from the underwater coffin he was marooned in."

"Oh for storm's sake, Lord Darius." I set down the remnants of my wine. Dealing with midshipmen's parents is a well-known ordeal of naval officers, and apparently, my first taste of it has decided to come calling today. "Vikon mouthed off—again—and received a backhand from the first officer for it. As for lost teeth and bruises, that happened two days earlier when he fell while skylarking in the rigging, which he had been warned against doing in foul weather at least twice."

Darius whirls toward me, finally condescending to acknowledge my presence. "You admit it, then."

I pinch the bridge of my nose. "Let us drop the veil and speak plainly. Your son has less discipline than a powder monkey and would have been bent over a gun long ago on any other ship. And if he thinks the midshipmen's berth is a coffin, perhaps a career outside the navy would better suit his sensibilities."

Darius locks eyes with Tam. "You heard her, Tamiath. A piece of Tirik filth laid his hands on my son."

I whirl on Darius, my blood pounding in my ears. "You are speaking of my first officer, sir. I will ask you to keep your tongue civil."

In the corner of the room, Bear raises his head, locks eyes with me, and whines.

My heart sinks into my stomach. *No.* Bear whines again, and Tam's eyes join the dog's in their concerned stare. I clench my jaw. I don't feel anything, not yet. But I know it's coming. Gifted. Magic. Elemental Attraction. All fancy names for a disease without a cure. And mine is choosing now to flare up. *Not now,* I beg my body. *Just give me a minute.*

"Civil?" Darius, plainly oblivious to the exchanged glances, is still continuing a now irrelevant for me conversation. Spittle flies from his mouth. "Civil?"

I'm barely listening. My hand clenches into a fist, my jaw grinding. I never asked for the bloody magic, never granted it leave to wreak havoc on my body. Bear alerts again and my heart quickens, the too-familiar dread already washing through me.

Putting down his glass, Tam saunters toward Darius.

The room spins before my eyes. Too quickly. It's happening too quickly.

"—You let a Tirik-bred dog aboard ship, allow him to give orders to a *royal-born* Felielle, and dare defend him when he can't keep his hands to himself?" Darius's voice builds to a crescendo. "I want this Quinn flogged. I demand—"

"You've given me much to ponder on, cousin." Tamiath puts his hand on the shorter man's back and nudges him out of the chair and toward the door. "I can't thank you enough."

I back away, getting clear of Darius's line of sight while I can still move. Fear replaces dread in my veins, coming and ebbing in waves that grow with each breath. A green light begins to pulse in my right eye. Its flash flash flash blinds my thoughts.

"But—" Darius starts to say. His words are distant, as if said on the edge of sleep.

"Let me discuss the matter with the princess." Tamiath pushes his cousin into the corridor, closing the door behind them.

My legs stall. I throw my arm out toward the table, my hand

aiming for its solid surface. I catch Darius's discarded wineglass instead. With no purchase, I fall hard to my knees, the shattered glass slicing into my palm. The green light multiples, the flashing speeds. With its next pulse, my whole body arches up off the floor. My teeth sink into my tongue, blood welling up in my mouth and trickling into my throat before darkness claims me.

CHAPTER 6

KYRA

*W*hen Kyra finally made her way to the docks, her oiled cloak wrapped as tightly against the rain as she could make it, she found nothing there except the distrustful glares of merchantmen skippers. The Felielle fleet and Princess Nile were out playing war games at sea, pitting their great guns against unsuspecting wine casks.

Kyra made a tour of all the newsleafs posted—the pillars having clever little ledges that kept the worst of the rain off the print—taking in the grim daily news: estimates of the Tirik force had increased, as had the number of battles fought and seamen lost. It was only a matter of time until the Tirik made landing and brought the war from sea to sand.

The rest of the day, as the rain died down, Kyra divided between earning pennies reading the same newsleafs to dockside visitors and silver crowns reading the fortunes of the wealthier marketplace patrons. Between the taste of the customers' emotions and the newsleaf updates, it was simple enough to concoct stories decent enough to buy her dinner. Together with selling the mushrooms, she did all right—though it was all a circle that never progressed anywhere.

Hunter's pin prickled Kyra's thigh through the pocket of her dress, refusing to let the morning's images rest. It seemed disrespectful to sell or toss the damn pin away, but Kyra little wished to keep it either, especially since her fingers kept slipping down to fiddle with the metal edges. She needed to leave it somewhere and forget Hunter altogether. Meddling in the world's business was what had gotten Kyra into trouble in the first place, what tempted her to sail from her home to a mainland that despised her.

Tomorrow. She would get all her business done tomorrow. Princess Nile Greysik would be done with the exercise by then, and Kyra would find her, plead her case, convince the young woman to hire Kyra on. With that plan firmly in mind, Kyra turned her coins over for a fish freshly caught and fried on heaped coals, and returned to her cavern to eat and think.

Except it wasn't working. By the time the sun had set and the moon rose to keep watch over Port Mead, Kyra's mind could see nothing save the butt of a rifle rammed into a man who did nothing to defend himself. Over and over and over. *Why?* Kyra demanded of the memory. *What broke, Hunter? What led to that?*

The distant toll of the port bell called two hours past midnight when Kyra gave up trying to close her eyes and ducked out of the cavern. She needed a walk to clear her mind. To help her sleep. She needed to know whether Hunter was here again, and she needed to make a decision. Kyra wouldn't delay leaving the mainland, but if she could help Hunter before she left, it would make her months in Biron worth something beyond empty misery.

It took Kyra an hour until she tasted him, but once she did, her chest tightened. Hunter *was* atop the ridge, but some distance from both the Spardic camp and the spot where Kyra had met him the previous night.

Picking up a stick, Kyra let her magic call to the heat until it coalesced into a small flame on the branch's tip, well away from her hand. The moon cast fair light, but Kyra wasn't about to climb up unfamiliar stones without a torch. This side of the rise might lack the cliff face facing the ocean, but it was steep enough to twist an ankle without trying.

Kyra's legs burned by the time she hauled herself to the top of the ridge and blinked at the empty space. Hunter had to be here. She'd felt him. She... There was no taste in Kyra's mouth, as if whatever had baited her to climb the stones was gone, melted like a mirage. Kyra turned about, careful to keep back from the cliffside drop. Her heart quickened, her blood rushing through her. Someone had been here. She was certain. Someone—

A knife pressed into Kyra's throat, a hard body rising like stone behind her. The smell of earth and steel filled her nose. Her stomach clenched, a scream escaping her lips as her torch fell and sputtered out. The bitterness of her own terror filled her mouth and throat.

"How did you find me?" Hunter's soft voice scraped against Kyra's ears. "How and why?"

Kyra's dry tongue refused to move, her hands trembling as they clawed at the arm holding steel to her neck. Idiot. Idiot. Idiot. She'd been tracking a wounded animal, never considering that it might maul her before she could set its leg. She'd meddled and fallen into her own trap. There was no one to hear her screams here. And even if there were, there was no one in Port Mead who'd care.

Hunter shook her so hard that Kyra's teeth clacked together, and for a moment, she couldn't squeeze a breath past her closing throat.

"Talk," Hunter ordered again in that same too-soft voice. "Now."

"I saw your dog," Kyra said, her thoughts racing to conjure an explanation. "I was curious—"

Hunter snarled softly, calling out Kyra's lie.

She froze. He could kill her if he wanted to. And he *had* killed, she was sure of that. He'd killed and he'd enjoyed it. The pressure from the knife increased, and Kyra's neck stung, a dribble of something warm and viscous slithering down her neck.

"I felt you," Kyra whispered. There had to be a wiser thing to say, but her mind refused to conjure anything but the truth. The man's weight shifted, and Kyra tasted his fury. He didn't believe her. He thought she was lying again. And he'd had enough. *Stars.* Her eyes stung, the words tumbling out of her mouth. "I can taste emotions. I felt you yesterday. And today. I'm Gifted. A flame caller. I felt you, and I—"

The blade withdrew, and Hunter pushed her away from him. Kyra stumbled, falling to her knees a pace away from the cliff's edge. Her breath halted. Too close. Much too close.

Hunter towered over her, his knife still in his hand, his other arm pressed against his ribs. He no longer wore a uniform, but there was a sword strapped down the length of his spine. That he was moving at all after this morning... "Name?" Hunter demanded.

Kyra opened her mouth to speak, but the only words she

could summon were ones she wouldn't stoop to say. *Don't hurt me, don't hurt me, don't hurt me.*

"I asked," Hunter said again—only to jerk toward the ocean as an explosion of fire bloomed above the port, shattering the darkness. Hunter twisted back to Kyra just as the first of the screams pierced the air.

"It wasn't me—" she gasped, her hands rising in surrender.

"Get to cover," Hunter ordered in a voice suddenly cold as steel. "Now."

Before Kyra could respond, Hunter gripped the cliff's edge and, in a smooth, feline motion, launched himself into the abyss below. Hunter's final words, thrown back to her over the cliff, echoed in Kyra's ears. "Get to cover. We're under attack."

CHAPTER 7

NILE

"*G*et up." Tam's voice reaches me through a haze.

I little remember falling asleep, but given the feel of a soft mattress beneath me and the velvety darkness, I've been out for some time. Everything hurts: my muscles, my head, my tongue. *Storms,* I must have bitten my tongue when the convulsions hit. In the distance, a bell strikes four in the morning.

"Get up," Tam says again. "There has been an attack at the port."

I bolt upright, the world spinning even as I catch the uniform Tam tosses into my hands. A quarter hour later, Tam and I are striding into the inn's common room turned command center and taking seats at a long wooden table stretching the length of the space. Early rays of predawn filter into the windows, drawing soft splotches of light on the rough wood. A steward distributes mugs of coffee, and I make the mistake of taking a sip before remembering the gash in my tongue and quickly spitting the hot liquid back into the mug.

Other officers filter in, quickly filling up seats. My chest tightens when Domenic strides into the room, giving me a curt professional nod before taking his place. No one else meets my gaze. Unlike Domenic, I'm too junior an officer to be included and too senior a royal to be excluded, thus efficiently upsetting everyone without even trying.

Admirals Pyre and Brice are the last to arrive, filing to their places with little ceremony. Pyre claps Domenic on the shoulder as he passes, saying something too quiet for me to hear.

"Aye, thank you, sir," Domenic says, ducking his head. Now that the Felielle navy has had their taste of him, Domenic is quickly becoming a favorite. A model seaman and officer.

"Gentlemen." Admiral Pyre pitches his voice across the silent room. "Thank you for rising from your beds at this hour. Approximately an hour ago, the People's Republic of Tirik used the cover of darkness to maneuver a small craft filled with gunpowder into Port Mead's dock. It appears that the crew then disembarked and concealed themselves before triggering the powder's detonation." Pyre pauses, his lips pressing into a tight line. "After bystanders and healers responded to aid the victims of the explosion, the bastards came out of hiding and launched a secondary assault with swords and pistols, tripling the body count until they were neutralized."

Pyre's words punch me in the gut. Bystanders. Healers. "The Tirik must have known the responders would be civilians," I say into the stunned silence.

Glares of thinly concealed exasperation shoot my way. *Felielle women do not opine on matters of strategy in the presence of professionals,* their eyes tell me.

"Of course they knew," Admiral Pyre says finally.

"Efficient bastards." Captain Zolan's words have a drawl to them, as if his thoughts are a few steps ahead of the present conversation. Of a height and age with Tam, Zolan has the same presence around a conference table as I imagine he has on the quarterdeck. His dark, wind-tousled hair frames strong cheekbones and skin tanned to the color of honey. "They had limited firepower and personnel at their disposal. The two-stage setup allowed them to minimize resources for the greatest damage. The Tirik didn't need to go to the crowd. They made the crowd come to them."

I tap my finger on the table, ignoring Domenic's warning glance about speaking out of turn. "The Tirik haven't targeted civilians before." My mind riffles through the puzzle of information and comes up empty. "Why start now, when they are winning again? When their flag is supposed to proclaim *power to the people?*"

Admiral Pyre sighs. "With due respect, Your Highness, the Tirik have been doing a great many things in the past three months that they haven't done before. And frankly, it's been working well for them. The Tirik are looking for body count. The question we are meeting to address this morning isn't about which bodies the Tirik targeted, but rather what it means for the Felielle fleet. That little cutter the Tirik blew to pieces didn't sail herself from the Tirik Republic—there is a larger Tirik ship somewhere nearby." He raises his chin and surveys the officers gathered. "Your thoughts, gentlemen?"

Captain Zolan leans forward, muscled forearms braced on the table's edge. "We end the fleet exercises immediately. Send all ships we can spare to support the Biron kingdom's patrols. Hunt down the bastards wherever they might be hiding and destroy them."

Admiral Brice, a potbellied man with a double chin and ample girth, stares at a spot just over my head. "What of the Diante? We've a shrinking two-week window. If we redirect our ships to support the Biron, how will we get to the Siaman?"

"The Diante can wait," I say, leaning forward. "We are under attack and can't spare ships to—"

"I see your point, Admiral," says Captain Zolan, talking over me without hesitation. "Perhaps we send a small squadron to the Diante Empire. Three or four ships, under a rear admiral's flag. We could convert a cabin to make it comfortable for Her Highness during the passage."

My face heats, but before I can utter a word, Tamiath's fingers beneath the table dig into my thigh hard enough to bruise.

"I would not venture to speak on naval strategy," Tamiath says smoothly, "but from a political perspective. I do not see the Diante Empire allowing a squadron of four men-of-war to enter its waters. You may recall that not a year ago, the Diante barred a Lyron Joint Fleet frigate from taking on fresh water at their docks. That they are inviting one ship is a great step in itself. Let us not push our relations by sailing a squadron into their waters." He shrugs. "We must also consider that the invitation was for one *Captain* Nile Greysik."

My gaze cuts to Domenic, sitting with his back straight and mouth shut. He won't speak unless addressed directly by a superior. Not even to voice support for me.

"The Diante didn't build an empire by being stupid," says Admiral Pyre. "They cannot truly expect an eighteen-year-old girl to sail herself halfway around the world."

I put my palms on the table, my voice hard as my body absorbs the insult. "You will recall that I was in charge of a ship when I met the Diante admiral who issued the damn invitation. Whatever—"

"To Prince Tamiath's point, it is unlikely the Diante worded the invitation lightly," Zolan says, barreling over me again. His voice is low and clear, and the men at the table turn to him obligingly. "If we disregard the invitation terms, we risk insulting the very people we are trying to gain as allies. What if the girl sails in nominal command while true seamen run the ship as the first and second officers? A Felielle squadron can still escort the principal vessel to the border, passing custody to the Diante upon the rendezvous, thus minimizing the risk to the princess."

Admiral Pyre nods along with the captain's words. "Satisfy proprietary and security without sacrificing common sense. Very good, Mr. Zolan." He drums his hand on the table. "Moreover, I've just the ship in mind—the *Helix*, frigate at the top end of a junior captain's possible command. She's coming out of dry dock in Port Lye next week. How quickly can you get her set to sail, Zolan?"

For the first time since the meeting started, Zolan's face creases. "Me, sir? I fear I fail to follow your meaning."

Admiral Pyre's brows rise as my stomach sinks. "I am accepting your idea, Zolan. Now I would like you to put theory into practice."

Zolan's lips press together. "With due respect, sir, I'm in command of the *Lily* just now. Not to mention the fact that it's been some time since I was a first officer on any sort of vessel." Zolan pauses and takes in Pyre's hardening gaze. For a heartbeat, I hang on to the hope that the captain will stand by his protest, but Zolan schools his face and bows in acknowledgment. "Of course. I serve at your pleasure, my lord admiral."

I sigh. "Gentlemen." I pitch my voice over the room. "I must point out that the efficiency of this discussion would increase exponentially if you acknowledged my presence at this table."

Silence. Dead heavy silence.

I raise my chin and meet each stare head-on, even as my heart pounds against my ribs.

Admiral Pyre is the first to speak, rubbing two fingers over sharp nose. "Forgive my bluntness for the sake of clarity, Princess, but your political station gives you no leave to influence the admiralty's decisions directly. You may, of course, recommend the removal of either me or Admiral Brice and endeavor to select leaders whose vision is more in line with your own, but that is the extent of your voice. As for your naval station... I hope you will understand me when I say that junior officers follow the orders they are given and that your recent gunnery trials performance raised concerns about your judgment."

Domenic's gaze cuts to me. *I told you so.*

"She seized an opportune gale to kick your protégé's rear end, Pyre." Admiral Brice's small eyes twinkle. "Not to detract from Mr. Dana's performance, of course, but scores are scores."

"And orders are orders," Admiral Pyre snaps back, his lips pressing together as he glares at his opposite number. Plainly, this isn't the first conversation the two men have had about my war game choices. Pyre's hand tightens around his coffee mug, his fingers bone from the pressure. "Mr. Dana," Pyre says in a light tone that has no one fooled, "you've had the honor of serving with Ms. Greysik previously, have you not?"

"Aye, sir." Domenic gives a half bow to the admiral, though the senior man's eyes remain on Brice.

"And in your personal experience, Mr. Dana," says Pyre,

"how would you describe Ms. Greysik's willingness to follow orders?"

Domenic shifts, his gaze brushing me for a moment before returning to the waiting admiral. "I have found Ms. Greysik to be a hard worker, sir," Domenic says in a carefully even tone. "Fully dedicated to her mission."

"Let me rephrase my question, Mr. Dana." Admiral Pyre's penetrating gaze swings to target Domenic. "If you were to order Ms. Greysik to do one thing, and she thought another option was preferable, would you trust her to carry out your instructions despite her personal objection to them?"

This time, Domenic doesn't look toward me before answering. "No, sir. I would not."

CHAPTER 8

NILE

*A*dmiral Pyre holds Domenic back after the meeting, and I leave without waiting for him or Tam, who is still exchanging casual conversation. The air outside the inn is too fresh for my racing thoughts, but it's better than being indoors. My pulse runs quickly, blood whooshing through my veins and setting every tight muscle aflame. Quinn, the ex-Tirik captain turned guard and friend, peels away from the inn's wall and falls into step beside me while Bear circles my legs.

"If you grow any bigger, I'll get a saddle and sell you as a pony," I murmur to the dog, who uses his head to bully me into an ear rub.

Quinn gives me a sideways glance. "The admiralty meeting did not go well?"

"It went fine." I set course toward the docks, wanting to see the site of the attack firsthand. I'm no expert in explosions, especially on land, but something about this one scratches at me. More to the point, I need something to occupy my mind just now. "We are sailing out to the Diante Empire aboard the *Helix*, with Mr. Zolan as my first officer."

Quinn makes a sound in the back of his throat. Unlike any of my other friends, with the exception of Domenic, Quinn has been in charge of a ship before. "And what is Mr. Zolan's take on the situation?"

My jaw tightens. "That he is in charge." I quicken my pace. If Catsper were here, I'd ask him to spar, but walking is all I have available just now. "Zolan has been at sea longer than I've been alive. The only argument against making him my first officer is that he is as overqualified for the post as I am for a scullery maid."

"I don't believe you'd make a very good scullery maid," Quinn says quietly, keeping pace with me. Dawn breaks around us as we walk, the fishermen families waking up to ruined livelihoods. Port Meade's perpetual grayness adds to the greyness, and even the occasional brightly painted house looks exhausted. The final sight of the attack will be worse still. Quinn puts his hands behind his back, ignoring the many stares of passersby. Quinn's combination of tan skin and thick sandy hair, cut short to brush the back of his neck in Tirik fashion instead of grown to hang below the shoulders, already mark him as unusual. Combined with his place by my side and his accent, Quinn turns as many heads as I do. "You might recall that I've served on a ship where someone else—a People's Commissioner, in my case—believed himself in charge. It's more complicated than you give it credit for."

Oh, I think it's plenty complicated. Made no less so thanks to Domenic's remarks. Saying as much aloud smells too much like wallowing in undeserved self-pity, though. Zolan is one stripped of a cherished command to play nursemaid to mine, not the other way around. "There is no such thing as a nominal command, Quinn. The crew of the *Helix* will be my responsibility no matter what Zolan or the admiralty or the gods themselves say."

Quinn grunts suddenly, his hand going to his shoulder as a rock the size of a chicken egg clatters to the ground.

"Die, Tirik dog!"

"Only good Tirik is a dead Tirik!"

"Rotting fish, rotting fish, who are you? I'm Tirik, I'm Tirik, that is who."

My gaze jerks to a group of boys, their thin frames and tattered clothes speaking of difficult times. Made more so last night.

Quinn steps toward them, and the boys scatter, all but the smallest lad with large blue eyes and an old, too-large sweater. Holding his ground, the boy trembles, but he faces down Quinn. Quinn isn't a large man, but after a decade on the quarterdeck, he's more than mastered the art of making himself formidable. The rock that struck his shoulder moments ago now bounces in his hand.

The small boy opens his mouth, his high voice quiet and shaking even as his eyes brim with hate. "Rotting fish, rotting fish, who are you?"

"I'm Quinn," Quinn answers, gravely holding out the stone on his open palm. "I'm a person, and I'm from the Tirik Republic. Would you like your stone back? I believe you've misplaced it."

The child kicks Quinn's shin and runs off.

Quinn lets the stone fall to the ground and turns about, marking the other boys. None dare to come out and face him.

My demons in the Felielle admiralty suddenly seem

negligible in comparison. I put my hand on Quinn's shoulder. "I'm sorry."

He nods. "I heard about the attack. Though..." Quinn's lips press together. "It doesn't make sense to me."

I wait for Quinn to say more, but don't push the subject. The ex-Tirik's loyalties are...complicated. I've given my word never to ask him to raise a weapon against his former countrymen except in self-defense, and that includes the blade that's his knowledge.

"Do you recognize the young woman watching us?" Quinn asks, jerking me free of my thoughts.

I frown, following Quinn's signal to a dark-haired girl a year or two older than me whose gaze indeed follows my every move from her post beside one of the wooden pillars plastered with newsleafs. She is petite and beautiful, with a dancer's lithe body, skin tanner than Quinn's, and large chocolate eyes. Her dress, a yellow and green too lively for Port Mead's usual leaning toward trout-brown and gray wool, is cut at an angle— shorter in front than back.

She holds a small metal bauble in her hands, her fingers absently worrying its shiny surface. Nothing about her looks familiar, however, and I'm about to dismiss her into irrelevance when our gazes meet and the magic in my veins gives a sudden start.

I draw breath. That sensation, one of my magic reacting to someone else's Gift, is sharp and familiar—though I've not felt it in over half a year. Not since my magic had mixed with my twin's and changed. Grew. Evolved.

If the odd girl feels a reciprocal jolt, she gives no sign of it. Instead, she bites her lip and turns away, as if having changed her mind about whatever it was she'd intended.

"Nile?" Quinn prods.

"Let's move out of here," I say, picking up the pace to put distance between myself and the girl. When Quinn catches up to stride beside me, I lower my voice. "She is Gifted. My magic feels hers, and I little wish to discover whether this sensation goes both ways."

"Your magic *feels* hers?" Quinn echoes. With the out-of-sight-out-of-mind approach to elemental attraction in the Lyron's six kingdoms, there is no such thing as an expert in Gifted and magic—but Quinn, with his history of transporting Gifted passengers and work in taming and training my own magic, comes as close as anyone in Lyron gets. "That's impossible."

"Yes, well, the list of impossible magical feats that have slapped me in the face over the past eight months is getting tediously long." I rub my temples. "Have you seen Catsper? Tam says Spardic Command won't release anyone to come on the cruise with me, but I want to hear it from him. Otherwise, it's just you and me, Quinn."

Not Domenic. He has the *Raptor* now. Even if he didn't, the admiralty has already filled my first officer's billet with Zolan. My chest tightens, two weeks suddenly seeming very, very short, and it's an effort of will to force air into my lungs.

"I've not seen Catsper, no." Quinn's words pull me back to the conversation. Hands still behind his back quarterdeck style, Quinn looks dutifully ahead, ignoring the hate-filled stares that follow his every move. "But I'm willing to lay coin that we'll find him at the explosion site."

Yes. If there is trouble somewhere, it's safe money to bet Catsper is to be found beside it. And—

"Nile!" As if having heard the reference to himself in my thoughts, Domenic catches up to us, Tam striding thoughtfully beside him. Bear separates from my side to ram into Domenic's thigh, howling with soft pleasure as Domenic rubs his ears. I say nothing. Despite the dog's joy, the air around us thickens with each passing heartbeat of silence. Domenic clears his throat. "You left quickly."

Quinn politely strolls a distance away to give Domenic and me privacy.

"I wanted to see the attack site for myself." Truth. I start moving again, as if it's possible to outwalk Domenic's unspoken question: *Are you upset with me?*

I am not. I can't be. Domenic was asked a question. He answered it. I lost what little credibility I'd built up. Those are the facts, but they are not his fault. Just as Admiral Pyre's patronage and *Raptor*'s command billet aren't Domenic's fault. The important thing is that I will have a ship and a crew. I will have the sea. I will earn my way toward the rest.

Yet none of that sounds quite right aloud. So I walk instead, nodding to Tamiath as the prince's long strides bring him up to our side, skirting around the large dockyard supply warehouse whose gray-green stone walls pierce the long pier like a thorn.

No. I skirt what used to be a dockyard supply warehouse but is now little more than a wall separating the eastern-side docks from the ravaged world on the western side.

Despite the ocean, the stench of burnt meat, gunpowder, and rotting death saturates the air. On my left, bodies and body parts are thrown into haphazard piles for victims' families to sort through. Ahead, the wooden pier is broken with gaps and holes spraying cold water with each wave passing beneath. I take a step, and one of the spitting holes vomits onto my boots, the cold wetness squishing inside the leather. "Storms."

Several heads turn to me, eyes vacant and angry. Clothes streaked with blood and soot. I step back, raising my palms, and the heads turn away. To rummage through bodies, to help clear debris, to look for family. Bear presses against my right thigh, and Domenic comes up to stand at my left shoulder, stopping just short of putting a hand on the small of my back.

The worst of it is still ahead, a gaping hole where the eye of the blast must have flared. What used to be a small wooden shelter is now a bit of charcoaled debris, and the sea is peppered with pieces of broken hulls and nets. The Tirik must have waded right into the center of where the fishermen tied up their boats before setting off the explosion, choosing to destroy many small crafts instead of targeting the bigger military sloop anchored some two hundred yards away.

True to form, Catsper is crouching beside the blast site, his blond mane of hair shifting in the light breeze. I call his name.

Lifting his gaze, Catsper uncurls to his full height. A slight jerkiness to his usual feline grace hints at an injury hidden beneath soot-and-blood-stained clothes. *Of course* Catsper was in the thick of the attack.

"What happened?" I ask.

"A suicide assault." The marine's mouth is set in a grim line. "The Tirik destroyed their one means of retreat before jumping out with swords blazing. They never intended to leave the pier alive. I don't like it."

"They also avoided a military craft to target civilian fishing boats," I add, my jaw tightening. "A blow to commerce and morale rather than a typical show of force."

"We've seen the Tirik choose death over surrender before," Tam says, his gaze like mine, on Catsper's ribs. "The People's Party punishes soldiers' families for 'cowardice.'"

The marine shakes his head, the motion tight. "This is different. This bunch wasn't fighting to the death. They knew they were dead before the slaughter started. When they realized I knew which end of the sword is sharp, they took human shields. But even then, they never planned to walk away from the battlefield. I could see it in their eyes."

"Waves and hail." I rub my face. "And that?" I jerk my chin at Catsper's ribs.

He shrugs. "Gunpowder went boom. Swords went clash. The usual. Where is Quinn?"

"He's—" I look over my shoulder, expecting to find the man trailing us, but find only the press of strangers.

Tamiath swears beneath his breath and spins around to retrace our steps back around the broken warehouse, Catsper, Domenic, and I falling in beside him. Rum, the squat, evil beast calling itself Catsper's dog, separates from his patch of dry dock and trots behind us, teeth bared.

The muscles between my shoulder blades tense as minutes pass without Quinn's face becoming visible along the pier. The crowd is thicker than it was earlier, especially around the wooden pillars with posted newsleafs, where I last saw the Gifted girl. I move closer, but the press of bodies is too tight to see through without active elbowing to burrow into their midst. Waves of fury rippling through the gathered men are palpable enough to spur my own pulse.

"Can you see?" I ask Domenic, but a voice from the mob's depths rises before Domenic can answer, others picking up the call.

"Murderer!"

"Filth.

"Die, Tirik pig!"

CHAPTER 9

KYRA

*I*t was madness. Madness and pulsing, mindless rage that spread like infection. One moment, the Tirik man who'd been with Nile was standing by himself, and the next, a trio of vacant-eyed fishermen were cutting off his retreat, herding him toward the newsleaf pillar where Kyra stood. The Tirik was in his mid twenties, with tanned skin almost as dark as Kyra's own, and intelligent eyes that hid his fear.

The Tirik didn't struggle, letting himself be led away from the royals, protecting them from getting swept up into what he knew was coming. Kyra stepped away, only to bump into someone behind her. Many someones. A whole crowd that was gathering with a bitter, single-minded rage potent enough to make Kyra gag.

Kyra knew the two fishermen holding the Tirik's arms. She'd read a newsleaf for them just yesterday, not knowing she was telling them of their sons' deaths until tears poured down their faces. They refused to pay her, but she wouldn't have taken their money anyway. They had too little to spare. After the attack last night, likely none at all anymore.

The third man, a thick-mustached brute who smelled of drink, Kyra hadn't recognized at first. The last she saw him, days ago, he was a proud, pipe-smoking merchant captain refusing to take her passenger. Today, he was soot and stains and anger. His ship must have been one of the crafts destroyed. And now— now, his arm swung back and punched the defenseless Tirik in the ribs so hard that the man choked on air.

Kyra gasped, looking toward the gathering crowd to pull the men apart.

The crowd cheered. It was bigger than before too. People flocking to violence like moths to flame. A shiver raced over Kyra's skin, the pulsing rage saturating the air about her. She clutched her dress, stumbling as the crowd thickened and jostled behind her. They weren't evil people. Rowdy and unwelcoming, but not violent. Not mindless. Not like this.

"Murderer!" someone yelled, cheering as the merchant struck the Tirik again, this time across the face. Blood beaded at the corner of the Tirik's mouth and ran down his chin.

"Filth!" A woman's voice.

"Die, Tirik pig!"

The merchant cocked his hand for another blow, though the Tirik was hanging in the fishermen's grip now, unable to find footing.

"Stop!" Kyra shouted as loudly as she could. No one heard. Not even the people bumping her back and shoulder. "Stop it!" she shouted again, only to hear a grunt of pain and more cheers as another strike landed. *They are going to kill him.* The realization widened Kyra's eyes, spurring her heart into a gallop.

People who weren't murderers were going to beat an innocent man to death.

An authoritative, military voice from the back of the crowd shouted an order for everyone to stand down, but the words fell as flat as Kyra's own had. Something needed to be done to get the people's attention, to snap them out of their rabid resolve to hurt.

Her hand still clutching her skirt, Kyra rushed forward into the small space that still remained around the Tirik and his captors.

"Leave him be! He's done nothing," Kyra called, not ordering, but pleading. She gripped the merchant's thick arm with her slender hands. The merchant knew her. The fishermen knew her too. If she could get them to listen, to stop for one moment, she could end this. "Please," Kyra said. "Stop. More violence will solve nothing!"

The merchant twisted toward her, his nostrils flaring in the chill. With a single shake of his powerful forearm, Kyra's grip fell away and she stumbled back, tripping over her own heels and landing on her rear. Breath caught in her chest, and she braced her arm on the ground, trying to stand.

Grabbing the front of Kyra's dress, the merchant hauled her to her feet, his bulk now looming over her and blocking out the light. Her heart stalled before starting into a gallop. No. No. He knew her. He—

She saw the back of the man's hand move in too familiar a way, and flinched even before it landed across her face. Pain echoed through her cheek, spidering through her face and scalp.

"What's this? A second Tirik pig?" A slur blurred the merchant's words and eyes, which flashed in satisfaction as encouraged murmuring answered him from the crowd.

"What?" Kyra shook her head, struggling to pull herself

away from the grip the merchant still had on her dress. She twisted her head toward the fishermen holding the Tirik man between them. "You know me. I'm not Tirik. But even if I was —" She gasped as the merchant's free hand clasped her chin between his thumb and forefinger, examining her tan skin.

"You look Tirik." He sniffed her neck. Four times her size, he could snap her in half with a thought. Not that there was any thinking happening. "You smell Tirik. You love Tirik."

And then Kyra was airborne, tossed like a rag doll against the very pillar she'd read news from the day before. Her back struck the hard wood first, then her head. A ringing filled her ears, mixing with the swoosh of blood racing through her veins. The crowd closed around her, their voices rising in competition. She slid to the ground, a pace away from where the fishermen held the Tirik.

The merchant cracked his knuckles.

"Hang them both!" voices shouted from the crowd.

"Burn them with our ships' remains!"

"Drown the rats!"

A dog's savage growl parted the crowd, the beast's muzzle soaked in blood that dripped from his snapping square jaw. The mob shifted from the animal with greater enthusiasm than they showed for humans, and a dockworker too slow to clear the way screamed as teeth closed around his calf. The man beside him, a Biron guard who'd been busy shouting for Kyra's head moments earlier, aimed his boot at the dog's side.

"No!" Kyra shouted at the guard. She knew that dog. And she knew the blond man who crushed the Biron guard's nose before that kick could land.

The dog's head swung toward Kyra, his muscular shoulders rising and falling with deep, powerful breaths. Dark canine eyes met Kyra's, and the dog's short-cropped tail gave a single wag before the beast went back to his business of ripping men to shreds.

The merchant in front of Kyra reached down to grab her.

Hunter's hands gripped the merchant's forearm in midswing. With a smooth shift of weight, Hunter ducked beneath the arm he held and came up behind his foe. A bare blade Kyra hadn't seen Hunter unsheathe flashed beside the merchant's throat.

"Call them off," Hunter hollered. "Now!"

Before the merchant could answer, the mob finally broke whatever line they'd held and closed in. Cursing, Hunter retracted his knife and threw his foe into the oncoming mob. A dozen legs tripped over and trampled the unexpected obstacle, the man roaring in pain as someone's heel crushed his hand into the pier's wooden planks. Blood flowed from the merchant's torn skin as he rose to his hands and knees, trying to stand. A stray boot kicked his temple, and the man fell motionless, collateral damage of the rabid army's assault.

Drawing up her knees, Kyra covered her head with her arms, bracing herself for a blow. Hunter disappeared from her line of sight, and the dog was working his savage way through the crowd. Through her arms, Kyra saw Princess Nile's familiar face as the girl elbowed her way toward her Tirik friend. Unafraid, determined, nothing like Kyra herself.

One of the fishermen was midblow when Nile came upon him, and savagely redirected his fist from the girl's head. Kyra's mouth opened in a wordless scream, but the princess pivoted away from the strike, sidestepping the blow even as her elbow collided with the man's temple.

The fisherman went limp and dropped to his knees.

Nile shook out her arm.

"Nile! Behind you!" a large man in a naval uniform roared

in warning, sudden fear pulsing from him as he fought his way toward the princess. His dark hair whipped behind him, his focus singularly, fully on Nile.

He was too late. As Nile turned in response to the warning, a pair of hands was already grabbing her from behind. Before she could react, Nile's attacker hurled her headfirst into the pillar Kyra crouched beside.

Nile shifted in the air, striking the unforgiving wood with her shoulder instead of her skull. A moment of frozen grimace, then the princess was gasping for air, her eyes wide. Gripping her injured shoulder, Nile tried and failed to rise.

Kyra reached out her hand, grasping Nile's elbow. "Are you all right?"

The princess recoiled as if burned, her dark eyes cutting up to meet Kyra's. And for the first time since the princess entered the fray, Kyra tasted Nile's fear.

CHAPTER 10

NILE

*T*he dull thud of impact echoes through my body a moment before the pain catches up to it. I gasp, then gasp again as the magic in my blood flares so violently, I wonder if lightning hasn't struck my skull. Above me, men pummel each other with rabid fury. Their homes have been attacked, lives and livelihoods wiped from existence overnight. They want—they need—for someone to pay the tab.

A pace away, Quinn struggles on his hands and knees while Domenic fights two men at once, trying and failing to make progress toward the pillar. Catsper dances in the middle of the riot's storm. His blurry form twists, kicks out behind him, recovers in time to block a club aimed for his head. I wonder whether he doesn't feel his injuries just now or simply doesn't care. The wild savageness in his eyes suggests the latter. I try to rise, but the ground tips sideways.

"Are you all right?"

My magic pulses, sudden and so hard that it takes me a moment to realize that someone is touching me, holding my elbow. Tanned, slender fingers pulsing with magic of their own. *Storm and hail.* The girl from earlier. Cowering at the foot of the same pillar I'd just been bounced against, she has a hold on my flesh now, her dark eyes staring into mine and her magic whipping my own into a frenzy.

I jerk away from her touch, fear washing through me. My shoulder screams, and my magic growls at the sudden separation. I manage to get my feet under me on my second attempt, blocking blows as I rise.

The girl remains down on the ground. Wrapping one of her arms protectively about her head, she presses the other against the pillar behind her. I'm about to haul her to her feet and pull her away from the pillar altogether, when my magic gives another start. At the wooden pillar's base, a few inches from where the girl's hand grips the wood, there is now a small trickle of smoke, a kernel of blossoming flame.

Understanding floods me. A flame caller. I've no time to contemplate the impossibility of a flame caller surviving into adulthood as I bring my knee and elbow together to block someone's limb and gently tap into my own magic. The kindling fire will take too long to grow into a noticeable distraction, but with help...

Sending a small breeze to billow the infant fire, I keep my eyes locked on the girl's even as I raise my voice. "Catsper!"

The marine grins, grabs the closest man with a heavy coat, and knocks him into the flame. The girl screams as fire grabs dry material, eating it with greater ease than the pillar's damp wood.

"Hold fast!" I command the other Gifted, my wind and her fire twining together. Catsper's victim screams and sheds the garment, which now crackles freely in the chill air. A tendril of smoke snakes into the air. Another.

"Fire!" someone screams, others picking up the call. "Fire! Fire!"

The rioters stop, their priorities shifting from violence to self-preservation as quickly as they'd tipped from civilization to murder. I breathe out a long, slow breath as, one by one, men leap away from flame. And from us. There is likely a better way of breaking up a riot than setting rioters on fire, but the fire works too.

"Time to leave," says Catsper, moving out of Domenic's way as the man strides to me. Dock workers with buckets and guardsmen with clubs are already replacing the rioters, and it would be best if we disappeared before questions begin. Tam has Quinn's arm draped over his shoulder and pulls the Tirik away. Bear, the overgrown little coward, comes leaping from wherever he hid during the fight and makes his rounds around the group, all wet nose and wagging tail.

"Can you walk?" Domenic's arm snakes around me recklessly, his steady body offering support to mine. There is a cut across his cheek and blood crusted on his shirt, but his eyes examine me with an intensity that pierces my chest. His hand rises halfway to my face before he gets control of it and curls his fingers into his fist instead. "Goddess, Nile. You look like hell."

"I'm all right." I swallow a wince. My body throbs, my right side a single screaming bruise. Inside me, magic vibrates like the lingering chord of a violin. Leaning on Domenic, I turn toward the fire-caller girl. She is still crouched on the pier, her once-yellow dress a mess of blood and dirt. "Who are you?" I ask.

"Kyra," she whispers as Catsper hauls her to her feet and motions us to start walking.

"Is there anyone whose business you don't stick your nose into, Kyra?" the marine demands, pulling her along behind us.

"You two know each other?" My voice is hoarse, and my mouth feels stuffed with cotton. The girl looks positively fragile with wide eyes and delicate, trembling fingers, which is about as far from Catsper's usual choice of company as one can get.

Kyra's gaze flickers to Catsper, who still has a supportive hold on her arm. "No. We just spent a night together."

Catsper snorts, and heat consumes my face.

THE ROOMS TAM and I share at the inn are strategically chosen to ease the approach and retreat routes for our respective lovers. Slipping a key into the lock, Tam now swings the back entrance open and ushers everyone inside and up the creaking staircase to the second floor. Unlike the pristine front entrance, wine stains decorate the wooden planks and a bouquet of smells ranging from stew to sweat hang in the poorly ventilated air. Another door leads directly from the back staircase into our sitting room. The lock obeys my keys with a click, and I stand back to allow the others by until Domenic takes the door from me. The change from the back staircase to the plush rug of our room is stark, the stale air changing to clean freshness tinged with a hint of salt from the sea.

My magic flickers as Kyra walks past me, waving to hers in happy greeting. This isn't normal. Nothing about my magic has been normal since Clay.

Tam settles Quinn onto a chair. "Are you all right?"

Quinn presses his lips together and nods. His left eye has swollen completely shut during our walk, and he breathes with a caution that speaks of bruised ribs. "It happened quickly. A few insults and shoves... Escalated until everyone with an opinion joined the fray."

"Why didn't you call out to us?" I press my back against the wall and slide down to sit on the floor. My magic settles to a low simmer, but the world at the corners of my vision still blurs and sharpens at disorienting intervals. I've no idea whether Kyra's presence or my body's recent encounter with the wooden pillar is the culprit.

"Besides not wishing to start a riot?" Quinn hangs his head, speaking to the floor. "If they attack me, it's a few upset hooligans swinging fists. If they attack you, it's Biron subjects assaulting Felielle royalty at best, and naming you Tirik sympathizers at worst."

"I don't think anyone's identity registered by the time the fighting started," says Catsper. His skin is flushed, anger seeping from his gaze. The marine's signature chill calm is nowhere to be seen as he wheels around to tower over Kyra. "What the hell did you think was going to happen when you stepped into the middle of a mob? A rational discussion on the philosophy of scapegoating?"

The girl flinches away from the marine, though her face flickers up to answer the challenge. "What was I supposed to do?"

Tam, who belongs to the wine-drinking school of disaster management, fishes a set of glasses and a bottle from his travel trunk. "People are getting desperate, especially in the coastal towns," he says grimly. "It was bad enough when the fighting happened out at sea. This morning, the Tirik struck land. I fear what happened on the docks is only the start. Something is happening in the Tirik Republic, something that is turning the war in their favor. And damn me if I know whether they've devised a new weapon or started pressing every able body into armed service."

Tam's words tear through me. We need the Diante, and when I fail to deliver them, the coming deaths will lie on my soul. My chin drops to my chest. I'm a sailor. Nothing more, nothing less. "We are setting sail in two weeks," I tell Catsper, my voice hollow and distant. Domenic shifts his weight. I swallow. "Did Spardic Command—"

"I'm cleared to sail with you," Catsper says, sticking his hands into his pockets.

Tam, Quinn, Domenic, and I all turn our heads toward him. Even Kyra looks over, though her gaze is more confused than incredulous.

"I was under the impression that Spardic Command said not just *no*," says Tamiath, "but *hell no*."

Catsper shrugs one shoulder, a flicker of rage touching his eyes for a mere heartbeat. "I can be very persuasive."

Kyra raises a brow, which Catsper ignores. Whatever night the two spent together must have been...memorable.

I cough quickly before my blush gives away the direction of my thoughts. Domenic and I are yet to touch that territory, with him—not me—holding the line. "We should start getting ready, then." I force my body to uncurl and straighten my back. "Two weeks is little time to prepare for a six-month adventure. Are you well enough to get home, Kyra? We can ask one of the guards to escort you."

"Actually..." Kyra swallows and looks at a spot on my cheek, just below my eyes. "The reason I was on the pier today... I was looking for you."

"Me?" My pulse stutters. Magic. Had she somehow learned of my Gift before this morning? Was it a plan to blackmail me that spurred her to seek me out, that makes her dark eyes wide now? A nightmare repeating itself. I brace myself for the inevitable threat, the one where Kyra promises to reveal my Gift if I fail to do her bidding. My voice tightens. If the girl so much as hints at exposure, I'll toss her into the bilges for six months to keep the rats company. "Why?"

Kyra frowns at me, as if she's somehow heard my thoughts and found them odd. "I'd heard you were sailing for the Diante Empire," she says in a thin voice, her teeth worrying her lip. "And I wanted to beg for employment aboard your ship."

Not a threat, an employment request. It takes me a moment to work through her words. Besides being Gifted, which Kyra might have been able to conceal if not for my magic's new trick, the girl is tiny and fragile. Her body is little suited for a sailor's labors, and she is too old to join the ship's youngsters in carrying gunpowder. Which, on further reflection, would be a horrid idea anyway. "You would like to enlist in the Felielle navy?" I say as neutrally as I can manage.

"Stars, no." Kyra blinks as if confused why anyone might desire such a thing. "I'm from Milan. It's—"

"In the far archipelago, I know." That explained the unusual accent and behavior. Until the recent earthquake temporarily made the resources of the Siaman archipelago vital, the islands there saw little to no traffic from the mainlands. It's entirely possible that before this morning, Kyra may truly never have witnessed what a mob of otherwise rational people could do when together. I motion for her to continue.

"I'd like to get back there, and no merchantmen will sail to the Siaman just now. But you are heading that way. So... I can cook, and clean and wash laundry." Her clear soprano quickens with each word. "And you would need to pay me nothing, just... just at the end, take me home. It won't be so very much out of your way. And I will work for as long as you might require. We—"

I hold up my hand. I don't need a cook or a laundress. What I need is secrecy and a bloody miracle. "The *Helix* is a fifty-four-gun man-of-war, Kyra. She isn't the kind of ship you imagine."

Kyra frowns. "I don't understand."

"What Nile means," says Catsper, crossing his arms, "is that we carry gunpowder and humans, and need you setting the ship aflame as little as we need you rummaging inside our heads." He turns toward me. "Kyra might have mentioned that, in addition to being a brilliant tactician and fire caller, she's also an empath."

Empath. *Empath.* A year ago, I'd never have believed such a thing possible. A lot of things changed in a year, me not the least of them.

"Please," Kyra says quickly, her words racing Catsper's. "I will do anything you wish. I know some physic too. I come from a family of healers. Doesn't your ship need a doctor? If you lot are going to be killing each other, you'll need someone to take care of you."

I watch her, waiting for the threat. She knows what I am, has to know after our magics mingled at that pillar. And my secret is the last arrow she has in her quiver.

Kyra closes her eyes. "Please," she whispers. "I've nowhere else to turn to."

My chest tightens. There is something to be said for a girl who protects a stranger, who respects the secrets of those she owes no loyalty to. And there is something to be said for her Gift too. The advantage of an empath when negotiating with the Diante could mean the difference between failure and success, and waves know I need the help.

I frown at Tam, whose face mirrors my own thoughts. Worry. Interest. A halting bit of trust. Domenic's face stays impassive, likely unable to mix the notion of breaking the rules to bring another Gifted aboard against the possibility that doing so may be right.

"The *Helix* has a doctor, Kyra," I say after heartbeats of silence come and pass. "But tell me about this head rummaging."

Kyra rocks back on her heels, her face suddenly guarded. "I can't read thoughts, if that's what you want."

"Can't or won't?" Catsper asks.

"Can't," Kyra snaps at him. For the first time, there is a bite to her words. She turns back to me. "And I *won't* be a spy. People's feelings are their business. Just as our Gifts are ours. If those are your terms, then I'll leave you be."

Ah, so there is the mettle that urged a powerless girl to stare down a mob. I raise my hand to calm the avalanche. "Not a spy," I offer. "And I won't ask you to inform on the crew to me. Only to advise me in negotiations with Diante officials."

Kyra cocks her head, considering my words. "Is there such a post on a ship? Would the crew not despise me if I did no work during the trip itself?"

Smart girl. I nod. "Can you read and write?"

"Yes," she says quickly. "And I speak a bit of Diante too. Milan had some trade with their merchants."

I tap my knee. Better than I thought. "Officially, you'll be a combination of my steward, clerk, and lady-in-waiting. It will mean caring for my food and cabin and clothes, and serving at any meetings I might have. You'll be privy to conversations and strategy, and by the time we meet the Diante, we should be able to work together smoothly. Does that sound fair?"

"Fire caller." Catsper enunciates the words for me.

"Gunpowder. Ship. Boom. Why do you think no merchant will take her?"

"Tirik. Winning." I spit the words right back at him. "No Diante, no survival. Her flame calling is thread thin—we can keep her away from the gunpowder." My head swivels back to Kyra. "And I imagine I need not tell you the importance of keeping your Gift a secret lest we have a mutiny on our hands?"

She nods, and I'm about to sigh with relief when an itch stirs my thoughts. I look between her and Catsper, choosing my words with care. "Are you two... I mean, is it going to be a problem that..."

"No," says Kyra.

"Yes," says Catsper at the same time.

CHAPTER 11

NILE

*K*yra, Quinn and Catsper leave the suite without looking at each other, leaving the prince, Domenic, and me behind. Tamiath surveys my face, then whistles to Bear. "Shall I let him out for you?" Tam asks me politely. "I believe Rum is outside terrorizing the servants, and Bear might enjoy cowering in the shadows while Rum works."

I touch his cheek. "Thank you."

The prince nods and kisses the top of my head with a nonchalant possessiveness. I should be grateful that is as far as the prince goes—Aaron would likely have slugged Domenic before leaving just to remind him who my friends are. Felielle men are protective by nature, but brothers are downright irritating.

Domenic steps away from the prince's path, keeping his

gaze piously on the window until the door closes. I walk over and slide the lock into place.

Domenic's shoulders shift to fill all the space before me. "Nile." My name rolls off his lips, the songlike Felielle accent clenching my chest. With us finally alone, Domenic's restraints release like a bowstring, and he has my face in his hands, gently prodding my bruised cheekbone, surveying every inch for signs of hidden injury, brushing stray locks of my red hair behind my ear. Soft, caring caresses, gentle grazes.

I snatch his wrist, lowering his hands. "I was in the same fight you were." I find Domenic's eyes, then let the energy his gaze releases into my blood rush through me. Rush through him as I lay my right hand flat on his taut abdomen. Low on his abdomen. "I'm all right, and I have better ideas on how to spend a stolen moment of privacy before we separate."

Domenic swallows, cursing beneath his breath. His body tightens as if it strains all his muscles just to keep still.

"We should talk," he starts to say, but I cut off his words with my mouth.

We've had enough talk. Enough play. Enough caresses that trace the curve of my hips but never touch the core. I want to be wanted, and we might not get another chance at such privacy for months. A year. However long my mission to the Diante Empire will take.

My hand slides to Domenic's breast, the beat of his heart thumping hard enough to pulse through my flesh. Salt and brine scent fills my nose as his coiled body springs free with a muffled groan, spinning me, pinning me greedily against the bedroom wall.

Domenic presses his lips over mine, their velvet warmth echoing through my veins. Within the confines of his arms lies a whole unexplored world, one that makes my heart stop and race anew with each shared breath. My nails dig into Domenic's shoulders, and his kiss deepens, claiming me with that predator's possessiveness.

I press my hips into him, my hand tugging at the laces of his shirt. Failing at that, I grip the fabric, pulling open the collar. The rip of tearing cloth thunders through the room, the walls suddenly too thin by half. My heart quickens. I've just *ripped* Domenic's shirt off. And it felt good. After months of occasional evenings stolen between duties, I'm done with slow gentleness.

The heat from his bared torso engulfs me. I break the kiss to run my hand over Domenic's collarbone. His chest. The tattoo snaking up his sternum. This man who stalks the quarterdeck with strict propriety and unwavering power is now mine to touch and explore. My heart thumps, this time echoing low into my body. Tingling in a way that makes me squirm against Domenic's chest.

Domenic's hand slides beneath my shirt, his fingers splaying across my scarred back.

I pull his wrist. Not off my body—*storms*, I never want to pull him off my body—but down toward the curve of my hips. Away from the ridges and valleys of ruined skin between my shoulders. He'd called my body beautiful, scars and all, but I'm hardly blind to a mirror's reflection. And I want this night, our only chance, to be perfect.

"Trust me," Domenic whispers into my temple, his hand inching back. Caressing my flesh. "I—"

"No more talking." I press my lips into his, silencing his words.

A moment, a heartbeat of hesitation, and his body responds to mine. His mouth presses back, claiming mine hungrily. His hand slides to my pants, a calloused finger caressing the waistline. Dips down toward quickly moistening thighs.

I groan my pleasure against his mouth, pressing my hips against him when he raises his face to draw breath.

Domenic curses. His hand, already at my waistline, makes short work of the laces holding my britches. Unlike my fumblings with his shirt, Domenic's motions are sure and experienced, and nothing tears as the knots loosen. Lithe, powerful fingers circle my belly button, slip lower. Lower. Slither back up.

I moan my protest at the retreat and hook my leg around Domenic's thigh. An odd movement given the state of my britches, but fortunately, Domenic solves the dilemma by clasping my waist and lifting me into the air, moving us away from the wall.

My breath hitches, my heart stalling and galloping alternately as I ride his motion and wrap my legs around his hips. We land on the bed, me on my back, my legs still wrapped about him. Domenic atop. My pants somehow brilliantly absent.

Domenic sucks in a breath and runs his hand up and down my thigh, the bulge in his own britches betraying his desire. The hand reaches beneath my shirt, cups my breast while his eyes watch my face. My eyes. I smile, and Domenic reaches to relieve me of shirt altogether.

"Don't," I breathe, my back flashing in my mind. A reflex. "This way. I want you this way."

A shudder runs through him, his muscles rock hard before they push away. Not just away from my shirt, but from me.

My soul shrinks. "What's wrong?"

Domenic sits on the bed, panting, his forearms braced against his thighs.

I rise up on my elbow, covering my naked legs with a blanket. "Why did you stop?"

"Because this is wrong," he snaps, wincing at his voice. He blows out a long breath and continues much more gently, "This isn't what your first time should be like."

My face heats. "So you know better than I what my first time should be like?"

He gets up from the bed. "I do have a bit more experience, Nile, not that this fact apparently matters."

"Storms and hail. You are this upset over my shirt? Really, Domenic?" I reach down to find my pants, feeling suddenly naked. If he doesn't want me, we shouldn't be here. I shouldn't be here.

Domenic sighs and returns to the bed, sitting on its edge. "I'm not upset over your shirt. I'm not upset at all. I want you to trust me completely when we join, and you need more time." He reaches toward me.

I pull away, moving to the opposite side of the bed. "We don't have more time."

Domenic rubs the heels of his hands over his face. "We do. That is what I was trying to tell you before..." He makes a vague motion to the bed. "Admiral Pyre held me back after you left. He wants me to go with you as the *Helix*'s second officer. He thought serving as a lieutenant under Zolan would do me good."

The world tilts, my thoughts spinning like the needle of a compass unable to find true north. We are staying together—as together as one gets on a ship with hundreds of souls and no privacy. Happy news. Joyous. Or should be. "Are you...disappointed?"

"Of course not." A lie.

I cross my arms.

Domenic's mouth thins. "I imagine I am feeling very much like you did when faced with the option of joining me on the

Raptor or staying in command of the *Eclipse*. Except you actually had a choice."

Ah. I lean away from him. My chest is tight, and I fasten my clothing with more care than required. I do understand. To give up a ship, your ship, whether she is as small as the *Eclipse* or a grand three-decker, leaves a hole inside. But our situations aren't the same. The *Eclipse* and *Raptor* are both too small for truly extended voyages like the one the *Helix* will take, and unlike me, Domenic will certainly get another command. The same Felielle navy that seeks any reason to deny me the quarterdeck is fawning over their discovery of Domenic.

Even if the vitalness of the *Helix*'s mission fails to soothe Domenic's pride, shouldn't the advantage of staying together tip the scales? I clear my throat and say the only thing I can. "It will be an honor to have you under my command."

Domenic shifts his weight, a ripple of cautious confusion touching his face. His shoulders, already spread wide, open a fraction more—his habit before issuing an unpopular order or announcing punishment, as if he is steeling himself against an inevitable, invisible assault. "Zolan's command, Nile. You heard Admiral Pyre. Your position will be honorary. Zolan will be in true command."

The spinning compass needle inside my mind comes to a stop so abrupt, I'd stumble from the recoil if I weren't sitting already. A deafening silence roars in my ears and spiders through my chest and gut. No. No, I couldn't have heard him right. Admiral Pyre I can begin to understand, but surely not Domenic, who knows me, who's seen me on the quarterdeck and standing before the enemy.

The Domenic who just this morning all but told the admiralty you couldn't be trusted.

"You were in the same briefing I was." Domenic's voice is

quiet, stoic. He isn't enjoying his words, but clearly he's not about to back down from them either. "The admiralty made its wishes known. Our duty is to execute those wishes, not contort them into ones you prefer."

I, not we. "I will be wearing a captain's epaulette, Domenic." My voice is low and even enough to match his, though my heart pounds against my ribs. "And I will endeavor to live up to them."

Domenic's fists tighten in his lap, and he forces his hands to open. "Goddess, Nile." His eyes pierce mine. "Enough. You are not qualified to command the *Helix* on a cross-continental cruise. There is no shame in it, it is just a fact."

Heat rises to my face, so strong it's a miracle the air itself doesn't kindle into flame. Not qualified to command my ship. Not qualified to decide whether I'm ready to lie with a man. Not qualified to judge whether and when the risk to my body is worth taking. I stand up and reach back to braid my hair, giving my hands something to do instead of punching a bloody wall. "Thank you for that vote of confidence, Domenic."

The bed creaks, Domenic coming to his feet as well. His chest rises and falls with deep breaths as if he's been running. "There is no voting in the navy, and even if there was, it would be the admiralty's vote to cast, not mine. And not yours either. Your scores failed to qualify you for the *Raptor*, much less the larger *Helix*. That's the truth of it, Nile. You may hold yourself so above rules and orders that you see nothing wrong even with cheating, but do not expect the admiralty to agree. Or me."

My hands fall, my pulse stalling as Domenic's words slap my face, each one stinging more and more until I'm numb. I say nothing when Domenic finishes, looks down, takes a step toward me with his arm outstretched, as if a gentle caress can trump his words.

"There is one regulation you seem to have forgotten, Mr. Dana." The voice is mine but feels foreign. Too cool. Too calm. Too final. "Intimate relations between officers in the same command is forbidden. You will be happy to know that we shall be keeping to that rule from this moment on. As for the details of how the *Helix* will be run, that is something I shall sort out with Mr. Zolan."

Domenic's eyes widen, and he rocks back on his heels as if struck with a rogue wave. "Nile—"

"Ma'am," I correct. "You are dismissed."

I hold my place until Domenic gathers his things and leaves. Then the tears come.

CHAPTER 12

KYRA

$\mathcal{K}$yra left Nile's suite through the same backdoor passage she'd entered, her mind spinning, her heart beating harder with each step she took. She'd gotten the ticket home she needed, but now, with the passage secure, the weights attached to her passage fee were chilling her blood. The princess expected Kyra to taste the Diantes' emotions on command, to thrive aboard a naval ship filled with too many souls in too little space. But emotions were tricky and as elusive as eels, often meaning something entirely unlike what they hinted at. What Nile wanted might yet prove impossible, but if the princess was willing to take the risk, Kyra was too.

"Where are your things?" Hunter—Catsper—asked, catching up to her. "You are relocating to the inn with the rest of the Felielle crew." A statement of fact not to be confused with a warm welcome. An order, perhaps? Was this man entitled to give Kyra orders? His personal opinion on the matter notwithstanding.

Making a mental note to ask Nile about Catsper's relative position, Kyra turned slowly toward him. She tasted nothing of Catsper's emotions. The last time that happened, the man had tried to slit her throat.

Stars take her, what *had* that man done to himself to lock his emotions so far down that Kyra tasted so little of them so often? People typically prioritized their feelings, letting some float closer to the surface and protecting others—but not everything and not all the time. Then again, typical people did not need to seek an abandoned ridge in the middle of a cold night before permitting themselves to feel pain.

With the fighting over, Catsper held an arm close to his side. The Spade commander must have cracked some ribs, if not broken them outright. And that was before Catsper threw himself into the middle of a brawl, taking blows as gladly as doling them out. As if he'd been seeking a beating as well as a fight.

Kyra's fingertips tingled, wanting to brush over the abused flesh and draw away the heat. The chill wouldn't knit the bones together, but it would help the swelling and pain. Then again, Kyra was certain that the man neither deserved nor wanted the pain gone. The question was *why*? If Kyra was to be Nile's steward, to take care of the princess, that duty started now. "Why did you lie to Nile about Spardic Command releasing you?"

Catsper's eyes flashed. "I didn't."

"Because you aren't a Spade anymore?" She wrapped her hands around herself. Catsper could snap her neck in two easily enough, but she didn't think he'd do it here. "What did you do that they kicked you out?"

Catsper cocked his head, thoughts racing through his eyes. Kyra's mouth filled with the too-familiar tang of hate and fury, though Catsper's calm posture gave nothing away. "Since you are so adept at scouting my private life, write your own narration. And while you are at it, fetch your own things as well."

Waking up at the inn the following morning, Kyra had to blink to orient herself. After weeks of living in a cavern, the tiny room felt skintight. The neighbor to her right was coughing again, and, judging by the smell, the servants scurrying down the hallways carried full chamber pots. It would be worse on a ship. Weeks, months, with no escape. But at least there would be a ship now. And home at the other end of its voyage.

A parcel awaited Kyra just outside her door. She opened it to find a pair of loose trousers and several shirts, along with a note from Nile about possibly finding these clothes more comfortable at sea. Kyra ran her hands over her dress. She'd washed it yesterday, and the yellow fabric was bright again, the stains nearly gone. She'd stay wearing it, if such was permitted.

Questions. Now that the princess had agreed to take her, question after question filled Kyra's mind. The merchant ship Kyra had taken from Milan to Biron had been small and disordered, nothing like the large naval vessels run by strict rules and barbaric traditions. Would she be required to wear a uniform? Pee where men could see? Would the men... Could the seamen strike her if she made a mistake?

"No," Nile told her in iron certainty an hour later, when Kyra ran into her and Bear outside the inn. Or, more accurately, when Bear found Kyra and, in his enthusiasm, toppled her into a puddle.

The princess was different than she'd been the previous night, her eyes slightly swollen and her emotion salty and jagged. "No on all counts," Nile said, her face stoic and tone considerate. "Only the officers wear a uniform. The seamen are issued clothes but may add to their kit as they wish, as may you. You will berth in a partition off my cabin and may use a private head there. As for laying hands on you, no. You are a civilian and will not be subject to discipline."

"And outside discipline?" Kyra's voice trips "Will..."

Nile stepped in front of her, cutting off her path. The princess was two years younger than Kyra, but half a head taller and strong as a man. The rumbling storm of emotion Kyra tasted from her a moment earlier disappeared behind a wall of granite certainty. "No one will lay a hand on you, Kyra," Nile said, finding her eyes. "I will not promise you a comfortable voyage, or one safe from enemy fire. But you have my word that no man on that ship will touch you."

Kyra blinked. Not at the words—she'd heard such before—but at the pledge that formed their foundation. The princess was making a promise, not just for Kyra's sake, but for her own. As if she needed to protect, thrived on it. The navy, its purpose, Nile's purpose—they were all intertwined inside her. All vital and perhaps as deep as her soul.

"Kyra?" Nile's voice became wary. "Are you head rummaging?"

"No," Kyra answered quickly, then winced. "I... Not rummaging, just speculating. I do that sometimes. Often."

Nile's brow rose. "And where does this speculation lead you?"

"Typically...into trouble."

A small chuckle. Then Nile's face changed again, back to hiding that salty, jagged glass, back to pretending those edges weren't slicing her to ribbons.

Despite the early morning hour, the streets around them buzzed with a sea town's morning chores, the men and women bundled against the foul weather. Fishing boats shoved away from shore, market tents rose; several tipsy seamen enjoying their last dregs of shore leave stumbled and sang as they pulled brightly dressed whores along.

And I've got meself my woman,
And I've got meself my ship,
And I've got meself—

"A sailor has a wife in every port," Nile told Kyra, nodding toward the seamen. "At least that's how the saying goes."

"Begging pardon, Your Highness." A boy of ten wriggled his way through the crowd, stopping before Nile to hold out an envelope. "A message for you, ma'am."

Kyra had never been important enough to have messengers combing the streets to deliver news into her hand, but Nile seemed impervious and dismissed the boy efficiently with a penny and a word of thanks. The seal cracked smoothly under the princess's thumb, the paper shaking open obediently.

Nile's jaw tightened.

"What is it?" Kyra asked.

"The *Helix* is docked in a post a day's journey south of here, and my first officer, Mr. Zolan, has apparently decided to head out there early this morning—incidentally before I might summon him to discuss the coming commission. He assures me that the ship will be prepared for my arrival in two weeks and requests that the *Helix*'s second officer, Lieutenant Domenic Dana, attend him presently to assist provisioning."

Dana. The large, broad-shouldered man who drank in

Nile's every move when he thought she wasn't looking. When the princess said Dana's name... To the world, Catsper and Nile might look similar in their matter-of-fact words, but to Kyra's empathic sense, the two were opposites. Whereas the marine tamped down his emotions so deep that even he couldn't touch them, Nile's feelings assaulted her with each breath. Not that anyone would know from speaking to the princess. "Do you practice saying things in a matter-of-fact way?" Kyra asked. "As if all pieces of information carry the same neutral weight?"

It was Nile's turn to blink. "Of course. A ship's crew takes its steadiness from their officers. On the quarterdeck, you must always be confident in your words, even if you feel anything but."

"Captain Greysik?" A boy in a midshipman's uniform rapidly changed course, setting it for Nile. "I've a message for you, ma'am."

The princess took possession of her second folded sheet of the morning just as another messenger appeared with two more.

Kyra touched Nile's wrist. If she was to be the younger woman's steward, she had a right to take care of her charge. "Have you eaten?"

The princess gave a dismissive shrug, already breaking the first of the seals. "This confirms it," she said, her eyes scanning the few lines of text. Accepting the midshipman's offer of ink and pen, the princess dashed a quick response, sealing it with a signet ring before sending the boy away. "We are Domenic-free for two weeks," she said with an attempt at a smile.

Reaching over, Kyra neatly plucked the remaining message from Nile's hands. "You shall read the rest over breakfast. If the past hour is any indication, the notes will continue coming for those weeks. Should you die of starvation, I will have no transport home."

CHAPTER 13

NILE

wo weeks. Two absurdly busy weeks. After sitting
with their thumbs up their rears for the past six
months, the Felielle Admiralty and crown suddenly have
myriad vital tasks to be attended to. I'm fitted for a new uniform,
one with a captain's epaulettes and a decorative trim worthy of
making a foreign appearance. A Diante language tutor appears
at my doorstep, his assistant pouring a stack of books in Kyra's
arms. A packet marked "Diante Sea Charts" is found to
somehow contain Eflian land maps at the same time as an
exasperated letter from Zolan states that he's discovered rot in
drinking water casks and is having everything removed and
inspected. My name is misspelled in the Lyron League's official
letter to the Diante. The letter is corrected to, this time, misspell
the name of the Diante admiral. When, the day before setting
sail, I learn that my Diante-Lyron translator has slipped from a

roof he's been thatching and broken both his legs, I finally explode with a string of curses that has several inn patrons stepping into the corridor in morbid curiosity.

"Shall I tell the translator to come along anyway, then?" Lord Vikon inquires when I stop for breath.

"No. I can manage in Diante well enough, and Admiral Addus is fluent in Lyron, thank the storm." I pinch the bridge of my nose. "Is there anything else in that stack of papers you are holding, Lord Vikon?"

The lord wisely stuffs the papers back into his bag. "No, ma'am. Just one quick question. Given my birth and our shared family ties, I thought perhaps I might do better berthing in the officers' instead of the midshipmen's—"

"Since what bloody storm are *you* coming along?"

Vikon draws himself up to his full height. "It was arranged yesterday. An invitation from Prince Tamiath himself."

Murder flashes through me, and I turn on my heel so quickly that Vikon jumps, dropping his papers. The door of my suite is still echoing when I grab Tam's shirt collar and describe my specific plan for dismembering him with a dull knife.

"I had no choice." Tam holds up his hands while Aaron, bastard that he is, grins. Tam winces. "It was all I could do to keep Vikon's father from making good on his threat against Quinn. Darius is neither powerless nor the imbecile he looks to be."

I let go, rubbing my temples as I drop into an empty chair.

"I know you hate hearing it, but a large part of the reason the Felielle navy is entertaining your position is because you are royalty." Tam's voice is apologetic but so damn reasonable that I want to yell at him all over again. "If my young wife is to enjoy the untold privileges of the Felielle royal name, then Lord Darius feels his son should as well. He wasn't demanding young

Vikon be put in charge of any vital ship's function. He knows the boy will never be an officer in anything but name, but that name is vitally important. And unfortunately, a certain common-born ex-Tirik under your command recently trampled over said name in muddy boots."

"Good fortune with all that," Aaron puts in before letting his grin fade and striding over to me. "Fair winds tomorrow, Nile," he whispers, pulling me to my feet. Our forearms clasp, foreheads touching together. "Come back safe, little brother."

"Last chance to leave *that* behind." Catsper motions to Kyra as she, Catsper, Quinn, Vikon, the two dogs, and I board the cutter that is to row us out to the *Helix*. The marine is the last to hop into the waiting boat, his gaze busy surveying the shadows for untold threats and lurking Tirik warriors.

Kyra snorts.

Ignoring them both, I slide over to make space for Bear and Rum. The latter, usually prone to sinking teeth into flesh for personal amusement, sprawls unabashedly at Kyra's feet. As if sensing my gaze, Rum lifts his head and growls.

"Get in line," I tell him. There is a whole ship out there that likely shares the dog's sentiment, from the first officer forced out of his own ship, to the Felielle seamen who think me a decoration. As for Domenic... My stomach clenches, my hand tightening on the side of the boat. "Take us about the ship," I tell the coxen. "I'd like to take a look at her before coming aboard."

Unlike my night journey to the *Aurora* nearly a year ago, today the sun is out. The fresh wind ruffles my hair, sneaking into my collar and filling my nose with the scent of salt and brine. Domenic's scent. Pushing that thought aside, I lean my chest against the breeze, offering my soul to the wind that makes my magic tingle with life and energy.

Before us, the *Helix* stands majestically on the calm seas, each sail and rope ferruled perfectly to regulation. Smaller than the three ships of Admiral Brice's squadron, which will be escorting us to the Diante territory, the *Helix* is the newest of the group. There is even a new coat of paint on her hull, which appears to have been recently scraped to clear it of minor debris and seaweed.

Vikon whistles, puffing out his chest like a rooster. His new uniform is well cut, the golden buttons gleaming in the sun. "A beauty, isn't she? Makes you long to run your hands all over her."

"I'm unsure who you speak of," says Kyra, "But might I propose that not all thoughts entering a young man's head need be shared in mixed company?"

Catsper snorts, and Vikon turns a delightful shade of burgundy.

"Mr. Vikon was referring to the *Helix*," I tell Kyra, pressing my lips together with some effort. "Ships are considered female."

Vikon clears his throat. "I'd say it should be smooth sailing so long as you stay out of Mr. Zolan's way, cousin," he tells me.

I grab Catsper's wrist before he can bury a fist in Vikon's nose, and glower at the middie, who opens his palm in a *what did I say?* inquiry that I don't bother addressing.

The boat pulls up to the *Helix*, and I rise, balancing my foot atop the seat until the hulls merge. The sea between boat and frigate boils, its whooshing song a death trap and a welcome. I draw breath, time my jump, and latch easily on to the grips. My heart starts to pound in earnest as I climb up to the deck.

The bosun's pipe starts the Felielle kingdom anthem the

instant my hat clears the rail, and Zolan's side party snaps to attention. I doff my hat until the music finishes, and Zolan strides to me, each step perfect and confident. In the sun, his tanned skin seems to sparkle and his dark eyes are hard as obsidian stone. Behind him, the Felielle seamen watch me warily. Domenic stands at rigid attention that would do a Spade proud, his eyes piercing a spot just over my head. His clean-shaven skin underscores the square cut of his jaw. The strong arms that will no longer wrap around me press rigidly against his sides. My chest clenches, and I force my eyes away.

"Welcome aboard, ma'am." Zolan's voice carries without seeming to have gotten louder. "Allow me to introduce the ship's officers and young gentlemen. This is Mr. Lorel, the sailing master." Zolan invites a man of ample girth forward to shake my hand.

Lorel gives me a small, polite bow, his handshake having something in common with a dead fish.

"Mr. Phal, the fourth in command."

Tall and reedy, the mustached lieutenant squeezes the bones of my hand together as he smiles into my face.

My hand is still screaming when Domenic approaches next, his face as even as the deepest sea. The familiar grip of his calloused hand sends lightning I shouldn't feel through my skin. "Mr. Dana. A pleasure to see you again." My voice is husky, and I turn quickly away to acknowledge the middies Zolan sends my way next.

I wonder what emotions Kyra senses just now and what she makes of the mess.

The introductions taken care of, I pull my orders from the inside pocket of my coat and read them aloud to take official charge of the frigate. At fifty-four guns, the *Helix* is by far larger than any ship I'd imagined commanding for years, and she looks as pristine on the inside as she did from the boat. The planks are sanded clean and dry, the ropes are coiled, the lookouts have their eyes trained on the sea despite the curiosities on deck.

I put my hands behind my back and mentally run through the list of pre-sail tasks. Check watch schedules, gun and sail drills, double-check the food stores before departing, especially the lemon juice we add to the seamen's grog to keep their teeth from rotting. Start—

"If it would be convenient, ma'am," Zolan says, interrupting my thoughts, "I'd like your approval for my drill schedule and your signature on the provisioning ledger. In my final inspection, I found us short three barrels of salt pork and have requested those be delivered into the hold. I've also taken the liberty of purchasing additional powder for the ship's guns to use during exercise. Unless you prefer an alternate schedule, I'd like to exercise the crews with live powder every other day, with dry runs and sail drill in between."

Right. Score: Zolan one, me zero. Well, at least I know now Zolan intends to balance my official captain's status against his unofficial directive to keep the ship under his reign—by running the ship so efficiently as to make me irrelevant. From what I've seen, the man is competent enough to pull it off. Checking my pride, I bow to the older man. "Of course, please carry on, Mr. Zolan and...thank you, sir."

Zolan turns away without acknowledging my words. "Mr. Dana, a moment of your time, sir," he calls, his voice cracking like a whip and sending the gawking crew scurrying about their business. "Front and center, if you please."

My neck tightens, though I make certain to keep my face neutral. I can count on one hand the number of times a commander called me to attention in the middle of a working quarterdeck, and the humiliation of each is still branded in my memory.

Domenic strides up, attentive but unsurprised. Not his first reprimand, then, and it's been only two weeks. What in the bloody hell has been going on? Domenic's back is straight as he finds his spot, his uniform pristine as always, with the neck buttoned all the way to the top. Only the small tap of two fingers against his thigh gives Domenic's unease away. And that, only to me. "Sir?"

"What is the status of our powder, Mr. Dana?" Zolan asks. Of an age with Tam and slightly shorter than Domenic, Zolan commands the deck without trying.

"Loaded and stored, sir." Domenic raises his chin. "I checked the bills of lading and accounted for both the allotted rations and the extra purchases."

"I am glad to hear that the *Helix*'s stores are in order." Zolan puts his hands behind his back. "However, when I want an accounting of goods, I will inquire of the purser, whose job that is. What I want to know from my second lieutenant is whether the powder in my guns has been checked and whether our Goddess-blessed ship is battle worthy."

A brush of red touches Domenic's face. He's too disciplined to move, but I catch the miniscule twitch of his shoulders, the tension in his jaw that's fighting to stay raised. To be called out before the crew, before *me*... It's what Rima used to do. And I think Domenic would rather take lashes than endure that again.

Striding forward, I place my own hands in the small of my back and speak lightly despite my racing pulse. "You will forgive the misunderstanding, Commander Zolan, but on Mr. Dana's previous assignments, there was either no purser or not one to be trusted. The lieutenant is thus accustomed to reporting on all details of ship's operations."

Zolan turns. Looks down at me from his greater height. Bows just enough to answer regulation. "Of course, ma'am," he says calmly. "But as Lieutenant Dana is no longer on those ships, I would appreciate it if he performed the duties of the *Helix*'s second lieutenant—unless, of course, you have other chores for him to attend to?"

Domenic's face reddens further.

The heartbeat of ensuing silence, interrupted only by Vikon's self-satisfied snort, is a well-aimed slap. As the ship's first officer, Zolan has full authority to make Domenic's life hell —and I can do nothing about it without stooping to the nepotistic dishonor Captain Rima has turned into an art form.

I force a dismissive smile to my lips. "Not at all, Mr. Zolan," I say, and do the one thing I can to smother the fire—remove myself from it. Taking up a spyglass, I walk to the opposite rail and turn my attention to the ocean and the three ships of Admiral Brice's squadron that stand at anchor beside us.

Zolan two, me zero. Sum wagered: Domenic.

CHAPTER 14

KYRA

*T*he ship was alive. The seamen around Kyra certainly thought of the *Helix* as a living being, and her constant creaks, moans, and shifts lent weight to the sailors' sentiments. It was dawn, and Kyra was shivering on deck because Nile was already up, fully dressed, and inspecting a crew that rolled their eyes at her back. The princess moved as if a wasp had flown into her shirt collar and now propelled her about without pause, checking the ropes securing the *Helix*'s black iron guns, offering a hand up to a fallen ship's body, ordering knots untied and redone, asking after the helmsman's family, inquiring how the gunner came to earn a scar across his cheek. Every time Kyra blinked, Nile was in a new place.

Except one, where she never ventured.

At the very front of the ship, Dana stood dressed in his full kit, as he had all last evening and the entire night. Ten hours now, by Kyra's reckoning. A punishment from Zolan for having done or not done something Kyra didn't understand.

For his part, Zolan stood at ease on the quarterdeck, sliding an occasional exasperated gaze over Nile and a more thoughtful one over Dana. The *Helix* had set sail a few hours earlier, the canvas sheets filling with such a pop that Kyra thought a gun had gone off by happenstance. Now, the *Helix* headed south toward the Diante empire, Lyron's jagged coastline slithering away on their left, the open ocean pulsating on the right, so large and vast, there was no end to it. A shifting, deadly blue cloth that went on forever.

"Clear off!"

Kyra jumped out of the way as a sailor wearing only white slop trousers and a neckerchief lumbered past with an enormous piece of wood balanced on his shoulders.

"Pardon me!" she called after him.

The man raised a free hand in acknowledgment, his rolling gait steady on the rocking deck even as a strong wave lurched the ship.

Kyra stumbled back, gasping out another apology upon colliding with a young man carrying a water pail. The sailor's eyes widened, the pail clattering to the deck and drenching Kyra's shoes. The man himself wore none, most of the seamen preferring to stay barefoot.

"Your ppp-pp pardon, mum," he stammered.

"Not at all, my fault," Kyra said quickly, seeking a better place to stand. Less than a day aboard, and she longed for anything that stayed still. The only place on the whole that seemed safe from rushing bodies was beside Zolan. Taking a breath, Kyra set course there.

"I would recommend against that." Quinn's soft voice

sounded beside Kyra, the man's open palm offering an alternative path, this one heading toward the rail.

Kyra's eyes widened.

"You will not fall overboard," he said with a small, kind smile. "Not in this sea. But I can stand beside you for a spell if you would like. I believe you will find the rail is a wiser place to take the air than the quarterdeck."

Kyra nodded, gripping the man's offered arm so hard, she likely bruised his skin. As Nile's guardsman, Quinn had no sea duties aboard the ship, and his eyes, however unobtrusively, never strayed far from the princess. "Might I ask you a few questions about the ship?" Kyra asked softly, hesitating until Quinn gave an encouraging nod. The questions sounded naïve even to her, but the issue was baffling. "Is Nile a lieutenant or captain? I've heard sailors say both."

Quinn chuckled. "Ah, the traditions of the navy. She *is* both. By rank, Nile is a lieutenant and would be junior to both Mr. Dana and Mr. Zolan outside the *Helix*. By position, Nile is in charge of this ship and is thus addressed as *captain*, just as she was on the *Eclipse*. While she is the *Helix*'s captain, she is temporarily superior to Dana and Zolan both. It is an unusual situation, but it happens."

"Are Dana and Zolan not captains as well?" asked Kyra.

"Lieutenant Dana was the captain of the *Raptor*," said Quinn. "Captain Zolan was the captain of the *Lily*. Since having two people with the title captain aboard the *Helix* would be confusing, Zolan has been temporarily demoted to commander."

Kyra brows knitted together. "And as the *Helix*'s captain, what is Nile supposed to be doing just now?"

"There is no one task," said Quinn. "A captain ensures

everyone on the ship is performing their duties, oversees discipline, makes decisions on how to handle the vessel. But truly, it is about directing the crew the way a conductor leads an orchestra. One must both keep the rhythm and know when to break stride—and ensure the musicians follow along with you when you do. "

Kyra flinched as a bit of salt spray bounced from the *Helix*'s hull and into her face. Some ways down the deck, Rum and Catsper made their appearance, the dog clearing space around himself without trying. Kyra looked back at Quinn. "And is Nile doing all that well?"

Quinn's jaw tightened, his words slow and carefully chosen. "Nile is attempting to show the orchestra players that she understands music, but she is fighting a headwind. The admiralty and Mr. Zolan have undermined her authority so deeply, the men see no reason to concern themselves with someone they feel little belongs on a man-of-war. Which—"

Kyra screamed as something very dead and bloody plopped down at her feet. Disgust tightened her throat, and the sudden copper tinge in the air made bile crawl up Kyra's gullet. Around her, men turned to see what the fuss was about, but Kyra little cared. "What... Is... That?" Kyra's breath came in gasps.

The bearer of the bloody dead thing, Rum, cocked his ear and blinked large brown eyes in confusion.

"A rat," Catsper, striding in Rum's wake, clarified cheerily. "It appears Rum took it upon himself to fetch you breakfast. Really, you should be honored."

A few paces away, the young seaman whose pail Kyra had toppled, whistled with appreciation. "It's a nice, fff-fat miller, mum. If you don't want him, c-could I..."

"It's all yours," Kyra rasped. She would not vomit. Not in front of all these men.

"Thanks, mum." The seaman knuckled his forehead and

reached for the kill, only to jump back as Rum bared his full set of glinting canines at the intruder. A snap of the dog's powerful jaws had the sailor find work in the rigging.

Catsper stuck his hands into his pockets. "I think Rum intends his present for you specifically."

Kyra's hand rose to her mouth, her dignity a forgotten asset. "Please...please get that away," she asked Catsper, who obligingly reached down and picked the dead rodent up by its tail, swinging it slightly.

"Mr. Catsper." The voice, strong and even, belonged to Zolan. Kyra hadn't noticed the commander approaching and now felt her muscles clench like a giant fist, though the first officer only made a polite leg in her direction. Coming to stand beside the marine, Zolan put his hands behind his back. "I could ask the cook to have the miller cooked for you, if you'd like. Meanwhile, my lieutenant of the marines has inquired about your expertise. I would consider it a personal favor if you might spare some time to share your thoughts with him and the others. Think on, please."

Zolan walked away as quietly as he came, and Kyra turned a questioning gaze to Quinn. "What was that?"

Quinn snorted. "That was a very well-worded 'quit fooling around on my deck and get to work.' It is typically accompanied by a suggestion that employment can be found if one has no task to occupy his time."

Catsper got a good swing on the rat's tail, whistled to the seaman who'd wanted the creature, and launched the rodent into the seaman's hands. The humor faded from the marine's eyes. "Does someone want to explain to me why a man capable of doing *that* won't extend a hand to a young captain so desperately trying to contribute to her ship?"

"To Nile and Dana both," Kyra said, nodding to the officer

still standing rigid. If Zolan was ignoring Nile, it seemed Dana could not take a breath without being punished for it.

Catsper shook his head, a slash of fury rising to the surface for a moment before he turned to walk away. "There is nothing similar about it," Catsper said over his shoulder. "Zolan will put Dana back together after he breaks him. Nile he might just leave in shattered pieces."

CHAPTER 15

NILE

$\mathcal{T}$he only task more difficult than pretending not to hear snide comments and see men sway their hips mockingly behind my back is pretending not to see that Domenic is shaking from cold and fatigue. Striding over to a gaggle of four middies tormenting trigonometry with chalk and slate, I study their work over their shoulders. Zolan had instructed the youngsters, all aged twelve to fourteen, earlier this morning and explained the numbers so well, I'm still rehearsing his approach in my mind. *Storms,* but everything about Zolan is bloody perfect. The ship's stores, the watch bills, the repairs, the discipline. Without taking more than an occasional stroll from the quarterdeck, the man leaves nothing undone.

The man leaves nothing for *me* to do.

No. That isn't true. Zolan leaves no *captain's* oversight

duties undone, but there is always work on a ship. If it comes to that, I'll scrub decks before I'll hide in surrender and leave the seamanship to the men. "Your setup is correct," I tell a freckled middie who is about to erase his whole slate in exasperation. "You simply forgot to carry a two here."

The boy erases the slate anyway and gives me an elaborate bow. "Your Highness. It is good of you to come up and take the air," he says loudly enough for Zolan, standing two paces away, to hear. "Shall I fetch you a warmer coat, though? The wind will pick up shortly, no doubt."

My blood heats, and I almost snap at a bosun's mate to bend the boy over a gun for insolence, but the satisfied tinge in Zolan's eyes halts my tongue. The boy is simply seeking Zolan's approval, and I'm not about to make a thirteen-year-old into a pawn between officers.

"Mr. Zolan," I say instead. "Might I impose on a moment of your time, sir. In private."

The man dutifully follows me down to the captain's cabin. The large space is by far the most luxurious I've ever had to myself aboard a man-of-war, with a tall window, intricately carved wooden chairs around a table large enough to accommodate ship's officers for dinner, and even a separate partition for the steward. I didn't bring enough possessions with me to outfit the space, though Kyra managed to arrange my books, journals, and weapons in a way that makes my lack of foresight appear artistically calculated. Instead of a marine sentry who would usually stand outside a captain's door, Quinn —who followed Zolan and me down the hatch—now takes the post.

I sit on a hard, high-backed chair, motioning Zolan to do likewise. Ten years my senior, Zolan fills the cabin with his steady presence, his dark eyes darting to the window to check the seas and sky even as he brings his attention to me. Unlike Domenic, whose uniform is forever perfect, Zolan's blue coat and white shirt look like quarterdeck veterans. Clean, well-fitting, creased to be comfortable. If Domenic wears his coat as the honored badge of office, Zolan's clothing is a second skin, the sea-hardened body inside it speaking for itself. "Could we speak plainly, sir?" I ask quietly.

"Of course, Your Highness," says Zolan and waits.

Right. My heart taps my ribs in a rapid staccato, but I'm empty of other ideas. Honesty it is, then. "I've never led a ship this size. Show me what to do, Zolan. Tell me how to earn the men's trust. How to earn yours." There it is. The truth laid bare. My breath stills as I await his reply.

It's quick to come and as matter-of-fact and even as Zolan's common tone. "This is a four—perhaps five—week cruise to the Diante Empire. That *might* be long enough for me to turn Mr. Dana into the officer he should be, but I don't have time to teach a girl to play captain, and I find the prospect a poor use of energy and resources. I promise that nothing is required of you on this voyage to ensure the *Helix*'s safe and efficient operation and respectfully suggest you spend the time preparing for the diplomatic aspect of your mission."

I swallow, absorbing the blow as I force my chin to stay raised, my voice to keep an even tone that matches Zolan's. "I fully understand you are capable of sailing the *Helix* without my assistance, Mr. Zolan. I'm suggesting that I can contribute to an already well-run ship to make it better, and that it would be more efficient if you shared your thoughts and expertise with me than if I continued reinventing the wheel."

"If you would like to contribute, then keep your steward and preferably yourself scarce on deck. I've a ship full of young men, and the presence of pretty young women is bound to create discipline problems. Whether they direct ungentlemanly remarks toward the two of you or start fighting amongst each other, the result is the same—floggings that do not need to happen. If you truly wish to help, Your Highness, that is the greatest service you can offer."

"SHOULD I STAY BELOWDECKS, THEN?" Kyra asks that evening when I tell her, Catsper, and Quinn of my conversation with the first officer over a shared late-night supper. Outside the window, the ships of Admiral Brice's squadron have hung their lanterns, which sway like fireflies over the darkness of the ocean.

"Absolutely," Catsper replies immediately, swallowing a piece of stewed meat as if he hasn't seen food in days.

I kick him. "No," I tell Kyra, tasting my own salty meal. Unlike the marine, I feel the need to chew before swallowing. "The men can find it within themselves to think with their brains instead of their breeches. If they do not, they will answer to me long before Zolan gets his hands on them."

Kyra's lips press together, and she sets a silver teaspoon spinning like a top on the table. "I don't like Zolan," she says quietly, her hand closing around a mug of tea. The stir of my magic tells me that Kyra is heating up the liquid even before the small bubbles of boiling water rush to the tea's surface. "He is too handsome for his own good. Handsome men are used to getting their way." Kyra pushes the now-steaming tea into my hands.

I'm poised to flinch away but find the mug itself only lukewarm.

"I focus the heat on a point well away from my hands. Keeps me from getting burned," Kyra says, her gaze on the still-spinning silver spoon. "Forgive my ignorance, but who is in charge of the ship now? Is it Nile or Mr. Zolan?"

I hesitate, taking a careful sip of tea to buy myself time.

"Nile is," Quinn steps in to answer, his voice confident. "She is the *Helix*'s captain, and Zolan will follow direct orders or risk being charged with mutiny."

Kyra stops her spoon and stares at me. "Then why in the stars' name do you listen to the bastard at all?"

I give Quinn a sidelong look. The naval structure is difficult to explain when it functions as intended and even more complex in this perversion. "Quinn is right—Zolan can't negate my power to give orders, but he can and does make those orders utterly irrelevant. Decisions a first officer would typically consult with the captain on—from setting sail to addressing conflicts within the crew—Zolan resolves before I even know enough to weigh in on. The small things left for me to do are, in the grand course of things, irrelevant."

Except one. Domenic. And I can't interfere with that. My stomach clenches, and it's a fight to keep my face and hands still. Domenic is the one who wanted to serve under Zolan, who thinks Zolan is the storms' gift to mankind. Domenic made his own bed, and there isn't room for me in it. Even if it's now filled with nails and nettle that he doesn't deserve.

Kyra's dark eyes pierce me. I've not told her about my relationship with Tam and Domenic, but I wonder whether she hasn't learned more than I think from sharing our company these weeks. Kyra's voice shifts from curiosity to instruction. "So order Zolan to stop deciding things without you."

I blow out a long breath, reminding myself that Kyra can't actually read my thoughts. We were talking about the crew; the question easily follows that conversation. "Zolan has the crew and ship tuned as perfectly as a violin," I say firmly. "I'm not going to break the *Helix* for the sake of my pride. I'll overrule Zolan if I feel the ship or its mission are in danger, but short of that, I'll follow the old-fashioned route—show the crew I'm hardworking and competent and worthy of their trust."

"Because that has worked so well for the past three days." Catsper stretches like a cat, pushing away his long-empty bowl. "If you are so intent on showing someone your skill, how about showing me whether you remember which end of a blade is the sharp one?" He glances over at Kyra. "Wouldn't hurt you to join either. With a year or two of training, you might be able to fight off a four-year-old child without help."

Kyra ignores him, and I sigh, shaking my head. I wish I could take the time to spar, but there are too many things to be done—whether Zolan thinks I need to do them or not.

THE WIND IS with us the following day, filling the sails and chasing clouds across the sky. I'm on my way to deck, walking past the officer's gun room—the one place on the ship where tradition prohibits a captain from entering without invitation—when Zolan's voice breaches the closed door and stops me in my tracks.

"Mr. Dana." The first officer does not sound happy. Again.

I stop, locating a problem with my boot buckles that must be attended to immediately. Yes, tradition also frowns on eavesdropping, but I'm not quite that pious. On the other side of the thin bulkhead, a chair scrapes as if being moved to let someone stand.

"Sir?" Domenic's tightly reined voice betrays no emotion.

"Return to deck and run the gun drill *again*," says Zolan. "Use the midshipmen. If you can't manage to get a basic broadside fired within a respectable time frame, you might need to reconsider your career choice."

Storms. Zolan has been tormenting that drill for three of the four days we've been at sea, and the crew's progress has already exceeded reasonable expectations. I'm in full support of striving to do better still, but surely, berating an officer for failing to deliver a miracle takes things too far. Especially after said officer had been made to stand watch all night again for giving too many orders when supervising the *Helix*'s change of tack.

"Aye, sir," Domenic answers, the deck creaking under a heavy step. "Rerun the gun drill."

"And Mr. Dana..." Zolan adds, the creaking stopping at once. "Prior to your arrival, the greater majority of this crew was able to wipe their own asses without step-by-step instructions. I would be obliged if they returned to that state."

"Aye, sir." In my mind, I see Domenic's tight shoulders, two fingers of one hand tapping against his thigh.

I wait for the creaking to start again, posing myself for a quick retreat, but silence reigns instead. And then the words that never, ever lead to good things.

"Permission to speak freely?" Domenic asks.

My stomach tightens. *Throw him a line, Zolan,* I beg silently. *Tell him* no.

"By all means," says Zolan.

Domenic's words are so low, I can barely hear them. "Ms. Greysik *is* the *Helix*'s captain. And should be treated with the courtesy due that rank."

I freeze, my heart leaping into a confused gallop. Then the boards creak again, and I'm out of the pass-through before the gun room door swings open.

CHAPTER 16

NILE

*D*omenic's words to Zolan notwithstanding, the following week passes in the same tone as the first days had. We are ten days into the cruise when a rolling beat of a drum echoes through the *Helix*, calling the ship to battle stations. For a moment, I think the call is a surprise drill of Zolan's conjuring but it is midday, close to the end of the crew's meal, and Zolan is too good an officer to interrupt the hands' sacred time without need. I check my impulse to sprint up to the deck, each slow step an effort of will as my body screams for me to hurry, to see for myself what's happened. All around, the pounding of running feet vibrates the ship around me and bosun's mates' voices call silence.

A figure streaks by me, heading in the wrong direction. I grab its wrist, spinning with the force of the momentum until I find myself staring at Lord Vikon's pale face.

"What is it?" I ask, letting go of the boy's sleeve.

"Mr. Dana sent me to, uh, get his pistols." Vikon trips over the words.

"Carry on, Mr. Vikon," I say, letting go. "With some dignity, please."

By the time I finally come up to deck, the crews already stand beside their guns, the netting stretches overhead to protect from falling debris, and the wooden deck planks are covered in sand for traction. One of the powder monkey boys is strategically laying out piles of rags and sticks to be used for tourniquets.

On the quarterdeck, Domenic is instructing a middie, who nods and rushes off to lay out signal flags. Zolan, also already at his station, turns and, for once, condescends to address me directly. "I have ordered the ship to quarters, ma'am," the first officer says with impeccable calm that is likely meant to soothe me along with the crew. "It appears the Tirik Republic wishes to amuse us today."

It is a good day for a battle, if there is such a thing. The skies are clear, the seas stretch calmly in all directions, and the wind is strong enough for maneuvering the ship without being a hazard. Of course, the enemy will enjoy the same advantage, which is the great equalizer that is the ocean. I call for a glass. There is no land in sight, just the *Helix*'s three sister ships and whatever vessels the Tirik Republic brought to the game.

"Three Tirik vessels off starboard, ma'am," Domenic tells me, the first words to me in weeks. Words that Zolan should be saying now. "All with approximately twenty guns apiece."

"We'll handle them easily," Zolan drawls, jerking his chin toward the companionway. "Take charge of the lower gun deck, Mr. Dana."

Instead of watching Domenic stride away, I accept the delivered spyglass from a middie and examine the horizon. Three, just as Domenic said. Approaching at full sail, though, faster than the Republic ships usually move. "Does it not strike you as odd that the Tirik would continue heading toward us given our greater number, Mr. Zolan?" I ask, focusing on the foremost ship.

Silence answers. I look up to find that Zolan is no longer beside me, but rather reviewing the signal midshipman's work. Fine. I return to study the coming ships, which are indeed approaching our much heavier force. As I watch, the two wing vessels break off, spreading out from their brethren as if to encircle us. Sailing at the back of our diamond formation, I suddenly find my *Helix* too close to the other friendly ships for comfort, our great guns too likely to hit one of our own number should battle break out.

"Helm," I call out, my voice ringing clearly over the hushed deck. "Bring us three points starboard."

The seaman at the helm begins to spin the wheel, only to have Zolan place a halting hand on the spokes. "Shall I signal the admiral with our intended target location, ma'am?" he asks with deceptive calm.

I curse myself, my face heating. Fighting as part of a unit under an admiral's command is not something I've done before. I've been a junior lieutenant on Captain Fey's ship, but even then, most of the *Faithful*'s orders brought us into solo action or missions. To fight under an admiral's flag meant yielding the larger decisions to a central commander—and that squarely includes maneuvering my own frigate into a different position until the admiral's flag commands it.

My face heats. Too late now. "Yes," I say, recovering much

too late. "Please inform the flag that I wish to maneuver for the weather gage."

Zolan purses his lips and nods to the middie, who immediately sends the signals up the mast. A few breaths later, another set of flags rises to the mast of the admiral's ship. *Denied, Helix. Keep formation.*

Right. Cursing myself, I instruct helm to hold our present station and, after counting to a slow hundred for dignity's sake, head for the hatch. Unless the Tirik sprout wings, nothing will be happening in the next quarter hour, and there is something I need to do before the killing starts.

After the sunbathed quarterdeck, my eyes struggle to adjust to the gun deck gloom. Just above the waterline and a hundred forty feet long, the gun deck hosts twenty-six of the *Helix*'s fifty-four guns, with thirteen of the great beasts posted on each side. The *Helix*'s heaviest guns, these black beauties will launch twenty-four-pound shot up to a mile if they fire well. The sailors stand in teams beside the weapons, the more experienced hands reminding the newer ones to tie kerchiefs around their ears to protect from the coming din. The middies scurry about, trying to make themselves look busy despite there being nothing to do just yet.

My appearance is marked with unenthusiastically knuckled foreheads and tugged forelocks, which I acknowledge with a curt nod, my attention suddenly and wholly on the broad-shouldered officer turning toward me.

The one who'd thrown me to the wolves at the admiralty, whose rise in rank came with a redoubled devotion to rules—a devotion common to those whom the rules benefit. The one who, behind closed doors, stood up for me before the most powerful man on the ship. My mouth is dry as Domenic steps toward me, my heart racing my mind for words.

With his height, Domenic has to duck beneath the low overhead beams, his movements smooth and practiced, as if his body remembers where the beams are and needs no reminders from his eyes. Those are steadily on me.

Stepping back into an empty corner, as much privacy as the gun deck allows, I put my hands behind my back. Not for formality's sake, but because I don't know what else to do with them. Domenic braces his arms on the overhead beams, his body blocking the rays of light sneaking through the open gunports. His salt-and-brine scent fills my senses, making the ship spin around me.

"Hello," I whisper. Three weeks since our last conversation, the one that ended *us*. It feels like three years.

He nods. Domenic was always better than me at hiding himself from the world. He had to be, to survive beneath Rima's rule. Just now, though, I wish he was a little less skilled at it. "Ma'am." His voice is low and musical.

Suddenly, no words come. *Storms*, I'm ridiculous. "I wanted to see if you were all right."

Domenic's jaw tenses. "Aye, ma'am."

My nails dig into my skin. We have so little time. None at all for games and formality. "You are a good seaman, Domenic," I say quickly. "And I don't want to let Zolan convince you otherwise. Tell me how to help."

Domenic's face lowers, and I don't know whether the darkness there comes from shadow or something else. He says something too low for me to hear, and when I prod—

"I said," Domenic's voice snaps, "that I don't need your pity."

I recoil. "Pity?"

"You think I can't endure a few hours without sleep?" Domenic's nostrils flare. "That I want the *Helix*'s great captain to step in and protect me from my commanding officer?"

The words hit me like ice water, stinging even after Domenic clamps his mouth shut. I should never have come here, should have known he'd little welcome my company after I pushed him out of my life at Port Mead. To Domenic, the value of being on the *Helix*—the only silver lining to the loss of his beloved *Raptor*—lies solely with serving under Zolan, not me. Even when Zolan treats him like a dog who'd messed the rug.

Thinking otherwise, based on nothing but a short phrase overheard out of context, might be the stupidest step I've taken yet.

"No, you are quite correct." My voice is tight, leashed as tightly as my magic. "Please carry on."

Domenic opens his mouth, but shuts it without speaking and silently touches his hat.

Returning to deck, I stroll to the rail to watch the ships and waves and skies. I do everything except feel. Deep in my blood, my magic blinks awake and pulls on its leash. *Storms*, but I wish I could let it out just now. Let it destroy something. Anything. Beyond the confines of our ship, the Tirik vessels continue their approach, as if ignorant of their inferior size and weight. As they get closer, the ships fan out into the familiar line of battle formation, readying to stand broadside to broadside with our small fleet. It's ludicrous. Suicidal. The small boat crew that martyred themselves at Port Mead at least took a chunk of their enemy out with them, but these ships will never get close enough to do real damage before we sink them.

The Tirik Republic has always been free with forcing its people into harm's way, usually by means of killing the families of officers they deem disloyal. That's kept plenty of Tirik captains from prudent surrender, but this... It's *proactive* stupidity. If this is the Tirik Republic's new doctrine, it's downright frightening. And sad.

After twenty minutes of tense silence, signals finally run up the admiral's mast. I've memorized the code and don't need to wait for the signals middie to read the flags from his code book. "Open the gunport, Mr. Zolan," I say formally. "But hold your fire until the signal from the flag."

"Aye aye, open ports but hold fire," Zolan says, relaying Admiral Brice's orders to the gun crews, who'd heard them perfectly well the first time. The repetition of orders down the chain of command is a tradition on naval ships, and at least Zolan and I can agree on that.

"Mr. Quinn," I call, bringing the ex-Tirik captain to my side for an uncomfortable conversation. The one single hard line of his agreement to defect and serve under my command was a promise never to be required to attack his former countrymen directly, never to have his knowledge employed against the people he called friends. With him and Catsper aboard in the capacity of personal guardsmen instead of naval sailors and marines, their official station during battle is as messengers— though there is no one aboard who imagines for a heartbeat that the Spade will be anywhere but in the thick of the fighting. Quinn, on the other hand...

Quinn's lips press into a hard line as he steps up beside me, and I try to phrase my question so as to respect the agreement between us. "If the Tirik were to order several captains on a suicide mission," I say carefully, "is there any way one might go about minimizing the lives lost on both sides?"

Quinn frowns, squints at the approaching ships, returns his attention to me. "Might I make use of your glass, ma'am?"

I hand him the spyglass and watch as Quinn hops easily

into the rigging, hooking an arm though the ratlines while he examines the approaching vessels from a better position. He returns a minute later, his shoulders tight as he meets my gaze. "Destroy those ships," Quinn says quietly. "Now."

CHAPTER 17

NILE

"*W*hat?" Of all the things for Quinn to suggest, slaughter is low on my list of expectations. "The Tirik—"

"Those are not Tirik ships," Quinn says. "Destroy them, before they get any closer, Nile."

The enemy ships break from the traditional broadside-to-broadside firing line and change tack to encircle us instead, their masts and sails straining. For all their speed and maneuverability, though, they are still small fish to go up against even the *Helix*, much less Admiral Brice's *Rose*, *Violet*, and *Thorn*—the latter of which has three decks of guns. "Brice must give them a chance to surrender, whoever they are," I say to Quinn. "We are a naval ship, not a pirate one."

In echo of my words, *Rose* and *Violet*—the two Felielle ships on the flanks of Admiral Brice's line—fire shots across the bows of the respective vessels trying to outflank us.

Quinn's jaw is tight. "Trust me. This isn't time for moral superiority. I will explain when there is time."

"I'm not going to become the very people we are fighting to protect our kingdom from based on *trust me*. You need to give me more than that, Quinn," I snap. "What are those ships going to do?"

"I don't know," Quinn snaps back, his brows pulled in a tight knot. "I'd tell you if I did. But whatever it is, you little wish to be on the receiving end of it."

My stomach clenches. My gut says to trust Quinn, but there is little I can do. I'm not ready to commit murder on a gut feeling, and even if I was, we are too far away to land our shot. "Mr. Zolan," I call over the deck. "Have the gun crews aim our entire broadside at the Tirik forty-two gunner who is vying to square off against the *Helix*. Track her full approach, but hold your fire." It isn't much, but it's something.

Zolan turns his head, his eyes dripping contempt as he echoes my order. Tracking a moving ship that appears to pose little threat will put a strain on the crews, and my demand must seem frivolous. A nervous captain making busywork, needlessly fatiguing the hands before a battle.

I pull my shoulders back. Zolan is welcome to his contempt. So are the others. So long as the crew stays alive, they are welcome to curse me to as deep a hell as they wish just now.

Ignoring the warning shots, the Tirik close and flank the Felielle line. The agile forty-two gunner who's marked the *Helix* as her target deftly skirts around *Violet*, establishing a clear path from its broadside to us. The other two Tirik ships put themselves in similar positions against the *Rose* and *Thorn*, like vicious little dogs yapping at a pack of mastiffs, unaware of their size and might.

Quinn's hands tighten on the rail, my own body tensing in reflex. "That forty-two is quicker than she should be," Quinn mutters. "Don't you think?"

I nod. I'd marked as much on their approach, to consider later. At this point, the ship's speed will be of consequence only if one of us flees and the other gives chase. Which seems unlikely.

"Breathe easy, lads," Zolan says from his place beside me. "That little frigate is too far to do us damage even if she were to land a shot. My only regret is that our escorts will blow her to splinters before we have a chance to exercise our guns."

As if in answer, a belch suddenly echoes from the Tirik guns.

Sprays of water rise from the ocean where iron balls fall short of their target, despite the Tirik's high aim to mitigate the distance. At the end, only one shot of the dozens fired even reaches a ship, plopping harmlessly onto Violet's deck. The frigate doesn't so much as buck from the impact.

She doesn't return fire either. Not until her fire would be effective.

"Might the Tirik be engaging with us for show?" I ask Quinn. "Demonstrating to the Republic Admiralty that they attacked the enemy as directed, without actually sacrificing their crews for no chance at victory?"

Before Quinn can respond, the Tirik forty-two reloads and fires at the Helix a second time, the shot flying just as high as before.

Quinn and I exchange glances and even Zolan frowns. Poor tactics, forced engagements, and occasional mistakes are one thing, but this pattern of apparent errors is smelling too much like cheese in a mousetrap.

My lips press into a line, my attention on the Tirik airborne broadside. Taking fire is never *good*, but these high-lobbed volleys should stand no chance of harming us where it truly counts, below the waterline. This time, one of the balls manages to breach the distance between us, landing on the *Helix*'s foc'sle with a dull anticlimactic thud, like a load of cow dung flung from the heavens.

Lieutenant Phal nudges the fallen shot toward the rail, ushering it overboard before it can roll over and crush a foot or hand. Nine pounds of lead can cause mischief even without great momentum, and—

The ball explodes, taking Phal's polished boot with it—both the boom of the blast and Phal's scream breaking the deck's silence a fraction of a second later. A cloud of shrapnel and an odd mist rise into the air, striking Phal's face as he bends over his mangled leg.

My heart thumps once, watching with a trained detachment even as my mind races to understand. Iron balls should crush, strike, bludgeon—they shouldn't explode. They.... My thoughts halt altogether as Phal's hands suddenly jerk from his leg to his throat, his fingers clawing his neck. A heartbeat later, the man falls retching to the deck, blood leaking from his nose, his ears, his eyes.

The deck and everyone on it seem to move in slow motion. A delay between reality and reaction. The men standing beside Phal double over, clutching at their throats, scratching their faces, writhing on the deck soaked in their own bloody vomit and piss. *Storms*, gruesome as shrapnel is, the gore from the metal debris is nothing compared to the horror of bodies gushing, drowning in their own fluids, gasping for air that won't come.

CHAPTER 18

KYRA

*K*yra hunkered at her assigned battle station, a dark, tiny hold deep inside the ship's bowels where she, Rum, and Bear were tasked with not getting dead. The air hung thick and stale, making her take shallow, halting breaths lest she inhale lungsful of mold and rat droppings. Blackness swallowed her fingertips. Above her, the *Helix* vibrated with the pounding of bare feet and carpenter's tools and occasional bellowed orders. And then silence. Silence and darkness and the never-ceasing *scrape scrape scrape* of the rats.

No one had explained anything. Kyra knew that this wasn't the usual daily drill only because the timing was wrong and there was an anxiety saturating the ship. And because it wasn't ending. Not when she counted to a thousand, or two thousand, or ten thousand. The walls of the hold closed in around her, her heart pounding against nothingness. Each breath was too small, the air threatening to end altogether while the ship hummed with tension.

The ship jerked as if struck by a storm. Or enemy shot.

Kyra's heart lurched into her stomach, and she screamed into the darkness. One of the dogs whined pitifully. Kyra's mouth dried, her fingers trembling as they wrapped around her head. Someone was firing at the ship. Iron balls designed to fracture hulls and masts and bodies. Would she even know that the ship was sinking before the water blocked the door of her hold? Would she drown quickly, or would she still be here, pounding on the planks of a ship that had sunk? Would she be dead and not know it for minutes? Hours? A day?

She rose, a hand on the bulkhead as the ship bucked again. Rum growled his displeasure, but she couldn't stay here in the darkness, helpless as the world exploded around her. She couldn't face death from inside a coffin.

Heart pounding loud as thunder, she pushed open the door of the hold. It creaked, but there was no one around to stop her, to usher Kyra back into hiding. The seamen were higher up, at their stations. Doing something to protect themselves. Breathing real air.

Trailing her hand along the bulkhead, Kyra felt her way to a ladder and climbed up through one hatch. Then through another. The air freshened and cooled the higher she went, light bathing her skin. She would go to the deck and stay out of the way. She would face death with the wind on her face and the sun and...

Screaming shattered the air as she reached the top of the companionway ladder, gagging on the blizzard of fear and pain, fury and excitement leaking from the crew. Men rolled on deck, clawing at bloody faces as their comrades moved to fill in the voids and man the great guns. By the rail, Catsper stood with his musket aimed at the enemy. The marine's hair whipped behind him, and his shoulders were open as if inviting enemy shot. Daring it to strike flesh.

Nile. Pulling her gaze away from Catsper, Kyra visually swept the deck, trying to find the princess amidst the carnage. Before she could, a misshapen iron ball plopped onto the deck several paces from Kyra's companionway ladder. There was a crunching sound inside, like the fracturing of a clay pot. Kyra's breath, which had gone still with the shot's arrival, returned. Thanking the stars for the defective projectile, Kyra took a step forward.

"No!" Catsper hollered, launching himself at her across the deck. The marine's shoulder hit Kyra's face, knocking her up and back and—Kyra screamed as she fell backward into the hole of the companionway ladder while another explosion echoed above. Her hands flailed, her left wrist screaming as it tried and failed to brace her body against the impact. The crack of wood against Kyra's back and shoulders and skull thudded through her body. Another weight fell atop her, heavy and hard as the planks beneath.

The weight lifted, coming to its legs with a feline grace.

Kyra fought for lost breath, but Catsper grabbed her arms, jerking her to her feet. Pain shot through her wrist and elbow.

"Move!" Catsper had her by the back of her dress, forcing her ahead of him. His grip stayed on her dress, shoving forward faster than her feet were willing to move. Her head pounded, echoing pain and noise inside her skull.

A second ladder. Kyra balked, digging her weight into the deck. She wasn't going down into a coffin. Not again. Not ever.

This time, the marine didn't bother with orders. His arm wrapped her waist, lifting her as if she weighed nothing at all.

She landed a kick against his shin as he cleared the ladder to the deck below and finally shoved her away.

"Are you suicidal?" Catsper growled.

Kyra was on her hands and knees, grasping for purchase in the gloom. "Are you homicidal?" she barked back. The illumination coming from the hatch was too weak to be of use, but Kyra thought she saw outlines of water casks and salt pork barrels. The air was stale with rat dung and mildew.

A click and a lantern sputtered to life.

"At the moment, very much so." In the haze, Catsper's chiseled form loomed over Kyra. His hair, streaked with either dirt or blood, was soaked with sweat, and his eyes flashed with a bitter-tasting fury. Catsper's hands opened and clenched at his sides as if it took all his willpower to keep from striking. "What the bloody hell were you thinking going on deck in the middle of action? Were you going to *feel* the enemy away? Or ask them to please stop and have a spot of tea instead?"

She scooted away from him. Catsper occupied the one bit of light, the one path between her and the ladder. His anger, his *fear*, barreled into her. Now. Of course it would be now that she'd feel him. The ship lurched, tossing Kyra like a sack of debris. This was her coffin all over again. Stale air and wild wind. No windows. No doors. Not enough air. Not enough light.

The magic inside her whimpered, absorbing Kyra's terror, the need to escape this place. Kyra's head pounded, and she reached out blindly, searching for hand- and footholds. She wanted to get up. To steady herself. To run.

Kyra's magic reached out as well.

The hanging lantern burst into flames, the tongues of fire reaching toward Kyra like snakes. Her magic pulsed, her blood alight with sudden life. *Stars.* Kyra's stomach cinched down on itself. She'd done this, set off a fire within a ship's sensitive belly. Just as the merchants had feared she would. She was as dangerous as the Tirik pelting the deck with iron shot.

Catsper swore, throwing his coat to smother the freed fire.

Kyra opened her mouth to apologize and thought better of it. There was nothing to say that would make the slip of magic anything but atrocious, and she doubted she could get any coherent words past her numb lips anyway. Her heart stuttered as the hold descended into darkness once more and the marine stepped toward her.

He was going to hurt her. Punish her for coming to deck, for making him leave the battle, for setting the lantern ablaze. Over the racing thud of her pulse, Kyra heard the boards creak beneath Catsper's boots. She pressed her injured arm protectively to her chest and braced herself.

Catsper's earthy scent filled Kyra's nose. Earth and copper. There was blood on him. His or someone else's.

"Kyra." Catsper's voice brushed her cheek.

She flinched.

"Kyra," Catsper said again, his voice low and even. "Would you consider burning the ship down later? It is a very long swim to shore just now."

She blinked into the darkness as if her eyes could adjust to see through Catsper's game. All she saw was the outline of a crouching figure. So very big and close. A breath's space away. A tendril of darkness reached for her. There. His hand. A small gasp escaped her, but she bit her lip to stifle the noise and raised her chin.

The darkness stopped. "Are you in danger of setting anything else alight right now?" the marine asked.

Kyra considered the question. Her magic simmered in her blood, anxiety and fear spurring it on in wild, unexpected bursts. Now that she was paying attention to it, however, she likely could ensure no further flames... She didn't think the marine would like the sound of "likely."

"I don't know," said Kyra. It was a struggle to keep her voice from shaking. "So long as flame doesn't already exist, my Gift has nothing to divert toward me. I can kindle *new* flame when I touch something, but that's an active process."

"So long as you aren't touching the hull, you won't turn it into a torch—correct?" Catsper asked. He wanted everything in tight, neat parcels. Direct answers to questions that weren't simple at all.

Kyra swallowed. "Yes," she said. It was close to the truth, but it didn't make them as safe as the marine would think. She would always be touching *something*.

Catsper moved faster than she could breathe. One moment she was crouching on the deck, her fingers spread on the wood— and the next he had her trapped against him, her back against his chest, his arms iron bands around hers and her feet dangling off the deck.

Kyra screamed.

"Oh for hell's sake." Catsper put his mouth close to her ear. "I'm not going to harm you if I can help it. But you aren't going to destroy this ship either. Understood?"

Kyra nodded quickly. "Yes. Understood. Let me go."

He snorted. "Not a chance." Without loosening his hold, Catsper lowered the two of them to the deck, Kyra's body tucked into his the entire time, no part of her free to touch anything but him. He settled finally with her in his lap, her arms pinned beneath his own. "Get comfortable," he said with that eerie even calm. "I'm not letting any part of you touch the *Helix* until I'm certain I won't be roasting my dinner on the embers of the ship's hull."

Kyra heard the words distantly, dull syllables barely audible above the roaring hold of a man's hands pinning her wrists in the darkness. Her body jerked. It knew that pressure constricting her muscles and tendons, knew what would come next too; thrashing hands pinned to the dirt, knuckles scraping stones, a weight so heavy that it was hard to breathe, crushing her chest. A familiar voice demanding compliance, ordering her to stop struggling before she made things worse. Before she made things hurt.

"Stop fighting," a very real voice said into her ear. Catsper. "You won't win."

Kyra didn't care. She wouldn't stay here either.

Kyra's arms were trapped, crossed over her chest, her left wrist throbbing with pain. But her right... Kyra opened her palm slowly, twisting and working the fingers into position over the marine's round bicep. Her magic shivered in joyful understanding, already savoring its coming freedom.

It took little heat to burn flesh at close quarters. The key was to ensure that only the marine's skin blistered and not her own—just as when she lit the tip of a stick without burning her own hand. Loosening the reins on her Gift, Kyra gathered the marine's own heat and focused it on a single point deep inside his bicep.

Behind her, Catsper's chest still rose and fell in a steady rhythm, his warmth seeping through his shirt into her back. That would change soon enough. He'd feel the cold first, a chill as his body heat shifted to answer her Gift's call. Then the heat inside the belly of his muscle. Then the pain.

Five seconds. Ten. Twelve.

Catsper tensed. Tensed but remained still, his grip unyielding. Even when a soft hiss escaped his lips. "I was wondering how long it would take you to do that," he said through clenched teeth. "I'm still not letting you go, in case you were wondering."

Kyra swallowed. "It will get worse. In case *you* were wondering."

"Better me than the ship." Catsper's heart beat hard enough now that Kyra felt it through her back, his inhalations slow and measured. *Stars,* his pain tolerance...

His pain tolerance. Not hers. Catsper had done nothing beyond what he'd said he would—kept her insulated from the *Helix*'s planking. Kyra swallowed, her thoughts sliding like pieces of a strange puzzle. If what Catsper claimed he wanted— to keep the ship safe—were true, Kyra should be tasting his anger now. Fury at her resistance, at her unwarranted assault.

Yet there was no fury. Only a bizarre mix of concern and pain echoed off him, lathered in a thin layer of gratitude. Who the man was thanking just now, and for what, remained a mystery.

"Are you... Do you enjoy pain?" she blurted, reining in her magic. Some people did. Perhaps...

A chuckle vibrated Catsper's chest. "No."

"You seek it out often enough." The cold night on the stones. The beating at the commander's hands. The stance at the ship's rail, all but daring the enemy to fire into his flesh. What he'd done just now. No, he wasn't *enjoying* it, but he was seeking it. Was grateful for it.

"What did you imagine I was going to do?" Catsper asked, all amusement gone from his voice. "When I grabbed you, what did you think would happen? And why?"

Kyra shook off the question. The general answer was obvious, the specific none of the marine's business. His reaction, on the other hand... "You want to atone," she whispered, more to herself then to him. "You did something, and you want absolution."

His emotions disappeared from her with a deafening explosion of silence. "I could teach you to defend yourself."

"Tell me what you did," said Kyra.

Catsper's arms, wrapped tightly around Kyra's body a moment earlier, loosened, dumping her unceremoniously on the deck. "You want to burn down the bloody ship?" Catsper said with eerie calm as he rose to his feet. "Get your head blown off by the Tirik? Do it."

Catsper's foot was already on the ladder when Kyra found her voice again. "I'm right, aren't I?" she called into the darkness.

"No." He started to climb. His final words, said so softly that Kyra was unsure she was meant to hear them at all, glided down the hatch. "There is no absolution for what I did."

CHAPTER 19

NILE

*A*nother iron-that-isn't-iron lands on our decks, this one condescending to explode on impact. More shrapnel and powder flies into the air. Zolan shouts for men to cover their faces, but neckerchiefs aren't enough. Nothing we have is enough.

Except me.

I fling my magic loose to the wind, the swooping gale racing through me so hard that I'm knocked backward against the mainmast. We can't protect eyes and flesh from the powder, but perhaps with enough air current, I can sweep the toxin into the sea and knock the incoming shot off its course. Not a small, controlled breeze, not even the tight burst of gale I called to move the *Eclipse* through the gunnery games—no, none of these will do. This wind has to cover one hundred forty feet of deck, blowing at once from port to starboard with an upward and outward trajectory, or else I'll be spreading the powder over the *Helix*'s own decks.

No, *storms and hail*. A direct port to starboard wind of that scale will capsize us outright. At a slight angle, then. Against the natural winds already blowing lengthwise along the ship. The absurdity of my calculation would make me laugh bitterly if I had the breath for it. I've unleashed a wild beast from a cage, and now want to neatly herd it down a convenient trail.

A twelve-year-old middie falls to his knees, and I'm done counting angles, fretting over my control. The boy doesn't have time for hesitation.

My arms wrap around my chest, uselessly trying to soothe my burning lungs as the winds howl through me. My heart pounds, my magic a raging beast fighting for freedom, for unchecked destruction. The hard wood of the mast behind my back is the only thing keeping me upright.

Zolan shoots me a glare of pure disgust. To him—to them all—I look like a cowering girl, too frightened to keep her knees from buckling, because the men can fathom no other explanation. And I don't bother offering one. I've not the energy to spare to worry about appearances, not if I want the middie now floundering on the deck to keep breathing.

And he is breathing, I realize. They all are now. Bending against the odd wind, holding on to ropes, but breathing. Zolan shouts orders to shift the sails, steadying the *Helix* against hard currents, setting course to get out of the Tirik's range.

My spark of relief dies as Brice's majestic three-decker moves against our attackers. The Tirik take aim at the admiral's ship, and the rain of shot they send upon it chills my blood. There are a thousand sailors on the *Thorn*, and no wind caller to clear the toxin. When that shot lands, the

Thorn's butcher bill will be ten times the *Helix*'s. A hundred times.

There isn't a choice. Trusting Zolan to keep the *Helix* afloat through my recklessness, I focus all my strength on shaping the magic's path to the *Thorn*. I am a sail, my tethers to the magic a set of ropes to control.

The *Helix* bucks under the sudden change of the wind's path, rocking to and fro on the gathering waves. My pulse rises, my knees shaking from the strain of holding the roaring magic. Time slows. Or speeds up, perhaps. Another Tirik death shot touches the deck and explodes. More shrapnel flies. More powder that I must clear before returning my attention to the flagship. More orders from Zolan.

I'm trembling. Even the magic is exhausted, burning my blood with its displeasure. There is a haze before my eyes, the world a blur of shapes and color too abstract for comprehension. All I know is that wind is life. Stagnation, death.

"Nile. Nile!" A man's face appears before me, though it might have been there for some time. Speaking. Shouting, maybe. I don't know. Jagged shards of glass cut my lungs with each breath. The man grabs my shoulder. "Stand down. It's over."

Another voice joins him, this one with a familiar songlike accent that sends a jolt of fire through me. "Get her out of here, Mr. Quinn. Now."

"Working on it, sir," Quinn replies. A hand shakes me again, then gives up, grabs my face, and forces my eyes to meet a familiar gaze. "Stand down, Nile."

Quinn's words finally penetrate, and I rein in the wind. My magic is half-furious at its sudden bridle, half-relieved at the reprieve. Darkness and light swim before me, my back pressing against the mast, my hands braced on my thighs. My eyes are as heavy as anchors as I lift them to the ocean, my wits slowly coming into focus. The enemy is fleeing, having delivered their horrors and received a taste of a Felielle broadside for their trouble. I'm not even sure which ship had fired. Whether the *Helix* had fired.

It doesn't matter. What matters is that we won. Or, at least, survived.

On the *Helix*'s deck, a half-dozen seamen howl still, blood coming from eyes forever melted shut. More lie motionless. The twelve-year-old middie isn't among the dead and wounded, though. Red-eyed, the boy is leaning on the rail and, like the others, staring at me with unhidden disdain. Their captain, who is panting and shaking, leaning against the mast in the wake of action.

Getting his arms under me, Quinn moves me toward the ladder leading down to my cabin. My mouth is dry, my body weak as a newborn foal's. And if I know myself, there is a convulsion riding in my shadow now, waiting for the right moment to spring.

Bear is waiting for me in my cabin, and I drop onto my cot, my head pounding and cradled in my arms. The dog hops up beside me, his worried wet nose nudging the back of my neck. Quinn hands me a glass of water, but my hands tremble so much, I spill most of the liquid before managing a sip.

"Eight months ago, you weren't capable of a tenth of this magic." Quinn eyes me with a mix of personal concern and professional curiously. "And you were already more powerful than any Gifted I'd ever met. I've no guess as to what price your body will demand for abusing it like you had to, but we'll take it one breath at a time."

I draw a shaking breath into abused lungs. On the deck above, the sounds of a ship recovering from battle start up slowly as the wounded are carried away and carpenters begin to take stock of the damage. Hammers strike bulkheads, debris splatters overboard, feet move about as crews put the ship to rights. Both my tail-tucked departure and current absence have been noted, the unflattering comments easily penetrating the *Helix*'s thick bulkheads. "What do I tell them?" I ask Quinn, waving my hand toward the overhead. "They all think—"

"The *Helix*'s crew is fortunate they *can* think," Quinn says, cutting me off. "The *Thorn*'s as well. Had you hesitated, you and your brave image would either be at the bottom of the sea or in an enemy prison. All of ours would be. I'm more worried about how quickly your Gift is scaling. Not that I'm ungrateful, but I can't imagine that the extra power is going to come without extra challenges."

A knock sounds against the door, which opens without further warning to allow Domenic into the cabin. Bear hops to the deck and wiggles his rear in greeting, though he refuses to stray farther than a step from my side.

My hand tightens on the edge of my mattress.

"Might we have the cabin, Mr. Quinn?" Domenic asks, waiting until his request is fulfilled before striding forward to crouch beside me.

My chest tightens as I struggle to ignore his salt-and-brine scent, now mixed with sulfury gunpowder residue. Behind my eyes, needle-sharp pain pierces my head. I want to curl into a ball around myself, but I force my back straight to meet Domenic's eyes instead. "Yes, Lieutenant?"

"How are you feeling?" Domenic's blue eyes search through mine. Unlike me, Domenic is as unruffled as always, minor things like near brushes with death granting no cause for a less than pristine uniform.

"Like I look, I imagine."

"You look like you should be dead." The back of Domenic's hand twitches toward my face, halts, returns quickly to rest on his knee. In the following silence, I hear the echoes of a seaman's voice inquiring about the *Helix*'s fearless captain, the answering throaty laughs cut short by Zolan's bark.

"The next man to make light of a lady—any lady—is going to find himself answering to me," the first officer is saying. "Am I understood?"

A chorus of contrite "aye aye, sir."

I rub my temple. For situational awareness, the captain's cabin is designed to have strong acoustics to the deck, but just now, I wish the ship's architects had been a smidge less diligent.

"Ignore them," Domenic says quietly.

Like he ignored all the seamen on the *Aurora* who thought him a sadistic, bloodthirsty tyrant. Maybe Domenic does have more mettle than I do. "Is there something I can help you with just now, Mr. Dana? I don't imagine Mr. Zolan would approve of your presence here, so let's be about your business as efficiently as we can."

"Really, Nile?" Domenic's calm voice finally snaps. "You think I came here on ship's business?"

My skin heats, my fingers flexing into fists. I'm too tired, too prone to do something I'll regret. Like grasp that hand that almost reached for my face. A tried and failed road. "I think I've little to say to someone who wishes to support me only in secret."

"They are *your* secrets." Domenic stands, crossing his arms over his chest. "Gifted aren't allowed to captain Felielle ships—so tell me, how do you wish me to spin what just happened? Suggest that you had simply been crouching to check your boot buckles?"

I throw up my hands. "You all but told the Felielle Admiralty that I wasn't to be trusted."

"You told the admiralty that yourself with your actions. And Admiral Pyre doesn't know the half of it, thinking your actions rooted in a snap decision to make the most of suddenly fortuitous weather—not premeditated insolence." Domenic's nostrils flare, his chest heaving with deep, solid breaths. "Breaking the law has consequences, and yours have just come to collect the bill."

"I believe the words you are seeking, Mr. Dana," Kyra's voice says from the doorway, "are *thank you for saving all our lives.*" The young woman holds her left hand tight to her chest as she walks forward and plants her small body between Domenic and me. "If there is nothing else, the captain needs to rest."

Domenic's whole body tenses, freezing for a moment before he touches his hat and strides out of the cabin. My heart continues to pound in the reverberating silence while Kyra tucks herself onto the cot beside me.

"Would you like..." Kyra directs her words to my blanket, her voice quiet. "Would you like to know what he is feeling?"

Yes. "No." I blow out a slow breath. "Domenic deserves his privacy like anyone else."

A small, relieved sigh from Kyra. "What can I do, then?"

I scrub my hands over my face. Exhausted I might be, but my gut says we aren't at the end of a disaster, but at its beginning. "Could you find Quinn for me, please?" I ask, reaching back to rebraid the hair that came loose during the gale. "I believe he has a few things to enlighten us with."

An hour later, I step from my cabin into a different world,

one painted bloody and dark with new knowledge. The deck is still a mess with blood, vomit, and urine staining the planks, but the wounded have been removed below. Eight seamen, including Lieutenant Phal, are laid out in neat rows atop their hammocks, their mess mates sewing the cloth shut over the bodies. Despite the open air, the deck smells of death. A harsh butcher's bill, but not as harsh as it could have been.

My legs still shake, but Quinn's words ring in my ears as loudly as the report of the great guns.

"Mr. Zolan," I call out the moment I clear the companionway ladder and stride onto the quarterdeck. Faces that I ignore turn to stare at me. I hold my back as straight as my bones allow, keeping up the damn illusions that are part of naval fabric. "Signal to the flagship. Helix *requests meeting. Emergency.* Then have a cutter lowered. You will accompany Mr. Quinn and me to the *Thorn.* Mr. Dana, you have the con."

Domenic spins toward me, questions plain on his face.

I ignore him and wait on Zolan, who, after a heartbeat's hesitation, touches his hat and executes my orders with a calm that sizzles in contrast to the fire raging inside me. With the seamen in motion, Zolan strides back toward me.

I turn away.

"A moment of your time, Captain?" Zolan says anyway, the words hitting my back. He closes the distance. "Might I know the reason behind the meeting?"

"I imagine you will discover it shortly, Mr. Zolan."

Zolan catches my arm, his voice low. "I would like to assure you that I will get you safely to the Diante Empire and back. If the battle—"

I jerk away, my balance faltering before I regain my footing. Any other captain in any other navy would have stripped Zolan's rank for the manhandling, even before the commander uttered his insults. Not that Zolan would have taken such liberty with a male commanding officer. Just now, however, I've more pressing problems. "You have no idea what is going on, Commander," I say, striding to the boat that sways rhythmically on the dark blue waves. A few yards away, a sea turtle surfaces and paddles on in blissful oblivion of our problems. "Get in."

CHAPTER 20

NILE

"*T*he ships you encountered are Bevnian." Quinn's Tirik accent echoes off the walls of Admiral Brice's deathly silent great cabin. The sun has begun to set in the time it took for all the captains to gather, the rays painting the water with orange and yellow hues. Beyond the window, the drizzle of light rain taps the ocean surface, sending splashes and ripples along the cresting waves. The sea doesn't care about the evil cruising across it. Despite having heard Quinn's story before, I tighten my fingers on the table's edge. Quinn's jaw tenses, and he draws a fortifying breath before continuing. "The Bevnians are a clan-based people from the northwest part of the Tirik continent. Bevnian lands are vast and hard, with severe weather and little fertile soil. Until now, they've stayed clear of the Lyron-Tirik conflict—"

"-*Conflict?*" the *Rose*'s pinch-faced captain snarls. "Is that what you call your people's bloodthirsty aggression? The People's Party's relentless murder, plunder, and destruction?"

There were few happy people in the great cabin to begin with, and the tempers are quickly rising hot enough to cook a deer.

Quinn stares the man down with quarterdeck-trained calm. "I have no commentary on the nature of the war, Captain. As satisfying as insulting me might be, might I suggest we focus on today's attack?" Quinn waits a beat, nods to no one in particular, and continues. "The Tirik seamen you've encountered before today were from the civilized, southeast part of the Tirik continent. That wasn't by accident. As of seven months ago, when I left the Tirik command, no one in the People's Party would come within shouting distance of Bevnia, much less allow Bevnians into the navy. The general Tirik population did not venture even that close, preferring instead to scare children with tales of their savage, but fortunately very distant, neighbors."

Admiral Brice, sitting with his ample bulk at the head of the table, rubs his upper lip. The small smile of welcome he offered me when I entered is now a distant memory. "Am I to understand that—in over a dozen years of armed conflict—the Tirik Command had consistently and purposefully ignored a whole source of able-bodied warriors? That the People's Republic was saving up these *uncivilized neighbors* for...what exactly? A stormy day?"

"The Bevnians are from the Tirik continent, but the People's Republic doesn't consider Bevnians to be Republic citizens. The Bevnians likewise consider themselves a separate nation, if clans can be called such. They are..." Quinn hesitates, as if searching for words. "The Bevnians have a different moral code from the one you are used to, sir. The Tirik People's Party has made several attempts to reform their Bevnian neighbors to a civilized way of life. All the attempts ended with the Tirik emissaries eaten."

A bone-deep silence echoes through the cabin, battle-hardened commanders at a loss for words. Even the *Rose*'s captain sits frozen, suddenly rendered out of his depth. We all are.

"Eaten?" Admiral Brice echoes, his voice slightly choked. "Eaten how?"

"Usually roasted," says Quinn. "Sometimes raw. And sometimes a bit at a time, keeping the victim alive for weeks to do it. The Bevnians are from a hard land. They do not like to waste food or risk it spoiling."

Even having heard this before, my stomach still turns at the image. Around the table, the men shift in their seats, the wooden chairs creaking beneath them.

Zolan recovers first, tugging down his uniform as he straightens his spine and nods to Quinn. "Please, continue, sir. I presume the Bevnians' dietary habits are not the only reason for concern over their entry into the conflict?"

"No," Quinn says grimly. "It is only a reflection of their approach, which is mirrored in all aspects of Bevnian decision-making. As another example, you may be used to warriors ready to give their lives in battle, but Bevnian warriors will *plan* their own death as part of basic strategy. It changes the calculations."

"What makes you so certain that the ships we encountered were Bevnian?" Admiral Brice asks shrewdly. "You'll forgive my suspicions when a Tirik—forgive me, an ex-Tirik—officer suggests that a new and horrific weapon is not really part of the Tirik navy's arsenal."

Quinn puts his hands behind his back. "I observed the ships' decks through a spyglass. The Bevnians look different from the other mainland citizens. Stark white hair, pale skin and eyes, as if the cold leached them of color. As for your real question, sir, I do not know how the Bevnians fit into the People's navy. After several failed attempts to unite the continent, the Tirik People's Party eventually concluded that civilized relations with the Bevnians were impossible. Perhaps the Bevnians truly deviate from other humans at some core level, or perhaps their harsh lands had bred conscience and morality out of them. Either way, for the past decade, the official Tirik policy has been isolation. It was thus when I left."

Zolan cocks a brow. "And the Bevnians respected the boundaries the People's Party drew on a map?"

Quinn shrugs. "Like other predators of the northern part of the continent, they appeared content to be left alone."

The captain of the *Rose* snorts. "I understand the People's Party little wishing to break bread with the Bevnians, but bringing them in to support an armed conflict is an entirely different game."

"The notion of bringing Bevnians into combat was discussed several times," Quinn says, not rising to the bait of disrespect in the other man's voice, "but the final conclusion remained the same each time. Namely, that would be as deadly as bringing hungry bears onto a street."

"It appears that the combination of an earthquake-ravaged coastline and the failed Battle of Siaman has led the Tirik to reconsider alliances," Zolan says dryly. "Though the Bevnian weaponry appears rather sophisticated for a pack of hungry bears."

"I said the Bevnians were barbaric and without conscience," Quinn answers. "I didn't say they were stupid or simple. It is quite possible they consider *us* the lower life-forms in this equation."

I lean my elbows on the edge of the table and speak for the first time since introducing Quinn. "However the Bevnians entered into the war, they are here now. And with them, the rules of war as we know them have altered. The suicide attack at Port Mead, the airborne corrosive, these are all just a start. We all felt *something* shift four months ago, and I'll wager my life that something has white hair and a taste for human meat."

"Agreed." Admiral Brice purses his lips, his gaze shifting from me to the others. "Let us call things as they are, gentlemen. If not for today's fortuitous winds, our ships might well be keeping the sand company just now. We need to reconsider our naval posture. Are you familiar with these...flesh-melting explosives, Mr. Quinn?"

Quinn shakes his head.

"If I may, sir," I inject into the pause. The light rain has morphed into a downpour, and I raise my voice to be heard above its beat. Above us, men scurry to gather foul-weather gear before the water drenches them to the skin. "Part of the reason for the Bevnians' near victory is our ignorance of the danger. The fox was dressed as a sheep. Might I suggest the *Helix* continue to the Diante Empire alone, leaving the *Thorn*, *Rose*, and *Violet* free to pursue other duties? Warning the league of the Bevnian threat and mounting a defense should take precedence over an honor guard."

Zolan's eyes narrow on me.

"I flatter myself to think that the squadron offers more value than an honor guard, Your Highness," Admiral Brice says dryly but without venom. He turns to survey the table. "That said, I fear Captain Greysik's point is valid. The *Helix* must continue on to the Diante Empire alone, while we return to the mainland. Push the ships as hard as the hulls and masts can bear, gentlemen, and gather everyone's observation of this

Bevnian hell powder. Let us hope we are the first ones to have witnessed its effects."

The boat ride back to the *Helix* passes in wet, hunch-shouldered silence, the pouring rain soaking us within moments. Zolan's gaze stays on the dark horizon while my own sinks into the ink-black waves. While we thought we were winning, the world had changed. In the old war, the Lyron League battled a people who, behind their guns, politics, and ideologies, were the same as us. Now that the Tirik joined hands with the Bevnians, we fight against evil.

"The squadron will be making its departure signals within the hour, I expect," Zolan says, his attention still on the horizon.

"Good." The memory of Phal's bloody body ripples through my thoughts. Before today, I never truly appreciated the power of surprise, which the Bevnians wield with ruthless effectiveness. "The sooner the better."

"Should another attack come..." Zolan cuts his eye to me, likely trying to decipher why his cowardly captain advocated sending home her protection detail. Rainwater pours in steady streams off the sides of his hat, like a mushroom caught in the rain.

I let my neck stretch back, tipping my face up to the rain. It's no wetter than, hunching my shoulders against the downpour, and it feels better than I expected. Cold but refreshing. Free. "Should another attack come, we'll have fewer Felielle ships to worry about losing," I say, not caring how little sense the words make to him.

Quinn is the first off the boat when we tie up to the *Helix*, and Zolan uses the moment to slide close to me, leaning in to be heard over the rain. "Someone wise once told me that courage isn't the absence of fear," he murmurs, "but a willingness to act despite it. You did well, Your Highness."

I turn toward him, the rainwater pouring beneath my shirt and making me shiver. "If you want to offer someone encouragement, Zolan, try a kind word to Mr. Dana. I'll take care of myself."

THE FOLLOWING DAWN, it's all I can do to haul myself out of bed. Two convulsions struck me overnight, and my body teeters on the brink of collapse. However I managed to get through briefing the admiral yesterday without falling unconscious, the bill for the magic has come due. With interest.

"I'll pass the word to Commander Zolan that you are indisposed." Kyra watches me spill my coffee all over the breakfast table and takes the cup away, cleaning up the mess with a rag. She holds her left hand close to her body, her wrist swollen from a fall taken during battle. The first of many to come, I think.

"You should see the surgeon." I jerk my chin toward the injury. Kyra blanches, and I quickly change course. Stepping into the hell of blood, amputation, and melted faces can do more damage than the fall had, especially to an empath. "Or Catsper. He has quite the arsenal of medical field knowledge. If—" A knock at the door interrupts my thought, and I force myself to sit straighter before calling the guest to enter.

"Your Highness." Standing at the cabin door, Zolan is the picture of naval courtesy. His pristine uniform cuts well over a body hard with years of seawork, his face clean-shaven, his hair combed. Ready for a new day, while I'm struggling to sit without collapsing. "A moment of your time?"

"Of course," I say, though the only worse time for this audience would be in the middle of a convulsion. Not that I can tell the commander that. "What can I do for you?"

"I thought you might wish to know that Mr. Dana was able to run a sail drill this morning with all haste and minimal noise. It was his best work yet, and the men noticed. As did I."

Ah. So he was listening last night. "Thank you." I long for another sip of coffee but don't trust myself to pick up the cup without spilling it in front of Zolan. "I would appreciate if you did not mention our conversation to him."

A small bow.

I wait for Zolan to leave, but the man pulls out a chair and sits without invitation. The small gesture is a gross breach of naval tradition, and the wood's creaks of protest beneath Zolan's muscled frame might as well be a trumpet's call. "I wanted to suggest, ma'am, that you take some time to rest. Recover. We all wish to see you at your best upon our arrival in the Diante Empire, and I wonder if you might not have some lingering preparation to yet complete on that score."

I raise my face, meeting the man's eyes. I may lack Zolan's quarterdeck experience, but I've been trained for command since I was eight—a fact the man seems to have overlooked. "You wanted to suggest, Mr. Zolan, that I stay off the quarterdeck because the crew little wishes to take orders from me," I say with unapologetic bluntness. "And you are of a mind with them. Especially after the cowardly display you think you saw from me during action."

A touch of color rises on Zolan's face, and I wonder when he was last in a conversation that failed to follow his plan. He shifts in his seat, adjusts his shirt cuffs. Coughs into a fist.

Leaning forward, I interlace my fingers on the tabletop. "You look like a man with something to say, Mr. Zolan. You might as well do so."

"The Felielle navy has centuries of tradition," Zolan says quietly but not weakly as he recovers himself and sets his course. Like my voice moments ago, his tone is also void of apology. Facts laid out on a chart. "None of those centuries involved females on the quarterdeck. It isn't something that changes in a day. Or something that should be changed now, when we've more important battles before us."

"I see." I tilt my head. "And is it my gender or my seamanship that has you so convinced of my inferiority?"

Zolan's chin rises, but his voice stays even. "Inferiority is your word, Your Highness, not mine. I would hardly call a mission to negotiate an alliance that would turn the tide of the war to be inferior to that of a naval captain. We need not all do the same job, ma'am. Let the men bring you safely to where you need to be, and you can secure allies to bring us all safely home."

And if I can't? My chest tightens, and it's a struggle to keep my hands relaxed, my face calm. I'm a sailor, not a diplomat, no matter how much Zolan and the world would find the reverse to be more convenient. "You've not answered my other question, sir," I say instead. I do not expect a repeat of this conversation, so we might as well cover all ground. "I'm Ashing trained. Do you find my education lacking? Go ahead and imagine me a man for the sake of your answer, if it's more palatable."

Zolan's lips press together, his gaze on a small scratch on my heavy wooden table. "From what I've observed, outside actual battle, you are a superb sailor for your age and rank. A few bad habits, like all youngsters, but as with Mr. Dana's, they are correctable." Zolan lifts his face. "The problem, Your Highness, is that to correct those habits, I'd need to stress you as I do Dana, and you can hardly bear to see him suffer through it. But even if you'd be able to bear it, and I'd be willing to treat a woman thus —which I am not—the fact remains that you cannot hold your head in battle. And there is no correcting that."

I wonder whether it's fatigue or dignity or the practical reality of this new war that finally snaps the tether of my control. Whatever it is, it sends a snapping shock through my nerves as I see myself rising to my feet. Slowly. Deliberately. My eyes locked on Zolan's.

Zolan's brows flicker, confusion brushing his weather-hardened face.

"You think you know what happened during battle, Zolan?" My voice is low and even, my feet wide apart and braced. "You think you have a read on me?" The magic in my blood perks despite our exhaustion, and with my next breath, a phantom burst of wind knocks Zolan's chair backward onto the deck. I stride forward, my red hair whipping around my face as I tower over the commander, who scrambles on the deck like an overturned bug. "Where do you think Admiral Brice's fortunate winds came from? The Goddess? Why are there so few *Helix* sailors with their eyelids melted shut?"

CHAPTER 21

KYRA

*K*yra pulled the sleeve of her dress over her swollen wrist and shifted the satchel slung across her shoulder. Despite the perfectly respectable reason she had to be standing outside the gun room just now, Kyra knew that really, she was doing it again—meddling in things that were not her business, in the lives of people who wanted to be left alone. Even if being left alone would destroy them.

Well, Kyra was here now. And so was the gun room. Bulkheads had a way of appearing and disappearing aboard the *Helix*, the carpenter and his mates thinking nothing of taking down a wall to relocate it to a more convenient location. A pair of seamen squeezed by her, ducking their heads under low-hanging beams and reeking of sweat. The non-officers were allowed fourteen inches of space to sling their hammocks, and the close quarters bred stench.

Kyra waited until the men were gone before taking a cautious breath of air. So what if she was meddling? Somebody had to. Squaring her shoulders, Kyra knocked.

"Yes?" The voice belonged to the *Helix*'s second lieutenant, Dana. The same one Kyra had thrown out of Nile's cabin earlier. Kyra's stomach tightened. Of course Catsper wouldn't be alone. And of course he would be with the one man who likely wanted to chuck Kyra overboard. He had certainly been unhappy to leave Nile's cabin.

The door opened, and Kyra's mouth filled with traces of Dana's sour concern.

"Yes?" Dana said again, his voice softer now that he was looking down at her. "Is Nile well?" The sour taste intensified as if Kyra had licked a slice of lemon.

"Yes." Realizing that she'd been standing in the pass-through despite having been the one to knock, Kyra shifted her weight and fiddled with the satchel strap as she sought out words. Giving her fingers something to do helped. "Yes, Nile is quite all right. I...I apologize for speaking brashly to you earlier."

Dana shook his head. "You were in the right."

Kyra rocked back, unsure whether it was the ship or Dana to blame for her sudden imbalance. That was the problem with emotions; they told only a sliver of the truth. Sensing that the pause had stretched too long for comfort, Kyra finally located her voice. "I was looking for Catsper."

Dana's brow twitched, his surprise tingling on Kyra's tongue. "You've found him." Dana bladed his body to allow Kyra free entry into the officers' sacred space. "For better or worse."

On the heels of Dana's words, a knife buzzed by Kyra's ear and stuck into the bulkhead behind her, the hilt vibrating with a melodic hum.

Kyra jumped, her yelp piercing the air.

Dana's solid hands caught her shoulders, steadying her from behind. "Pay no attention, lass. We keep waiting for that one to grow up, but it might be a lost cause." Dana cleared his throat. "What can we do for you?"

Blinking to clear her vision, Kyra found Catsper sitting atop the long table that stretched the length of the gun room. He'd already acquired a second knife and now tossed it in one hand, letting the blade spin in the air between catches. His green eyes stared at her in a silent demand to explain the intrusion.

Coming here was a mistake. But, since it was already made, Kyra might as well ride the full wave of the doomed exercise. She made herself meet the marine's eyes. He *had* saved her life. "I burned you yesterday." Her voice carried more confidence than she felt. "I came to check after the wound. I brought some salve for it too." She tugged on her satchel by way of evidence.

Catsper leaned back on his arms, the muscles of his chest and shoulders shifting beneath his clothes. If the burn pained him—and it bloody had to, didn't it?—the discomfort plainly bothered him little. Catsper continued holding the silence for several more seconds, weighing Kyra with his gaze for each stretched moment. "So then... You want me to take off my shirt?" he drawled finally, his brow rising as he cocked his head. "What about my pants?"

Dana shut his eyes, his face reddening.

"I'm confident saying that we'd all prefer if your clothes stayed on." Kyra pressed her lips together, glancing at Dana. "The lieutenant especially, I think."

Catsper snorted.

Kyra crossed her arms over her chest, wincing at the sudden lightning shot of pain. She hadn't really expected the marine to let anyone near his injuries, and now at least Dana knew what to keep an eye on. Not that she was done with Catsper yet. "Nile also said you could take a look at my arm. Given that you are the one who injured it, I thought it a fair request to make."

Sliding off the table, Catsper walked around to its other end, where a pot of ink and some paper lay ready. Sheathing the knife in his boot, the marine picked up the pen and began writing.

"What are you doing?" Dana inquired.

"Explaining the difference between a doctor and a guardsman to the *Helix*'s good captain," Catsper replied without raising his head from his work. "Would you say 'keep your pet empath *on* a leash' or just '*leashed*' is better form in formal correspondence?"

"Excuse me." Dana slid the latch on the gun room closed, cloistering the three of them inside. With three long steps, he reached the marine's side, snatched up the paper, and crumpled it in his hand. "As I said," Dana told Kyra without the slightest hesitation in speech as he pulled a chair out for her. "We try not to pay this one much mind if we can help it. What happened to the arm?" His voice softened, and he crouched as if to make his large frame less intimidating. This from a man who strolled the decks as thunder incarnate. All Nile's associates wore masks, it seemed.

Pulling back her sleeve, Kyra carefully displayed her misshapen wrist. Despite having braced for this, her breath quickened, a gasp escaping her as Dana's fingers connected.

"I'll take care of it." Catsper's voice, suddenly beside her, made Kyra jump for the second time. When she could move again, she found Catsper towering over her and Dana both. The marine glared at the officer, as if the other had laid claim on marked prey instead of offering assistance.

Dana put up his hands and backed away toward the door. "I

believe the weather is shifting. Excuse me while I check on the sails."

The door clicked open, then shut. Perhaps Kyra should have gone too.

Catsper crossed his arms. "A day ago, you were trembling with fear that I'd snap your neck in two. Or worse. Now you come to me injured? A bloody rat has a better sense of self-preservation."

Kyra shifted. This was it, the shot across the bow, as Nile would say. The reason she came. "Oh, I've a very solid concern over my hide. You, on the other hand?" Her voice was soft but not weak. Not in this. "You court death and pain as if answering a siren's call. And I've decided I'm not letting you."

Catsper blinked. Then blinked again. "Are you insane?" he asked, his voice filled with genuine curiosity.

Kyra rubbed her bad wrist gingerly. "Do you imagine I enjoyed being thrown down a ladder yesterday?" she asked. "Being terrified? Being held prisoner in a cargo hold while the ship threatened to tear apart?"

"I imagine it saved your life." The note in Catsper's words suggested that he might be regretting yesterday's actions already. Too late now.

"Oh, it did," Kyra agreed readily. "*You* did. And now I'm going to return the favor. I don't expect you to find the experience any more pleasant than I did."

Catsper took a step forward, using his height and bulk to claim the space around Kyra. "Let us get a few things straight," he said quietly. "In addition to your theory being of no consequence, you are also in as much a position to *let* or *not let* me do something as that bulkhead over there is. The one with my knife still in it. Go find someone else to save. Are we clear?"

Kyra tilted her head up to look at Catsper. He was strong

and used to the implicit intimidation that power brought. Whether Catsper's victim cowed or squared up to match force with force, the marine won the home ground advantage. So Kyra did neither.

Reaching with her good hand into the satchel, she pulled out the small bit of metal that lay beside the salve. Pinching the pin, she twisted it in her fingers.

As light refracted off the pin's surface, the tsunami of Catsper's emotions, so well blocked until this moment, hit Kyra full force. Fury. Dread. Pain. Kyra gasped, and the storm disappeared at once, whatever shield Catsper had learned to put up inside him snapping into place. Too late, though; Kyra had the scent now and was prepared to stay the course. "Why are you letting Nile believe the Spardic Command gave you leave to go with her?" she asked, dropping the pin back into the satchel. "Why not tell her the truth, that you stopped being a Spade the day before the Port Mead assault? That is what happened, isn't it?"

"You came to get your arm fixed?" Catsper said.

Kyra paused. "Yes."

Catsper snatched Kyra's injured arm into his grip, his other hand trapping the swollen joint between his thumb and forefinger.

Kyra's heart pounded against her ribs, but she made herself raise her chin. Being injured made her safer, not more vulnerable in Catsper's presence. She was sure. A shiver raced through her. A test. This was another test, another game that Catsper played to make her scurry away like everyone always did.

But he hadn't run from her. Not when she stood near an explosive that melted shut others' eyes, not when her magic shattered a lantern, not when she burned him for fear he'd do what others had. When Kyra's life was in danger, he'd not left.

"Shall we continue the fascinating discussion from earlier?" Catsper asked casually. "Or are other things occupying your mind just now?"

Kyra bit her lip. He wouldn't hurt her. A game. This was all a game.

The pressure on Kyra's arm increased slowly. First a sting, then a flame of agony shooting down through her elbow and wrist. She bit her lip as tears welled in her eyes and spilled, one by one, over her cheeks. *Stars. Stars. Stars.* Catsper's hand moved, and the pain doubled. Tripled. Kyra whimpered, the nails of her free hand pressed so deeply into her palm that blood welled in the cracks of skin. Catsper's hand moved again, this time over her swollen wrist, and the heavy dread of surrender washed over Kyra's blood. She'd wagered and lost. She—

The room tilted. Kyra jerked back her arm, but the marine held fast.

"Stop." Kyra's voice rang clear and loud through the gun room. "You win. All right? Just stop. Let me go, and I'll leave you be too."

Catsper's hands stilled. His face swung toward her, and for a heartbeat, triumph rocked his gaze. Then the triumph was gone, and Catsper's jaw tightened. "I'm almost done," he said gruffly.

"Almost done with what?" Kyra shook her head, trying to clear it. She pulled back on her arm again, gasping when he refused to let go.

"Bloody hell, Kyra," Catsper muttered as if annoyed with himself, "I'm setting your damn wrist, not tormenting you for my amusement. As you asked me to do thirty storms-damned seconds ago. Aren't you supposed to *feel* when someone intends to use you for target practice?"

"I rarely feel you at all." Kyra breathed the confession, which seemed very much a secondary concern just now. "I thought you knew. You shield against me. Please let go now. It hurts very much."

"Of course it does. It's dislocated." His voice hardened to an order. "Draw a breath."

Kyra shook her head.

"Your call," said Catsper, and Kyra's wrist exploded flame. The agony morphed into a dull thumping ache a moment later, and the marine stepped away. "Is there anything else you desire before you return my belongings to me and get out of my life?"

Kyra rubbed her arm, her heart still pounding from the pain. Somewhere in the confrontation with Catsper, the advantage had shifted, and shifted again, until she was no longer sure who held the upper hand. But one thing was certain: had the marine stopped when she'd asked, her wrist would still be deformed and throbbing.

"Three questions," she said, searching his face. "Answer three questions, and I leave you in peace."

He spread his hands and hoisted himself atop the gun deck table, his face a stone.

Kyra cleared her throat. "What was the horrid thing you did for which there can be no forgiveness?"

His green eyes were glacier cold, his voice cooler still. "I killed nineteen children."

Kyra froze, her words suddenly gone. No. No, that was impossible. Except that the man was telling the truth. Kyra was as certain of it as she was of sun. And yet... There had to be more. "How—"

"We're done." Catsper was on his feet, his movement

predatory as he ripped the satchel from Kyra's hands. After pulling out the pin, the man threw the bag back at her. "No more questions. Get out."

"No." The answer came before thought.

Shouldering Kyra from his way, Catsper left the gun room instead, the slammed door vibrating in his wake.

CHAPTER 22

NILE

olan's neck bobs as he swallows, my wind beating his face and hair and body. "Stop," he manages. "Please."

I rein my magic back, though it bucks and fights me like an enraged beast. For a moment, I forget Zolan in the fight with my own storm, but the haze clears after two heartbeats of panic, and I return my attention to the commander.

Zolan is still on the deck, though now crouched in a fighting stance. Not that there is anything to fight now. Not anymore. He stares at me. Silent. Frozen. A veteran sea god at a loss.

I extend my hand to him and am as surprised as Zolan himself when he takes it, letting me pull him to his feet. Silence hangs between us again, now laden with repercussion. Because... Because I just threw everything into an abyss.

"Storm and hail," I whisper, my chest still heaving with exertion.

"A fairly accurate sentiment," Zolan says finally, righting the overturned chair. "Might... Might I beg for a cup of coffee? Or something a bit stronger if you have it."

I motion Zolan to the wine and collapse into my chair while he pours himself a glass, drains it, and refills it again. He places an identical goblet before me, but I little trust myself with liquid —much less glass—just now.

"How long?" Zolan asks finally. "Have you always... Or...Um..."

"I was wounded in *Faithful*'s final battle. The fever that came following that awoke the Gift. My twin is Gifted as well." *Faithful* Clay. The words sting. "Though his Gift manifested years ago."

Zolan's eyes widen, and I can practically see the calculation walking across his face. The Battle of Siaman, my Goddess-blessed escape from Rima's ship, the war game gunnery trials. All things I've done with my wind-calling. And done in secret. "Is this why you wanted to send the convoy away?"

"In part." My voice is flat. "I wanted to warn the continent as I said, but yes, I also know I cannot protect four ships. *Storms,* I don't know that I could have protected the *Helix* if the bastards had expected any countermeasures."

After a short eternity, Zolan drops his forehead into his hands. "This is why you appeared on the verge of collapse in action. You were occupied saving our asses."

"Yes."

"And the reason you couldn't contradict the crew's perception of your action."

"Yes," I say again. "Those centuries of tradition keeping

women from the navy keep Gifted away as well. I imagine one dose of an upside-down world is quite enough for the hands."

"I must beg forgiveness," Zolan whispers, genuine regret saturating his words, "but now that I know..." He trails off for a moment before raising his face to meet my gaze squarely. "By the Felielle Articles of War, a Gifted cannot command a naval vessel. I *must* relieve you of command, Your Highness. You know that, I expect."

I snort, though my shoulders feel laden with boulders and it takes me a breath to fight off the stinging in my eyes. *You can hardly lose what you never truly had to begin with,* I tell myself, but it little helps. "Yes. I do. As the *Helix*'s captain, my first duty is to the ship." I force my shoulders to square, my voice to stay even and strong. "And in this new world the Bevnians have written, protecting the *Helix* means calling the winds to her aid. I thought I could command the winds and the ship at the same time, but I can't. As for later, when this is all done, none of us are returning from the cruise the way we set out. The Bevnians have made sure of that." Reaching up to my shoulder, I unpin the epaulette marking me a ship's active duty captain and slide it across the table to Zolan.

No piece of cloth has ever been so heavy. Pushing myself to my feet, I stride toward where my sword hangs on the wall and extend that to Zolan as well, as is tradition in surrender.

"Keep it." Zolan's voice is even again as he nods to the sword. Another naval tradition, a mark of respect between one captain and another in permitting the weapon to be kept.

I swallow and nod in gratitude.

Taking the captain's epaulette, Zolan tucks it respectfully into the inside of his jacket. "Might I ask you to remain indisposed for a few days while I decide how to announce the change of command to the crew? We might well have a mutiny on our hands if they learn of a Gifted aboard." He rubs his eyes. "Not to mention that the Diante are expecting a *Captain* Greysik to attend them."

I nod numbly. "Provided there is no attack, I will use that time to recover. Point of fact, I don't believe I can stay upright much longer."

"Of course." Zolan—Captain Zolan—rises quickly, catching his unsettled wineglass at the last moment. His free hand braces the table. "And Your Highness... Thank you."

"Just so I'm clear," Kyra says, folding herself into a chair opposite mine. "Bad people attacked, you saved the ship, Zolan took away your command and confined you to quarters."

I prop my head on my hand. I'd fallen asleep the moment Zolan shut the door behind him, waking up the next day to the sun flying high above the horizon, a mildly upset sea, and the sounds of a crew running a full-force storm drill, as if expecting an imminent rogue gale. The convulsions that struck me overnight somehow strained a muscle between my ribs, making breathing uncomfortable. "It isn't quite like that."

Kyra slides a mug of hot tea—it's remarkably convenient to have a flame caller around when one likes hot drinks—toward me and takes out a chessboard. "Which part am I mistaken about?"

I massage my temples. "How is your arm?"

"Better." Kyra holds up the limb in question, her gaze weighing me like a cook assessing the best attack vector against a particularly troublesome chicken. "Dana is worried about you," Kyra says, pulling chess pieces out of their velvet bag. "He won't come near the cabin for fear of spilt blood, but he's worried."

I frown, trying to ignore the tightness in my chest. My ribs are too sore for this conversation. "Weren't you the one who said you would not spy on the crew for my benefit?"

"I'm not spying, I'm observing." She sets the pawns out one by one. "Are you two...entangled?"

I cock a brow. There'd never been much hope in keeping my history with Domenic a secret from an empath who shared my berth, but I'd little counted on the subject coming up now. I sip the tea, the hot liquid soothing against my throat. Holding the cup in my hands, I watch the swirling liquid. "If by entangled you mean whether we share a bed, the answer is no." As it has always been. Let Kyra's empathic sense work that one out. "Thank you for the tea, but I'm not in the right mood for chess just now."

"I'm not in the right mood for fishing words out of you one at a time." Kyra sets down the rook, finishing the setup. "And you are easier to deal with if your mind is divided between tasks. Black or white?"

"Kyra—"

She cuts her eyes to mine. "Is there someone else aboard you'd like to speak with? Because from where I sit, it appears we've enough problems with the Tirik and Bevnians without the *Helix*'s officers killing each other off themselves. Black or white?"

I sigh. "White."

She turns the board, and I obligingly move out my pawns, the opening gambit calming my frayed nerves—which, I imagine, was Kyra's intention. I wonder whether the girl is reading my emotions as we play.

"Well?" Kyra asks, her attention on the board where we both fight for control of the center space.

I shrug. "Domenic and I are not in danger of killing each

other off." Mostly because that would require more time in each other's company than either of us is capable of civilly handling. "Besides that, my head hurts as if an ax splits my skull in two, and the pressure building behind my eyes threatens to pop my eyes from their sockets."

"Sounds like an awfully small price to pay for keeping four ships alive." She moves her rook. "Shall we discuss what's really eating you? Has Zolan decided when you can leave your cabin and how he'll announce the change of command to the crew?"

"Not yet. Though he is apparently hardening the ship against any accident I might have. *Storms*, that sounds like I might wet the bed, not summon a hurricane." I flinch at my own words and set them aside to simmer somewhere just beneath conscious thoughts. I focus instead on the game, on Kyra's delicate hand hovering just above her queen. "You are going to lose that piece if you keep sprinting her all over the board."

Kyra smiles and shrugs a shoulder as if to say *maybe, but she'll be amused until then.* The girl is the most undisciplined player I've met—but she doesn't lose nearly as much as she should.

"Your insistence on slicing raw topics open and pouring salt inside, is that a Kyra trait or an empath trait?" I ask. "Just so I know what to avoid in the future."

A corner of Kyra's mouth twitches. "So far as I know, I'm the only empath and likely the only Kyra. So does it matter?"

I lean forward. Without a solid defense, offense suddenly seems a wiser strategy. "Did you and Catsper really spend a night together?"

Kyra's hand pauses in midair, then returns to the table to roll one of the taken pawns in a circle. "To use your terms, we've not shared a bed, no." She tucks her legs under her, smoothing her yellow dress over her knees. "How well do you know Catsper?"

I keep my eyes on Kyra's black queen, the one in danger of falling from the game. "Catsper is one of the most loyal, reliable, and steadfast people alive."

Kyra makes her move, and I counter quickly. She bites her lip. "Where is he from? Why did he join the Spades? Why is he so good at setting bones?"

I frown. "He's from Spardic, he joined because that's what Spardics do, and he can set a bone because the Spades' training is more brutal than any battle." Put that way, my knowledge of a friend does seem rather shallow. I bristle. "When I met Catsper on the *Aurora*, I had many secrets I wished to keep. He honored that and never pressed for more information than I wished to offer. It's only fair to extend him the same courtesy."

Kyra makes another of her amusing moves, and her knight suffers for it.

"If you didn't share a bed, then why—no, don't tell me." I shake my head. Catsper is a panther incarnate, with sculpted muscles, sharp knives, and a sharper mind. Between Kyra's physical delicateness and empathic power, a meeting of the two could end with nothing but disaster. And I don't know which of them I worry more for. "I can't begin to understand how your mind works, but please don't hurt him."

Kyra blinks her long lashes in exaggerated innocence. "Hurt him? That one bathes in pain and angst. I could smack him upside the head with a rock and he'd thank me." She clasps her queen between her thumb and forefinger and knocks my white queen off the board. "Your move."

"Mr. Zolan's compliments, ma'am," one of the middies announces, stepping cautiously into my great cabin on day three of my confinement. "And are you well enough to join him on deck?"

Sentencing time. Even though I've already surrendered my command, I can't think of the coming announcement as anything different. The point of no return when I shall officially become little more than an exotic weapon. My heart stutters, a jolt shooting through my limbs. "Of course," I tell the boy, making my dry mouth work. "Tell the commander I shall be there in a moment."

My hand has a white-knuckle grip on the companionway ladder, and my pulse pounds as if I'm fish bait watching her first storm approach. Three days. It might as well be three years. Thirty. After ascending the *Helix*'s quarterdeck as her captain, I'd left it as her coward. The crew, the ship, none of them need Captain Nile Greysik. *Storms,* none of them *want* Captain Nile Greysik. And they are about to get their wish.

My first steps on the open-air deck are loud as thunder in my head. The *Helix*'s three masts stretch seventy feet toward the clear blue sky, where a pair of far-from-home terns circle the rigging to the amusement of several young skylarking ship's boys. Patches of green and turquoise water warn of coral reefs beneath while a large turtle swims happily beneath the sun. Unlike my last bloody sight of it, the *Helix*'s deck is sanded clean. A perfect, happy ship. Happier than it was under my command. Bile rises up my throat, and my hand tightens on one of the ropes while I draw a deep breath of chilly ocean air.

At the stern of the ship, a seaman with a sandglass casts a knotted rope into the sea, counting the number of knots that pass through his fingers while the sand falls.

"Eight knots," the man sings out, the information

meticulously passed along to the sailing master, who notes the speed in the ship's log.

Zolan and Domenic stand together on the quarterdeck, talking softly. One of the older middies, a gangly sixteen-year-old youth, approaches the officers with caution. Both men offer the lad a warm greeting along with an explanation of a mathematics problem, if the snippets of conversation that reach me are correct. I even catch sight of Domenic laughing, before his eyes find mine and the laughter dies.

The eyes of other seamen dart to me as well, dart and look away quickly, trailing with contempt.

My stomach clenches.

"Captain on deck," Domenic tells Zolan, his voice dry and proper. He doesn't know, then, not yet.

I force my chin up, my shoulders square.

Domenic turns his back to me.

My jaw clenches, and, as I stride forward, I take up a friendly breeze's offer to knock the man's perfectly positioned hat off his head. The tiny dance with magic feels as good as Domenic's bewildered start.

Domenic grasps for the dropped object, cursing when it skitters along the deck, just out of his reach. Domenic tries again.

The hat hops along, the little breeze carrying it past the ruffling coats of nearby seamen, who pragmatically keep a grip on their own loose articles.

Domenic's third failed attempt to snatch the rogue object finally draws several poorly hidden chuckles from the crew, and Domenic's face darkens.

A smile just begins to form on my own lips, my magic poised to tickle the wind again, when a dagger nails Domenic's hat to the deck. The crew shuts its collective mouth as Catsper strides down from the poop and retrieves his weapon with apparent disinterest. He tosses the blade over his shoulder, and the deadly projectile lodges itself in the mast, a few inches away from a gawker's ear.

The silence and speed with which the crew finds employment after that rivals a battle drill.

Raising a brow, Zolan looks from the hat to Catsper, then Domenic, then me. "It appears I was not the first to the party," he says drily. "I believe a visit to the gun room is in order, if you all find it convenient just now. Is there anyone *else* we should invite?"

I swear I hear Zolan utter a prayer as he leaves the deck to Vikon and leads the procession to the gun room, where he claims a chair at the head of the long table. My heart pounds. Taking my seat, I slip my hands beneath the table to conceal their trembling. A quarter hour ago, I thought the wait would kill me. Now I think the actual conversation might.

Kyra and Quinn join Domenic, Catsper, and me, Zolan greeting each member of the little conspiracy with a thoughtful gaze and nod. Once everyone is settled, the commander surveys the faces a final time and begins in a voice that's anything but hesitant. "To call this situation unusual would be the understatement of the century, so let us begin with facts beyond dispute." He holds up his hand, extending fingers one at a time. "Princess Nile Greysik is a Gifted wind caller. Felielle forbids Gifted on its men-of-war."

Each word hits me like a lash, and it's all I can do to keep from wincing. Across the table, Domenic's eyes widen, his gaze piercing me so hard, it's a miracle it fails to draw blood.

You told Zolan you are Gifted? Domenic's silence demands of me.

I nod and markedly shift my attention away from him.

Catsper takes in the news with the marine's usual nonchalance. Kyra and Quinn, who both settled themselves at the far end, watch and listen intently.

Zolan unbends a third finger. "Had we obeyed Felielle's law from the start and kept Nile ashore where she belongs, we would all be dead now." He spreads his hands. "When the law was constructed, no one had a notion that a Gifted's wind might one day save us from an enemy the breed of which we'd never encountered. More to the point, our mission here is diplomatic, and destroying a chance at an alliance for the whim of protocol is the height of foolishness."

"Shall we continue on as before, then?" Domenic asks, his voice tight, betrayed at having been blindsided by this turn of events.

"Ms. Greysik surrendered her command to me three days ago," Zolan says flatly. "That is why she hasn't been on deck."

Domenic tenses, his fingers pressing into the tabletop hard enough to turn the nailbeds white. I wonder whether he's more unhappy over being kept ignorant or pleased about the rules finally catching up with my antics.

My own hands, concealed from view in my lap, tangle together.

"The dilemma," Zolan continues, "lies with what to tell the crew and the Diante. The latter is the easier solution, I believe. The Diante invited a Captain Greysik, which all the official papers and correspondences confirm Her Highness to be. Once we make contact with the empire, I will temporarily revert the *Helix* to Ms. Greysik, who will in turn place me back in charge as soon as she steps off the ship. It isn't ideal and perhaps stretches the spirit of both Felielle policy and the Diante invite, but there is no reason to air our laundry before the empire."

Nods come from around the table. Zolan is right, the

solution isn't ideal but should hold water well enough. I let out a long, slow breath that catches short with his next words.

"Now, with respect to the *Helix*," says Zolan.

I go still. Domenic leans forward.

Zolan's dark eyes sweep over us. "Even setting aside the law, Ms. Greysik cannot command a man-of-war and harness the wind at the same time. That much we've seen. Just as we've seen her wind magic save this ship and every soul aboard her." He turns to me and gives a small, respectful nod. "My original inclination to treat Ms. Greysik as a civilian passenger was a folly, for which I beg her forgiveness."

My mouth dries. Words fail to come. Which is good, since Zolan isn't done speaking.

"The question thus becomes simple: if Nile is neither a civilian passenger, nor the captain, where does she fit into the *Helix*'s hierarchy? The answer is likewise simple, for the tradition of the navy has answered it long ago. An officer's place in the command cadre is based on rank. As a junior lieutenant, Ms. Greysik will fall just under Mr. Dana and will answer to him."

CHAPTER 23

NILE

he table, the room, the world are all silent. I struggle to catch my breath, not trusting my voice to so much as utter acknowledgment of Zolan's words. I'd been prepared to be confined to my berth for the remainder of the voyage or be relegated to an auxiliary status similar to that the ship's surgeon enjoys. A narrowly skilled outsider. But what Zolan is laying out instead, a true place among the Felielle's officers and crew, it changes everything. Gives me a chance to remain the sailor that I've trained my whole life to be. How exactly that will play out under Domenic is a separate matter altogether. I swallow.

"What will you tell the crew?" Kyra's innocent words bounce along the tabletop.

"That due to Princess Greysik's turn of health and need to prepare for her vital diplomatic duties, she has appointed me to captain the *Helix* in her stead. As for the Gift..." Zolan shakes his head. "The unfortunate reality is that sailors are a traditional and superstitious lot. The same men who will happily thank the Goddess for rogue winds will as likely piss themselves as mutiny should they learn that those winds were called by a Gifted serving at their side. Thus..." Zolan turns to me, his gaze flickering to Domenic's hat and back. "Ms. Greysik, you will make no unauthorized disclosure of your Gift from this point onward. Understood?"

"Aye, sir." I touch my hat.

"Furthermore"—Zolan's attention swings between me and Domenic—"Mr. Dana, the ship's command must have a full understanding of Ms. Greysik's abilities to be able to direct her actions during battle. We will do well to have the winds synchronized with the ship's maneuvers, not battling against them." Zolan pauses and surveys the group one last time. "That is all, then. If there are no questions, everyone is dismissed."

I scrape back my chair, rising with the others, my heart still a pounding storm. Zolan has given me a chance, maybe the first *true* chance in the Felielle navy—

"Sit down, Nile." Domenic's voice freezes me halfway to the door. "I've not dismissed you."

A chill prickles my skin.

Zolan turns, opens his mouth to say something, then catches himself and strides from the room instead. A captain letting his officers sort out their own problems. Kyra, on the other hand, puts her hand on her hips, rooting herself into the deck until a quiet word from Catsper has her following the others out. With the door shut behind Quinn, who is the last to leave, I take a seat back at the table as Domenic instructed.

"You never told me that you revealed your Gift to Zolan."

I straighten my spine and wait. Domenic and I aren't

friends. And that's a good thing. This would be more difficult if we were.

"Well?" Domenic prods.

"My apologies, sir, what is the question?"

Domenic's jaw tightens, a vein pulsing along its defined side while the silence stretches between us. A call announcing the *Helix*'s speed as nine knots echoes from the deck above. Finally, Domenic shakes his head, his hair swaying, the sparkle of hurt in his eyes flashing once before disappearing behind a naval mask. "Very well, if you do not trust me to partake in decisions such as whether to tell the Felielle navy about your magic, that *is* your prerogative."

Yes, it is. I sit, still and patient. Just as Domenic ordered me to.

His large hands splay on the tabletop, stalling another heartbeat before he speaks. "In light of the new chain of command, I would like to make my expectations of you clear."

Storms and hail. I keep my face still and keep my silence. Domenic has a right to this conversation, this tone, this superiority that's clawing at my bones. He could have chosen to welcome me, to let me mourn my loss of command while helping me find footing in my new role. He chose this route instead.

And now I'm choosing not to give him the satisfaction of seeing me flinch. "Which part of duty do you believe I need a reminder of, sir?" I ask evenly.

"The part where you obey my orders," snaps Domenic, his tightly buttoned facade finally cracking. "As I'd obeyed yours."

I open my hands. "I've served under you before, sir."

"Aye. And as I recall, the last time you were under my command, you hijacked the bloody ship to follow the gut feeling of a Gifted prisoner you were ordered to stay away from."

"That was different."

"And the war games a month ago, was that different too?" He shakes his head. "For someone raised in the navy, your notion of command structure leaves enough maneuvering room for a fleet to get by on either side."

Right. We are back to that. Except Domenic now seems to have gotten it into his head to reform me. If I ever doubted my decision not to follow him to the *Raptor*, I do not anymore. I raise my chin, tilting my face up toward his. "I have one ongoing reminder of what happens to those who disobey you and am not anxious for another one. So, yes, I take your meaning, sir."

Domenic sighs and rubs his hands over his face, the cold steel in his blue eyes faltering. "You don't need to call me *sir* when we are alone," he says quietly.

"Aye, sir." I wait a heartbeat before looking toward the door. "Might I be dismissed to my duties?"

THE FOLLOWING THREE days remind me of a dance, with neither partner being quite certain of the steps. Domenic alternately finds fault with everything I do—from how quickly my watch turns out for inspection to which midshipman I send up to the lookout platform—and tells me to stop worrying about the deck and focus on meditation and controlling my Gift. If the former is frustrating, the latter fills me with resentment. Domenic has a right to ask after my magic's evolving capabilities and limitations, not to direct how and when I hone my body.

Unfortunately for Domenic, this isn't the first time in my life where I've answered to a superior I little wish to serve under. The secret is to show no emotion at all, give no indication whether their request to pass the logbook affects you more than a demand to run three hours of gun drill.

"Aye, sir, sound the well to check for water levels."

"No, sir, no problems with the crew to report."

"Aye, sir, the day appears clear."

"Let's go." Catsper kicks my boot as he walks past, a pair of practice blades in his hands. "Unless you've changed your mind about being used for target practice?"

"It will be the highlight of this cruise, Catsper," I say dryly, though it may well be. The one advantage of my new rank is that I finally made time to spar, which I've missed more than I dared admit. Plus, I'm curious to see what the crew will make of me with a weapon.

"What of you, Kyra?" Catsper calls as we approach the raised poop deck at the ship's stern. The hands part before him, their gazes morphing from intrigue to sordid amusement. After seeing Catsper take on two or three of the *Helix*'s marines simultaneously, the notion of him crossing swords with a princess must seem as absurd as the fact that said princess wears an officer's uniform. "If you have finally decided to expand your defensive arsenal beyond talking an attacker to death, you might consider joining Nile and me."

Standing at the poop's rail, Kyra's large, dark eyes narrow on the marine. She crosses her arms. "If there is a world where I'd allow you to beat me with a stick, it is yet to be discovered."

"Pity," says Catsper. "You make it sound delightful."

I press my lips together. The mirth fades, though, when a wiry topman slithers down the ratlines to land just beside the poop deck ladder I'm set to climb.

The man, Joran, smiles to display his lack of two front teeth, his eyes taking in first the practice blades, then me. "Goddess bless me, entertainment with the afternoon grog?" he says quietly enough that only Catsper and I hear the remark. "Must be holiday routine. I'd have prefered whores myself, but this circus will do."

I feign deafness, as I have daily since Zolan announced the change of command to the crew. There is little else for it. Any acknowledgment of having heard the remark would force an official report, which in turn will end with Joran at the grating. A whip would put an instant end to insolent comments but only fuel the sentiment. Plus, it is something I refuse to do—and, storms take me, the hands have somehow worked this out.

Centuries of tradition, I remind myself firmly. I'm up against centuries of tradition. Once I can earn the crew's trust, this pettiness will iron itself out.

Joran snorts.

Catsper stops in his tracks, the flash of his green eyes making Joran retreat a step, his eyes widening with the realization of how deeply he'd miscalculated the marine's attitude on lobbing insults at me.

"Keep going," I mutter into Catsper's ear. "It's not worth it."

The marine twitches his brow. With his loose pants, hair tied back into a bun, and a shirt sleeveless despite the chill, Catsper looks ready to take on the entire complement of the *Helix.* Now the marine twirls one of the blades in his hand, his attention skipping over the gathering crowd.

The remaining color drains from Joran's face.

Don't do it, Catsper, I think furiously at him.

He doesn't. He does something much worse.

"Mr. Dana," Catsper calls, his voice lazy but loud enough to breach the four paces of quarterdeck to where Domenic and Zolan are standing. "I'm feeling indisposed today, and Ms. Greysik is in need of a sparring partner. Since you are presently off watch, I was hoping you might accommodate us."

Domenic freezes, staring at us like a deer caught unawares.

"What the hell are you doing?" I ask Catsper quietly through clenched teeth. Domenic disliked crossing swords with me even when we were on speaking terms.

"Reminding several morons that you are an officer," Catsper murmurs with equal quiet, though a great deal more mirth. "Plus, since you and Dana seem unable to converse like human beings, you might as well bash each other's heads with sticks instead."

Storms and hail. Catsper is the Spade version of a meddling hag, and I will strangle him. Just as soon as I dig myself out of the current mess.

"Mr. Dana." Zolan's voice barely reaches me. "Your time is your own, but might I suggest against using it to strike a lady."

I don't flinch, even though my heart stutters, Zolan's words stinging more than Joran's insults. Zolan might call me an officer, but he has not changed his mind about a woman's place in battle. If Domenic agrees, the crew's opinion will be rooted that much deeper.

Turning my back to the quarterdeck, I stretch my arm across my chest and try to imagine something pleasant and impossible—like how good it might feel to actually land a blow on Catsper.

"You are quite correct, sir," Domenic's voice calls behind me.

I'm deaf. Deaf. Deaf. Deaf.

"But I do believe in this case, the invite was to practice with Ms. Greysik the second lieutenant, not Ms. Greysik the royal lady." I turn in time to see Domenic remove his coat and hand his hat to one of the middies. An act of charity to shield my dignity. I should be grateful, but I hate him for it. Three steps have Domenic at the ladder, climbing up to the poop. "Plus," he calls to Zolan over his shoulder, "I would not wish to get on Catsper's bad side by refusing the offer."

My teeth grind.

Catsper tosses a practice sword into my hands, throwing a second to Domenic. I let my fingers brush the polished wood, its cool, slick feel soothing to my quickening pulse. Raised in Ashing with an eye on the admiralty, I've studied swordsmanship since early childhood—an officer's weapon to contrast the common seaman's cutlass. Domenic, who'd risen to officer rank from the lower decks, has little such training. Technically speaking, I'm the stronger swordsman. Practically speaking, Domenic is twice my size and strength.

And then there is the crew. If my appearance with blades drew grins and sneers, the sight of two senior officers squaring off against each other like ragged hyenas is quickly bringing the deck work to a halt.

"Let's get on with it," Domenic murmurs, settling his weight onto his back leg and blading his body into a fighting stance. His face is dark, as if he'd been forced into this somehow.

I raise a brow and swing my blade in a circle, letting myself settle into a world of pure physicality. Voices and glares fade away to make room for the feel of my weight shifting to the balls of my feet, the rhythm of the deck swaying beneath me, the way the sun reflects off the green-blue waves, occasionally flashing into my eyes.

"Start," Catsper commands.

I step forward. Slow and careful. Circling Domenic, forcing him to follow my movements. Hoarding the boat's rhythm for myself.

Domenic is larger and slower, his attention still in part on the deck around him.

That's a mistake, and I tell him so with a quick lunge, the tip of my blade thrusting just below his ribs. A fleshy, satisfying recoil echoes back to my wrist.

Domenic winces in surprise. And pain.

I step back. Circle. Plan my next assault. Closing the distance quickly is a solid approach, a way to turn Domenic's longer reach from advantage to liability.

Eyes locked on Domenic's hips and shoulders, I let the deck bring me down and up, using the surge to close in and swing my blade at his head.

This time, Domenic parries. The impact of our blades ripples up my arm, through my side. *Storms,* he is strong. Instead of standing my ground, I let the force help me twist, turning my back to Domenic for a fraction of a second before my elbow slams into his solar plexus.

The crew chuckles.

I slide away, circling, waiting for Domenic's answering blow.

Nothing. Just a fighting stance tracking my movements, a face blank of emotion despite the hint of a flush rising on Domenic's cheeks.

My next attack is a cut along his side, deliberately slow. Easy to parry.

He does, dipping the hilt of his practice blade so my weapon strikes wood instead of rib. A decent block. But nothing more. No attack, no finesse, no strategy. This isn't a fight, it's a child's game. A streak of hot anger rushes down the column of my spine. "Did you come up here to spar or look pretty?" I demand, pushing closer until I can hook my sword arm around his. Our bodies press together, the rise and fall of Domenic's chest pushing against mine.

"I came up here out of respect for your feelings after Zolan's opinion of a woman's place." Domenic's words are a low hiss. "Whose brilliant idea was it to call me out? Yours or Catsper's?"

The coal-hot fury in my spine chills to ice.

"Mine," I say firmly. As if I'd ever lay blame on Catsper. Throwing friends to the wolves is Domenic's habit, not mine. "If you think crossing blades is a kindness you are granting me, you'll find the truth unpleasant." With that, I hook my heel behind Domenic's leg and dump him unceremoniously onto the deck.

Domenic's arm shoots out to brace himself against the fall, and Catsper curses him for it even before the pain makes Domenic grimace.

"Should have taken that fall across the back," I pant, kicking that poorly placed hand right out from under him, letting the crew chuckle. "Pay attention."

Color rises to Domenic's face, and the next several strikes fall with more force than necessary. I turn Domenic's overcommitments into invitations to rap the wood smartly against his wrist, his thigh, his neck. My next attack has me dropping low to bring my blade almost vertically up to Domenic's jaw. A stupid showmanship move that would have earned me severe reprisal from Catsper, but leaves Domenic befuddled.

I pull the blow, putting enough theatrics behind it to ensure that watching hands know I did so. As if I'm so much better than Domenic that I must contain myself. As if the first officer of the *Helix* is too weak to bear the strike of a practice blade.

"Nile." A low warning growl from Catsper. "Dana appears to be blind this afternoon, but I don't suffer the same ailment."

"Dana, is that who I'm training with?" My voice is just loud enough for the crew to hear without sounding like I intend for the words to carry. "I thought I was fighting the mizzenmast. Certainly he's no more hostile than a piece of wood."

Whatever control the crew kept on themselves snaps to a howl of laughter. Someone—Joran, I think—opines on whether the first officer hadn't accidently put on a man's uniform when he was seeking a woman's dress.

I'm too busy gloating to see Domenic's blade snap into a mighty arc. Not pretty or technical, but backed with every ounce of power the dozen years at sea have drilled into his muscles.

My breath catches, the bodies and practice blades suddenly moving in slow, viscous motion. Too late. I'm too late to parry a strike that's bound to snap my ribs. With a last-ditch hope, I lift myself to my toes, making my body light enough to fly with the blow instead of absorbing its force.

The attack catches me on the uprise. I'm thrust back a foot before landing, pain spreading from just beneath my ribs through my body. *Storms and hail,* had I reacted a hair slower, Domenic would have injured me. Badly. My jaw clenches, blood pumping hard through veins and pain. That wasn't amusing, or safe, or acceptable.

The crew is silent.

Something snaps inside me. I roll to my feet, hissing but not cowed. And not holding back either. Rushing through Domenic's open side, I slam my knee up into his groin. My chest heaves.

Domenic barely manages to shift in time to take the blow across his hips, his eyes flashing in blue fury. Gripping my shoulders, he throws me to the deck, his body following, his knee pinning my left arm.

There is nothing around me but the crushing pressure on my forearm, the roar of blood singing in my ears, the crack of the deck slamming into the back of my head. I'm going to get the arrogant bastard off me, and then I will make him pay. I will make him hurt. And, storms take me, I'm going to enjoy him screaming while the world laughs. My body tightens, a red pounding haze blocking pain and thought. I swing my right hand, aiming my sword hilt into Domenic's temple.

Catching my wrist in motion, Domenic bends it so hard, I release my sword with a howl. With the next breath, Domenic is fully atop me, straddling my body and holding my wrists, his bulk grinding me into the deck. The air rushes from my lungs, and Domenic's weight cinches viciously down on my ribs, making it impossible to draw breath. I swallow another grunt of pain. His nostrils flare, his muscles already shifting to cock his fist, the knuckles aiming for my cheek.

But the air I have, it isn't just in my lungs.

Tapping my magic, I punch a cold thin wind into Domenic's eyes, shove it up his nose and down his gullet.

Domenic recoils, and I arch my hips, trapping his right arm and leg to roll us over. To get on top. To crack my fist into his jaw before he tosses me off like a sack of grain.

Domenic's hair is wild as we scramble to our feet, his breath ragged and hard. Both our hands clench into fists and—

—and find themselves trapped in the iron grips of Zolan and Catsper.

"Gun room," says Zolan coolly into the heaving silence. "Both of you. Now."

CHAPTER 24

NILE

*M*y chest heaves, the *Helix*'s deck around me coming slowly into focus. My heart, still pounding away to feed my fighting muscles, now sounds too hard and fast for the absurd quiet calm. Eyes watch me. Zolan. Catsper. Kyra. Joran. The other hands. Not Domenic, though, whose gaze for once lingers at his feet.

Gun room. Right. I move in a daze. Down the poop deck ladder to the quarterdeck, down farther belowdeck. Follow Domenic through the narrow passageways of the swaying ship. My wrist hurts, as does my abdomen. Domenic has a bulging bruise over his left eyebrow from a blow I don't remember landing.

Except for the bruise, which is a remarkable shade of purplish red, Domenic's face is ashen, reality likely catching up with him as vividly as it is with me. *We started a brawl in full view of the crew.* I wonder if Domenic has ever strayed this far from naval discipline before. Of course he hasn't. Domenic's version of rebellion is opening the top button of his waistcoat.

Stopping at the gun room door, Domenic pushes it open and steps aside to let me enter first.

"A wee bit late for manners, don't you think?" I say dryly, walking inside.

"I'm sorry."

"For opening the door?" I wince over my bruised ribs, realizing only now that Catsper and Zolan had not followed us down.

Domenic makes no retort. His head is down, his shoulders tight, two fingers of his left hand pulsing against his thigh. Considering how badly I wanted to hurt him a few minutes ago, I don't know why this bothers me.

"Are you all right?" I ask.

Domenic drops into a chair, his forearms braced on his thighs. Sweat drips from his hair onto his face, the drops sliding down the angled set of his jaw. For a heartbeat, it seems like he's decided to ignore me, but then his head gives a single, firm shake. No.

No?

I blink, studying his face, his body. He has to be all right. Of course he's all right. We both are. A bit bruised but...but Domenic is stripped bare. I can feel it. To me, the mayhem on deck was just an errant confrontation, another day of proving myself to the crew. But for Domenic, for him, it was something else entirely. As if he's stepped over some invisible line of demarcation and shattered something that can never be repaired.

I'd wanted to inflict pain. But not this much. Not this way.

I pull a chair up beside him, though I doubt we've much

more time to speak. "It was just a fight, Domenic. Zolan is not turning this whole ship around based on a fistfight in the middle of a bloody war. And he won't strap officers to a grating the way he would a common seaman."

"I hurt you." Quiet words, said toward the deck.

I snort. "You hurt me a great deal more before you ever swung that practice blade. Let us not confuse a few bruises with reality."

"The reality, Ms. Greysik," says Zolan, striding into the gun room, a tense Catsper at his heels, "is that two officers of a commissioned man-of-war in His Felielle Royal Majesty's armada acted like a pair of snot-nosed midshipmen and disgraced the uniform I wear."

Domenic and I rise to our feet, standing shoulder to shoulder while Zolan picks up a stray pen off the table and taps it against his thigh as he paces.

"Sir, I take full—" Domenic cuts off at a flash of Zolan's eyes.

Step. Step. Step. Zolan's feet measure the length of the gun room, his face blazing. He stops finally a pace away from Domenic and me, and places his own hands behind his back. "When I was concerned that a woman's presence on a ship of war would lead to discipline problems, I wasn't imagining it being you who would swing the punches, Ms. Greysik. Nor did it ever occur to my imagination, Mr. Dana, that a Felielle officer, a *captain* of a frigate, no less, would raise his hand against a lady. I am disgusted." Zolan's nostrils flare. "What have you to say for yourselves?"

I keep my face raised and chin high. Domenic is as ashen as I've ever seen him, so much so that I'm unsure he could speak even if he wanted to. *Storms and hail.* Less than a quarter hour ago, I longed to slam my fist into Domenic's face, and now my treacherous hand wants to brush his in reassurance.

"Well?" Zolan demands, starting to pace before us again.

"It felt good. Sir," I blurt. Which is stupid and idiotic, but at least has the advantage of being true. Domenic's head jerks toward me. Behind Zolan, Catsper presses his lips together.

Zolan freezes. Stares at me as if recounting the words in his mind. "It. Felt. Good?" he clarifies.

"Aye, sir."

Throwing his pen into the air, Zolan drops himself into a chair, mumbling, "It felt good," beneath his breath. "It felt good."

"And is this your recollection of the event as well, Mr. Dana?" Zolan asks.

"No. Sir."

"Mr. Catsper," Zolan snaps, making the marine straighten his back. "You are Spade trained?"

"Aye, sir," Catsper answers with some caution.

"Excellent. Since you orchestrated this disaster, you shall have a hand in cleaning it up. I want the overabundance of energy Mr. Dana and Ms. Greysik ail from to be channeled into an educational exhibition before the crew. By the time you finish, I expect Ms. Greysik's good feelings to be such a distant memory that she can't so much as *think* of them without falling over from exhaustion." Zolan's eyes narrow on the marine, his voice dropping to a chilling rumble. "Should I find your efforts falling one hair short of a Spade's notion of discipline, Mr. Catsper, not only will I put both your friends to the grating, but I will make you wield the cat. All your uniforms be damned. Am I understood?"

Ice grips my throat, and the usual amused gleam is nowhere to be found in Catsper's eyes as the marine bows. Catsper flashes Domenic and me a single apologetic look before striding out to lead the way on deck.

SEVENTY-FOUR. Seventy-five. Seventy-six. My lungs burn as I sprint across the poop to touch the deck by the starboard rail, then the port, then back again. Eighty. Eighty-one. The ten paces of moving deck are longer with each sprint. I can't feel my feet, and the incessant cramp in my hamstring threatens to topple me utterly. Ninety.

Domenic vomits over the rail.

No one laughs. The hands' mirth had ended two hours ago, sometime between the second time I slipped in my own blood, which trickled in a thin, viscous thread from my nose, and Domenic heaving up the little water we've been allowed.

Ninety-nine. One hundred.

"Enough." Catsper booms, nothing of my friend lurking behind his cold green eyes. "Bring the boat in."

My stomach clenches, a chill gripping my spine. A ship's boat, lowered to tow along on a line attached to the *Helix's* hull, looks innocent enough—but hauling it in over rough seas makes every muscle scream. During our last attempt, the waves had ripped the rope from my hands, taking skin with it. The red stains where I gripped the line last beacon mockingly.

Domenic stumbles up behind me, gripping the line. His body shakes, but even the tiny body heat we share standing beside each other is a luxury.

"Haul!" Catsper orders.

We throw our weight against the rope, make no headway against the waves. Not now, when just standing is enough to make me dizzy. My foot slips, and the deck slams into my side before I even realize I've fallen.

"How long can you keep them at it?" Zolan asks.

"Are you asking how long until I run out of ideas, or until I kill them?" says Catsper.

"Presuming neither of those will come to pass, how long until they collapse?"

Catsper's voice is low and hard. "I can keep them on the verge of collapse without actually destroying their ability to move for three days, Mr. Zolan. By the middle of day two, I will require safety monitors. So you tell me, sir, how long do you want them at it?"

Days. I grip Domenic's arm, and he gives me a reassuring squeeze back. He heard too.

"One more hour," Zolan says, putting his hands behind his back and returning to the quarterdeck with due calm, letting the marine's "Aye aye sir" hit him in the back.

Relief floods only long enough for Catsper to twist around, finding me still on my knees.

"Since 'haul' and 'nap' sound alike to you, we shall all wake up with a swim," Catsper says, taking off his boots. When I blink, exchanging an equally befuddled look with Domenic, Catsper points to the rolling waves of the ocean below. "The sea is the large wet thing three paces to starboard. Shouldn't be too difficult to find. Dive. Now."

"Sip it slowly." Kyra frowns, placing a mug of hot tea into Domenic's shaking hands.

Wrapped in blankets and sitting on the cot beside me, Domenic accepts the mug and promptly sloshes the liquid over his fingers. He stares at the steaming drops now hanging off his skin.

"Would you like some help?" Kyra asks him.

"I would like to lie on the deck and never move again." Domenic eyes the deck of the great cabin, which Zolan had insisted Kyra and I keep. "Ever. I don't ever want to move again."

"The deck is all yours." My teeth chatter, and I press my burning palms close to my chest. "I claim the cot." The words hang in the air between us as my mind catches up to my mouth. I'd just meant I was tired, not that he wasn't welcome to share my sheets. Which he isn't. But *that* is not what I meant to say just now. I... "May I have some tea as well?" I ask Kyra.

"Let me see your hands first."

My palms give a painful throb as I pull the blanket closer about me. The wounds can be tended...later. Much later. When I'm not teetering at the edge of endurance. For now, the thought of looking—much less tending—to the stripped skin makes me dizzy all over again.

Domenic sets his mug down, his forehead creasing. "What happened to your hands?" His long arm breaches the two feet of space between us, gently pulling out my wrist. "Let me see."

I tense. "I'm fine."

"I know." The feel of his hand on my skin is enough to make my heart stutter. *Storms* but I miss this touch, the strength and comfort of his arms wrapped about me, the scent of sea that always clings to his clothes. I miss it so much that I let Domenic bring my burning hands into the open, willing to bear the pain just to have him clasp my wrist a little longer. After four hours of dizzying work, I've earned a few moments of illusion.

The illusion shatters.

Broken red marks. Oozing blood and a clearish fluid. Several flayed flaps of skin. *Storms.*

Kyra turns her head, then steps away to retrieve a rolled bandage and water.

I glance back at my palms, and the cabin sways.

"It's all right." Domenic brushes his finger along the healthy outside edge. I jerk my hand back, but Domenic's grip on my wrist is unyielding despite a soft voice. He rubs a small circle on the inside of my forearm, covering the sensitive skin beneath my elbow. A distraction from my skinned palms. "A rope burn." Domenic's voice caresses my face. "I've done as much as a middie, sliding down the ratlines. It's all right."

Kyra clears her throat. "I brought some—"

"I'll take care of it," Domenic says, holding his hand out for the bandage without ever glancing from me. His eyes, blue and addicting, warm me more deeply than any blanket.

Which is ridiculous and goes to show just how bloody exhausted I am.

Kyra obediently hands over the rolled cloths and steps out of the cabin.

"Can you move closer?" Domenic asks.

My heart rattles. I want to move closer. I shouldn't move closer. Closer is warmth and strong arms and the scent of salt and brine that wraps around me. Closer is judgment and betrayal. "Closer?"

Domenic holds up the bandage. "I can't reach your other hand from here."

Right. I slide over beside him, my face tingling, and lay my hand in his lap just to show that I wasn't ever thinking he'd meant anything different. The next moments are quiet as Domenic wraps my hands, his own gentle and precise, as if something colossal depends entirely on how neatly the white cotton layers overlap each other. Tying off the wraps with knots only a seaman would think of using on bandages, Domenic hesitates, finding small strands of cloth to tuck a bit more neatly into place, waiting for me to pull away.

"This is a very strange day," I whisper instead. The blanket has slipped off from Domenic's shoulders, revealing a bare torso, the dark ink of his tattoo stark against chilled skin. He'd slipped into a pair of dry trousers, but the extra effort to don a shirt had seemed too monumental when we came. I only wear clothes because Kyra helped me into them. I rotate my hands so my fingers rest on Domenic's wrist, just above his pulse. "What with near drowning, and seeing Catsper in his full tormented Spade glory, you trampling a regulation—I'd sooner believe the Tirik are allied with an evil cannibalistic race."

"Aye." Domenic swallows. His dark hair, still wet, glistens in the sun rays coming through the great cabin's window. A drop of ocean slips over Domenic's forehead, bouncing playfully onto his eyelashes. He shakes his head the way Bear might to get the water off, and I laugh. Domenic touches a finger to my lips. "I do believe Quinn is standing guard outside the door," he whispers. "Let us not give him the wrong idea."

"Let us not give each other the wrong idea either," I whisper, catching Domenic's forearm as he stiffens at once, staying him before he can lean away. My eyes leap to his tattoo, to where a small scar cuts through the inked rope wrapping an anchor. My body remembers tracing that rope, the way that small bump scrapes my finger pads, how Domenic shudders when touched there because it's one of the few places he is ticklish.

My heart is trotting and my skin tingles, the aching, tired muscles adding to a reality-dimming fog. Beneath the naked tips of my fingers, Domenic's muscles coil to match my own tightening chest. I bite my lip. "Today...today is just an odd day. Today is just today. All right?"

Domenic's hand tentatively brushes my hair, the calluses on his fingers tracing the outline of my brow, my cheekbone, my jaw, making my skin blaze from the touch. "Today is just today," he whispers back, leaning his face down toward mine. Domenic's lips part, his warm breath caressing my face, a shudder rushing through him. "I can't hold off much longer," he breathes.

"Then don't." I bring my mouth up to meet his, and the chill lingering on Domenic's lips brushes against my skin. His mouth grazes mine tentatively before pulling back to linger a hair's width away, letting our breaths mix through parted lips. Domenic's palm finds the back of my neck, fitting into the groove with familiar perfection.

I shudder, my body suddenly hot despite the cold feel of Domenic's skin. A soft moan escapes my throat, and I part my lips wider in invitation. In demand. In anything that would make him press hard against me.

Domenic exhales a warm breath over my ear, the tip of his nose nudging my earlobe in a way that shoots a jolt of energy down my core. The bit of rough stubble on Domenic's chin scratches the front of my throat, so close and yet not nearly close enough.

Domenic shifts to kiss my upper lip, his mouth, now divinely warm, pressing around tender flesh for heartbeats before pulling back once more. The deprivation makes me vibrate with need, and yet the bastard makes me wait longer still, nipping the edge of my ear before kissing my neck. The angle of my jaw. The corner of my mouth.

"Please," I rasp, my arms pressing against his sides. "Please."

Domenic's hand tightens on the back of my neck with sudden raw savageness as his mouth finally covers mine, and we connect in a kiss that is an explosion of flame and desire.

CHAPTER 25

KYRA

*A*ll in all, they'd been fortunate. In the weeks since the Bevnian attack, only two forces threatened the ship: boredom of routine—though Commander Zolan proved a deft hand at concocting chores to attack that particular problem— and the possibility of spontaneous combustion, which surfaced anytime Nile and Dana shared breathing space. While the two did not try to dismember each other again, their forceful attempts at proper courtesy made even routine pleasantries taste like wartime negotiations. Fortunately, Zolan separated Nile and Dana between different watches the day following their spat, reducing their time in each other's company to a few tense minutes a day when they handed the quarterdeck to each other.

For now, it was Catsper who worried Kyra more. Since taking Dana and Nile for that final forced swim, the marine had been more aloof than usual, dividing his time between silently monitoring Nile when she was on deck and training with the ship's marines at all other hours.

"I can't sense anything from Catsper lately," Kyra confided to Nile over supper—which the princess ate only because Kyra forcefully replaced Nile's Diante cultural text with a bowl of soup and forced a spoon into Nile's hand. Though Nile would never admit it, she needed a keeper. "I think he has started to shield against me consciously."

"Is that possible?" Nile asked, her mouth full. "Because I'd like to."

Kyra snorted. "Certainly," Kyra said, moving the hard tack that passed for ship's bread closer to the other girl. "You've learned how to hide emotions from the crew. Just multiply that a hundredfold, and there you have it. As for Catsper, I think the debacle with the sparring match and aftermath bothered him more than he let on."

A spike of embarrassment flared from Nile as it always did when someone brought up the incident, but the girl tamped it down efficiently. "Have you marked Catsper's notion of a relaxing afternoon? The bugger probably just doesn't wish to admit that he enjoyed sweating us." Nile grinned, absently knocking a piece of biscuit against the table. "Jesting aside, I do think you are overthinking Catsper's silence. We always think that the one thing we do not see or know must be vitally important or interesting—but that is a logical fallacy."

Kyra turned her face to avoid watching the weevils crawl free from Nile's food. "Has he spoken to you about it?"

"No." Nile dunked her biscuit to let it soak in the broth. "But that is because there is nothing to talk about. And no harsh feelings. There never were. Catsper was following orders—and so far as naval discipline goes, Domenic and I were very fortunate. All three of us know as much." She frowned as the ship's bell sounded, calling her back to deck.

"You've barely started supper."

Nile shrugged into her coat, threw the remaining biscuit to Bear, and gave Kyra's forearm a squeeze. "I'm not starving to death, and Catsper is not wallowing in despair over overseeing some sprints and push-ups. I promise. Stop fretting. Your time is better spent learning what you can of Diante than watching me eat anyway. You know where the books are."

With a fortifying breath and a smile that tried and failed to hide Nile's fatigue from Kyra, the princess was gone and the ship continued humming its day. As Nile suggested, Kyra spent some time at language and culture study before leaving the cabin to take some fresh air above deck. Now that things had settled into an odd sort of normal, the *Helix* no longer felt as small and hostile as it had when Kyra first stepped aboard. Strange, superstitious—the crew teetered on the verge of panic when a midshipman almost ordered rum added to water instead of water to rum in the preparation of their grog—but homey as well. Nile was the kind of sister Kyra never had and secretly always wanted. Kyra's own siblings—

Kyra stiffened, a sensation so potently rotten filling her mouth that she choked. For a moment, Kyra thought the taste came from the memory itself, but footsteps behind her proved a different reality. She spun, pressing her back against the nearest bulkhead.

"Kyra." Lord Vikon's smile split his face. Although three years younger, Vikon was a head taller than Kyra, and his muscles, while less developed than most sailors', were still honed by days on deck and weather. His slicked-back brown hair and upturned nose gave him an air of arrogance that never quite disappeared. "You are a hard woman to find."

Kyra's heart pounded as her dry tongue formed words. There was no outward reason for the reaction, nothing except the taste that could be a memory. Vikon stood two paces away, his hands clasped behind his back, his head inclined with more courtesy than her station was due.

"Why were you looking for me, my lord?" she asked.

His gaze raked her. "I wasn't." Vikon shrugged a shoulder. "It was just a figure of speech. The ship can be a lonely place despite the bodies pressed together like pork in a barrel."

"I need to go," Kyra said, but didn't move. Couldn't move. Not without turning her back to Vikon, and everything inside her screamed never to do that.

Vikon's smile widened. A python swaying above his prey. "Of course," said Vikon, making no move to step aside. "Don't let me keep you from your duties."

Kyra swallowed.

"Vikon." Catsper's voice rang out on Kyra's other side, and the marine's lithe, shirtless form approached with long steps. The vile taste in Kyra's mouth mixed with starchy undertones of displeasure. "If you have trouble finding something to do, I'm in need of a sparring partner."

Vikon's jaw tightened, and Catsper raised a brow in silent response. Snorting, the boy touched his hat and finally strode away.

Catsper's attention focused on Kyra. He must have been working with the ship's marines, for beads of sweat escaped his tied-up hair and rolled down the groove of his muscled chest. The man was certainly not shy about removing his shirt and would change now only to look respectable while Nile stood watch. Catsper shifted his weight, the skin stretched taut over lean muscles showing a horrid collection of scars, both clean and jagged.

"I killed nineteen children."

Maybe Catsper deserved his scars. Maybe he deserved more of them than he wore.

"Did something happen that should not have?" Catsper's voice was dangerously quiet.

"No," Kyra answered truthfully. Nothing did happen. Nothing at all but phantom memories.

"The offer to train—"

"No." Kyra crossed her arms. "Do you seriously imagine I'd voluntarily subject myself to your notion of time well spent?"

"No. You would not." A muscle tightened along Catsper's shoulder, his face darkening. "I quite see your point."

Stars. No. She'd meant Catsper's own training with the ships' marines, not... "Nile isn't upset over what happened on deck," Kyra said quickly. "She said it was the best of alternatives. That Zolan would have done a great deal worse if you'd been easier on her."

Cold green eyes met hers. "Why are you telling me this?"

"I thought you'd want to know." Kyra raised her chin. "On the odd chance that you were concerned what effect driving your friends to the brink of collapse might have had on them."

Catsper's hand braced on the bulkhead an inch shy of Kyra's ear, lethal violence clinging to him like perfume. "Stay. Out. Of my head."

Putting a hand on his chest, Kyra pushed Catsper back, wrinkling her nose at the marine's sweat now transferred to her palm. "I'm not in your head." She wiped her hand on her dress. "I just have eyes in mine."

Catsper snorted and turned away toward the gun room and —presumably—a clean set of clothes.

Kyra's heart jumped. "Wait." The word was out before Kyra could stop herself, even though she knew she was being stupid.

Vikon was long gone, nothing had happened, and the ship, for being stuffed to the gills with men, was safer than any town on land. Certainly safer than her own house back in Milan. Just now, though... "Would you mind walking me to the great cabin? I find myself under the weather."

Catsper twisted at once, motioning for Kyra to walk before him. He asked no question, the only sound a whistle summoning Rum from the ship's shadows. When the marine left Kyra at the great cabin, the dog proudly invited himself inside instead. Curled into a ball atop Kyra's cot, Rum gave a soft, self-satisfied sneeze and started snoring.

By what had to be a miracle of the stars, the *Helix* suffered no further mishaps as it passed through something called Bottleneck Juncture and approached Diante waters. The bit of well-overdue good fortune also put the *Helix* at station a day forward of schedule, which left the crew and officers with a great deal more time to stare at the horizon than either had anticipated. Kyra found little excitement in the exercise until the masts of three Diante ships suddenly finally blossomed from a distant watery abyss.

Then it hit her.

Where an hour earlier there was nothing but the rolling waves, now there was a nation, a people, a fleet of ships. "Do you think the Bevnians' entry into the war will make a Diante alliance more or less likely?" Kyra asked Dana as he helped her focus a spyglass.

"I don't know." The officer's voice was quiet. "But I imagine that without Diante support, there may not be a Lyron League for us to return to in a few months' time. There is a great deal more riding on Nile's diplomatic success than any of us should be comfortable with."

Kyra looked sidelong toward Nile, who now clasped her hands behind her back and stood at the rail. Outwardly, she appeared as calm as Zolan and Dana, but the anxiety pouring off her was enough to make Kyra's own stomach clench.

Nile's gaze darted to the skylarking middies. No one in her right mind should *want* to climb suicidally high into the shrouds to satisfy curiosity, but Nile never claimed sanity. Kyra wondered whether it was the dignity of the girl's position or pragmatism over convulsions that kept her rooted to deck now—whatever it was, Kyra was grateful for it.

It was because Kyra was already watching Nile's face that she caught the sudden widening of the girl's eyes. And then the princess swore very, very colorfully.

CHAPTER 26

NILE

Standing at the *Helix*'s rail, I watch with bated breath as the approaching Diante ships take form on the foggy horizon, the filled sails rising toward the clouds with power and dignity. The weather has taken a chilly turn, and the wind nips my skin. The seas, however, are calm and clear, lapping the ocean surface gently. The first of the three vessels I recognize immediately as Admiral Addus's *Wave*, the Divine Squadron's flagship aboard which I'd once found unexpected aid. The warm hand of memory strokes the back of my neck, and I allow myself a smile. Somewhere between fighting wars, clashing cultures, and cajoling allies, there will also be the simple meeting with an old and wise friend. One whom I've missed more than I realized.

The other two ships are new to my eyes. One is a seventy-four-gun ship of the line, holding a subordinate post to Addus's

Wave. But the third... Swearing soundly, I lower my glass, snapping it shut against my thigh. I'd think this a jest if the Diante had any sense of humor.

"What is it?" Kyra asks, and I try not to wince as she steps onto the quarterdeck, which is sacredly reserved for ship's officers. Seeing her, Zolan throws up his hands. The girl is so honestly oblivious to naval custom that after a month at sea, the crew forgives her the same trespasses they allow Bear and Rum.

I point to the third ship. As large as the battleships beside it, the vessel appears to lack broadside armament altogether—or the square rigging of a man-of-war. "That four-masted monstrosity is a barque. A bloody glorified merchie."

"Is sailing a barque the equivalent of an insult in naval tradition?" asks Kyra.

I sigh. "No. But it is a very plain signal of peace—the Diante's preemptive countermove to any attempt to talk them into joining a war."

"So barques are a naval sign of peace?" Kyra clarifies.

"No. It's—"

"It's that she carries no guns to speak of, and her sails are rigged differently from ours," Domenic injects, placing his hands into the small of his back as he comes to stand beside Kyra and me. I move over to make room. Domenic might look dignified just now, but I know his back is so straight at least partially because it hurts to flex it. "Her sails can be managed with a smaller crew than ours require, but there is a maneuverability cost. She is awkward, unarmed, and very, very expensive. No kingdom in Lyron would dare put a ship that size into the sea for fear of losing it. She is too tempting a target for the enemy, and her loss would be too crushing in lives and gold."

"The Diante flaunt her to show just how distant they are

from violence," I say, reclaiming the conversation Domenic hijacked. "And that they wish to remain so." *And damn me if I know how I'm going to convince them into a war. Might as well chat with the sun about changing orbit while I'm at it.*

"Mr. Dana, back sail and hold position," Zolan calls, breaking up the conversation. "Mr. Vikon, make our number, if you please."

"Aye aye, sir." Domenic touches his hat and retreats from my side. He is a different officer than he'd been a month ago, speaking more quietly now and using fewer words to direct the crew. The rope's end is gone from his grip, and even the bosun's mates under him are rare to deliver stinging chastisements. He's orderly and efficient, and the seamen look toward him with respect instead of fear as they'd had to on the *Aurora*.

I'm unsure what the crew makes of me. Part of me is too sore and worried to care.

"Lord Vikon," Zolan says in a too-patient baritone, "have we an interpretation of our host's return flag signal yet?"

"Aye, sir. The... Deee—"

"*The Diante Empire*, I imagine," Zolan snaps.

"Right." The middie fiddles with the code book. "The Diante Empire welcomes Captain... This last one is spelled out, sir. N-I-L-"

"Good Goddess," Zolan murmurs before raising his voice. "The Diante Empire welcomes Captain Nile Greysik. And if I'm not mistaken, they are already lowering a cutter. He turns to me, formally touching his hat. "I believe this is where I turn the *Helix* over to you, Ms. Greysik. *Captain* Greysik, begging your pardon, ma'am."

I nod and bow toward the Diante flagship, my heart pounding with the knowledge that many spyglasses are trained on me. My back is straight, my chin lifted. I'm feigning the type of confidence a crew would expect.

Domenic gives me a small nod.

Vikon, for storms know what reason, scurries belowdeck.

"Our hosts appear enthusiastic to start our acquaintance," I say, forcing a smile to my face while the boat starts its long row to us. The lowered cutter is another wordless message, one informing the *Helix* that she is not to cross the invisible lines into Diante waters. The Diante Empire might have agreed to a meeting, but it is to be held squarely on their terms.

"It is time to go, then?" Lord Vikon's high-pitched voice sends homicidal thunder rolling through Zolan's face. Emerging from the companionway ladder onto deck in his full dress uniform, the boy looks ready for a meeting with the emperor himself.

"You, Mr. Vikon—"

"-Have been requested to attend Her Highness in this meeting by members of the royal family," Vikon retorts, his chin in the air. "Sir."

Zolan's nostrils flare, and for the first time since coming aboard, I see the man's iron control finally on the edge of snapping.

Two long strides bring me to the commander's side, and I grab the man's wrist. I never imagined myself pulling Zolan out of a fire, but it is a day of firsts, it appears. "Whatever you'd like to do to him, sir, it's not worth your career."

Zolan's eyes narrow, his voice so low that even standing inches away, I can barely make out the words. "Perhaps it is. Is he telling the truth?"

"If by 'members of the royal family' he means his father, then yes." I sigh. *Storms,* this is poor timing for this conversation —a fact which, I've no doubt, played into Lord Vikon's calculations. I study Zolan, the entitled middie, and the approaching cutter, my mind racing as quickly as coherent thought allows. "But this is the last card for the boy to play—once you note in the log that he was granted the ultimate honor of initial encounter, you can lock him in the midshipman's berth for eternity and none can claim he'd been slighted."

Zolan draws a deep breath in what must be a vain attempt to curb his fury. "Mr. Dana," he barks before I can stop him. "Get changed. You will be accompanying the party as well. I will expect a full report on our young gentleman's conduct upon your return."

I open my mouth to protest, but Zolan shakes his head.

"If you must take a rabid dog over there, the least I can do is put it on a leash," Zolan says with finality and steps away before I broker further argument.

By the time the Diante cutter pulls up on our lee, Zolan has a side party assembled and ready. The bosun starts piping the official welcome the instant the first of the Diante seamen appears at the entry port. The men come up one by one, identical in their burnt-orange uniforms, trained motions, and perfect hand-to-heart salutes. Within moments, two columns of six sailors with slanted almond eyes and shoulder-length, rust-colored hair form a walkway on the *Helix*'s deck.

Only then does their captain come, the gold epaulettes adorning his shoulders sparkling like miniature suns. My heart sinks.

Of a height with me and fifteen years my senior, the Diante officer's familiar face is just as cold as it was the first time we met. Even the crow's feet imprinted at the corners of his eyes are harsh as frost. His Greatness Captain Bassic, the captain of Admiral Addus's flagship and a strong critic of female officers in general and me in particular.

I step forward, and the men snap to attention with a resounding clap of palms against thighs. No signals. No words. Just a single smooth movement of a dozen bodies.

"Captain Bassic." I bow. My Diante is stronger than when we'd met last, and I am grateful for the last half year of language training. "It is an honor to see you again, sir."

"And you, Your Highness," Bassic answers in Lyron, slyly ignoring both my position and improved language skills while still blanketing the meeting with courtesy. "I trust your journey here was uneventful."

"I wish I could say it was." I obligingly switch back to Lyron and bow again. The Diante like bows. "But I fear the Ardent Ocean is not without its battles. It would please me to share anything you might find to be of use to your own ship."

Captain Bassic's answering smile is ice cold. *I care nothing for your war,* his eyes say without apology. *Do not try to sway me with tales of hardship.* "It will be my pleasure to listen to any tales you deem my ears worthy of," Bassic says aloud. "Admiral Addus is awaiting us on the *Stardust*, where a small reception has been prepared. It would be my honor to escort you."

"The *Stardust*?" I clarify, following Bassic's gaze to the four-masted barque. "Not the *Wave*?"

"The pleasure barque is the most luxurious vessel in the empire and was chartered specifically to welcome you to the Empire, Your Highness." Bassic's hard tone leaves little doubt of his opinion of both the extravagance and its waste on me. "Is that of concern?"

"Not at all," I say with another polite bow despite my clenching chest. There is nothing *wrong* with the captain's invitation. Nothing at all except that it puts an armed Diante ship of the line right between me and the *Helix*.

CHAPTER 27

NILE

The Diante cutter rocks its displeasure at the sudden intrusion of passengers as Domenic, Catsper, Quinn, Kyra and Vikon and I join Captain Bassic's crew. The fresh wind ruffles my hair and tempts my magic. My heart gives a nervous thump in reply. I would little like to fall to convulsions in the middle of the deck, and without Bear, I'll have little forewarning of an oncoming episode.

Gods touched, that's what Diante call the Gifted. Vessels chosen by higher powers to carry magic. It is a more dignified image than the cripples the Lyron kingdoms name us, but the end result is the same despite different dress: a general belief that Gods touched should keep to themselves, focus on little beyond their magic, and endure the costs without complaint.

Passing the invisible demarcation line into Diante waters, marked by a shift in the sea current, sends a shiver through me.

The cutter settles on the calmer sea, swinging around the majestic *Wave*—where hundreds of seamen stand in perfect rows to salute our passage—and turning toward the floating welcome reception. The *Stardust's* ladder is larger and easier to climb than a fighting frigate's hull, with extra safety ropes lowered to assist landsmen. I motion for Kyra to make use of those while I hop nimbly onto the swaying footholds and, to Captain Bassic's clear disappointment, mount the deck without mishap.

In place of hundreds of seamen, *Stardust's* greeting starts with...children. Two lanes of boys twirling ribbons of every shade of blue and green while a quartet of violins breathes life into the silken ocean. The music and children build to a storm, the sea parting to acrobatic dancers twining themselves into impossible shapes.

"Stars." Kyra clutches my arm as the dancers braid themselves together to make a single great beast. Wonder fills her voice, sweet and ripe. "Have you seen anything so beautiful before?"

"No." Not with a dozen years of war weighing on Lyron kingdoms. Even Felielle, landlocked and fat and central to arts and learning, has no funds to waste on training performers of the caliber the Diante Empire sent out to amuse us at sea.

The dancers finish, and I am about to offer prescribed applause when the quieting music whispers back to life and a rich *bom bom bum* of a gong sends all the performers kneeling on one knee. The hatch to the companionway opens to herald a troupe of two dozen young people—male and female both—ranging from ten to twenty years in age. The newcomers are clad in the bright colors of the rainbow, the girls' faces painted like butterfly wings. The four youngest of them sit on pillowed litters, silver bells adorning their ankles and wrists. The group comes toward me and bows, sending my magic into a sudden tornado of desire.

Gifted. Gods touched. *Storms.*

Bom bum bum, the gong calls again. Louder. Stronger. Stronger than it should be. Louder than is natural. *Bom bom bum.*

The sound grows with each strike, amplifying more and more until the vibration of the one single instrument fills all the air around as. As the music reaches its peak, two of the Gifted step forward and bow their heads to a shower of applause. I bring my hands together with the others, even as my gaze surveys the waiting performers.

There are twelve of them in total, six male, six female. Four standing apart from the others, as if afraid of being accidently struck. Water callers for whom a bruise can mean death. Looking closer at the litters at the wings of the semicircle, I realize that the performers sitting atop the pillows aren't children but adolescents with the tiny bodies and weak muscles of stone callers.

Magic is never free, whether we are called cripples or Gods touched.

"Look!" Kyra's gasp calls my attention back to the show, where fountains of water are arching gracefully through the air. One. Two. Three. A whole corridor soon rises above the deck, pearly beads of ocean sliding along invisible rails from port to starboard.

The gong calls again, and instead of smoothly riding through the arches, the streams of water crash into each other, erupting into a fine mist that rains down on us. A volcano of beauty and power.

A thunder of applause rolls over the deck, a background fiddle and several more instruments adding their voices to the celebration. All the performers return to the stage for bows and cheers before dispersing into informal dancing spurred along by the music's call. On cue, stewards appear bearing flat trays with bits of fruit, sticky pasties filled with a sweet reddish-brown paste, and small tumblers of a clear alcoholic drink, served warm, with vapors strong enough to make my head spin. With the exception of the few women and girls among the Gifted performers, the rest of the *Stardust*'s complement is made up of men. Men who make the *Stardust* sail, men from the naval ships, men dressed in colorful, high-collared shirts who are plainly here to enjoy the ship's hospitality rather than to make my acquaintance.

I stay where I am. Beautiful as the performance was, it is not the reason I'm here. Sure enough, five minutes later, a limping man in his fifties strides toward me. His hair, braided and tied into a bun, is lined with silver, and his intelligent eyes study me with kindness while all the other Diante part to let him through. Even Captain Bassic retreats from the man's way.

Warm recognition spiders through my chest. "Admiral Addus." I too bow low, and mean it. "It is an honor to see you again, sir. On behalf of all the kingdoms of the Lyron League, I thank you for the kind invitation."

"The honor is all ours, Captain Greysik." Admiral Addus switches from Diante to Lyron, likely in deference to my approaching companions, and inclines his head toward Quinn. "Your friend looked rather different the last time I had the pleasure of seeing him." The admiral's voice, though still warm, is tinged with question. The last time Addus saw Quinn, the latter was bound and kneeling, having recently been discovered with a hold full of Diante Gifted.

"Mr. Quinn has resigned his Tirik commission and kindly agreed to enter my honor guard," I say with practiced ease. I sweep my hand toward Catsper, Domenic, Kyra, and Vikon, introducing them each in turn.

"The performers were divine, sir," Kyra says with unbridled awe as her name sounds. "I cannot thank you enough for the opportunity to see their skill. An experience of a lifetime."

"The *Stardust* is a ship of balance and art," Addus tells Kyra, though I know the words are meant for us all. "It is the first of many of the cultural treasures of the Diante people I hope to share with Captain Greysik."

Cultural treasures. Not ships and guns. Nothing about the Diante welcome is accidental, and my own response must be as nuanced as theirs. Admiral Addus knows what I need. And he's telling me not to ask for it.

Stewards with food and refreshment encircle us, and my conversation with the admiral falls to the usual course of seamen's talk. The weather. The winds. The change of currents brought about by the great quake from around ten months past. We are just circling back to the earlier performance when Vikon rolls his eyes.

"Enough of women's talk." Vikon drains his wineglass and looks between me and Addus. "Is no one going to tell the admiral about the Bevnian attack? I thought we were here to negotiate an alliance, not chat about winds and fashions."

Admiral Addus busies himself with his drink while heat slowly rises to my face. Silent, deafening thunder rolls across us, so forceful that even Vikon seems to realize he's stepped too far off course. Instead of backing sail, however, the middie doubles down. "Ignore me all you wish," he says, slamming his empty wineglass onto a passing steward's tray, "but I'm the only one around here who isn't playing games."

Catsper moves before I can find my breath. One moment, Vikon is standing straight in his tailored uniform, and the next he is kneeling on the deck and moaning as the marine bends the boy's wrist onto itself.

"Let us tour the ship, Lord Vikon," Catsper says nonchalantly, as if he isn't threatening to collapse the boy's joint. "I would welcome your professional expertise on matters of...the deck planks."

I wait until the two move away, but can still think of nothing more diplomatic than straightforward apology. I offer it with a deep bow that makes my sore muscles protest.

"You likely overestimate my control of the Lyron tongue," Addus says with unwavering politeness. "I fear I've no notion of what the young man said."

I start to bow my gratitude, but Addus isn't done speaking.

"I must beg your indulgence to attend a few personal matters," he says, returning his drinking glass to a passing steward. "Please enjoy the *Stardust*'s hospitality before we leave here tomorrow to continue to the capital. I had the pleasure of visiting Ashing some years back, and it is an honor to extend a similar experience to my host's daughter."

I watch the admiral stride away and can't help feeling that I've already failed. Though what I could say to entice my hosts into abandoning their life of abundance to join my war still utterly eludes me.

"You should congratulate the performers," Kyra murmurs. "I think they worry they failed to please you."

Right. Kyra should be the diplomat, not me. I don't even *want* to congratulate the Gifted on their performance, not when coming close to them makes the magic in my blood buzz.

"Nile." Kyra's voice is stern now.

Obediently, I force a smile to my face. Feigning happiness is perhaps not so different from feigning fearlessness, and I've certainly done my share of the latter. With Kyra in tow, I make my way to the closest group of performers, who all stop talking and bow in perfect harmonious unison at my approach.

"It was a wonderful display," I say, choosing a wind-caller girl close to my age to address. Like the others, she wears loose silk trousers, tapered at the ankles, and a top that—while rising modestly to her neck—is tight enough to draw ongoing attention.

The girl blushes and looks to her male companion to answer.

"We are pleased for the chance to share the show with you, Your Highness." The boy's eyes are clear and guileless, and much younger than his age mates in any Lyron kingdom.

Kyra nudges me with her elbow. Apparently I'm not done with this conversation yet.

I clear my throat. "Might I ask how often you practice?"

"Every day," the boy says, the others nodding in support—though the girl waits to take her cue from the boys. "Two hours in the morning, four in the afternoon, and some after dinner."

His whole day. His whole life, really. "Have you...have you ever wished to do something else? Something that little touches your Gift?"

The boy looks confused, and I'm starting to think my Diante is poorer than I thought when he echoes the question. "Something else? I'm terribly sorry for not understanding. The gods have chosen this path for me. How could I do something else?"

"Very good point, sir. Of course." I nod and move on, the boy's voice still sounding in my head. He was born to a path and expects nothing different. Starting a conversation with another Gifted, I watch it follow a similar pattern. Yes, they love what they do. Yes, they work hard. No, they've never considered deviating from the gods' calling. As for the convulsions and muscle loss and unmanageable bleeds, those are all shrugged away as tributes. To be endured gracefully. Just as a Diante medicine woman once told me I must.

When a touch of orange brushes the horizon, I am surprised to find Admiral Addus standing at the rail beside me. We are quiet, the sounds of the revelry behind our backs at odds with the lap of waves before us. The sun is starting its journey to bed, the backlit clouds singing a lullaby to the journey. To the southeast lies the Diante heartland, where no Lyron subject has stepped foot in over a decade, the closest any of them having come being the coastal post at the Siaman, where I'd seen the Diante healer woman. Where the *Aurora* was not allowed to take on water.

"It is a pleasure to see such happy people," I say, my eyes on the horizon. "Happy and comfortable with themselves." The last time the admiral and I met, I'd presented him with dozens of Diante Gifted freshly rescued from a Tirik snare. Men, women, and children who'd surrendered their livelihoods for an ill-fated promise of a cure for the Gods' touch they bore.

A hint of a smile touches the corners of Addus's mouth. "These youth are from prominent families." Now that we are alone, his tone is soft and his words direct. "It would be foolish to deny that privilege of birth ripples through all people—artists, soldiers, Gods touched. We all want a better life for our children."

"Is that why you arranged for the *Stardust* to meet me, sir?" I ask quietly. "To show that my experience with your Gods touched we found heading to the Tirik Institute was...singular?"

Addus shakes his head. "You are a child of war, Nile. These are children of peace. They study beauty and develop their magic, while you perfect the practical. I wanted to show you that they are fulfilled too, just as you are."

"They are children of peace because someone else bears arms on their behalf." The words spill. For this short, private time, I can tell the admiral my true mind, and I savor every second of it. "Nothing is free, sir. Not food, not clothing, not peace and freedom."

"True," Addus agrees. "Which is why I and mine stand guard to protect their beauty and innocence, and we are happy to do it. If you give it a chance, there is much our kingdoms can learn from each other that is not rooted in war."

"May I ask you a question, sir?" I wait for his considered nod before clearing my throat. "If you truly believe the Diante Empire can avoid armed conflict, why is your navy as strong and agile as it is?"

Addus chuckles. "I said we were peace loving, not daft. Our navy is a defensive force. It is our hope never to fire a shot in anger, but should we need to do so, we little wish to miss." He glances sideways at me. "I must perhaps thank you for the opportunity to fly the Ashing flag a few months back. It was an important experience for my officers and crew to see what true battle entails—neutralizing the occasional pirate in the Diante West Corridor notwithstanding."

"They fought admirably." I mean every word. The Diante saved us once. Perhaps it's unjust to request it of them again.

"I have a daughter," the admiral tells me, flowing the conversation smoothly to less treacherous ground. "She is a few years your senior and studies to be a healer. I look forward to introducing you."

"The honor would be mine." I smile. "If she takes after her father, I imagine she will do great things. Find a cure for the Gods touched even. Unlock the Metchti Monastery." I'd once went to sea to find the legendary place, only to learn that it existed only in dreams.

"Mmm." Addus shrugs. "Perhaps. Though perhaps the Gods touched don't need to be cured."

"I imagine everyone would want to give up the side effects at least." I open my palms. "I'm yet to meet someone who enjoys convulsions, unstoppable bleeds, or muscle decay."

Addus chuckles. "Is that not a bit like wishing for commerce without money? A market where you only take and never pay?" The humor leaves his voice. "What was it you told me a few minutes back about nothing being free? The tribute the Gods touched pay would have to be borne by someone else if not them. How else could the balance be maintained?"

I have no answer, and we stand shoulder to shoulder in companionable silence until, some time later, the soft beat of Captain Bassic's boots sounds behind us. Admiral Addus stiffens, and I belatedly realize that he must have given orders for us not to be disturbed, for no one had spoken to either the admiral or me since he'd joined me at the rail bells ago.

Bassic stops a few paces from us. His face is tight and his bow too brisk for diplomacy. My heart skips a beat as the Diante captain straightens before his superior. "Forgive me, sir, but the *Wave* is signaling. Sails off starboard."

CHAPTER 28

KYRA

*K*yra was not jealous, not when the water-caller girl she was speaking with required two attendants just to ensure nothing accidently damaged her flesh. Physical contact was forbidden as a matter of course, and even the conversation they were having required at least a full pace of distance. And yet...and yet everyone smiled and laughed, their emotions a light melting sweetness of powdered sugar. The water caller, currently amusing both herself and Kyra by making animal shapes rise from the ocean waves, was neither ashamed nor private about her power. She went through her day without the cloud of pity and fear that all Gifted on the Lyron continent cowered under.

Stars, Nile lost her command for the simple fact that she could call the wind.

Kyra thanked the stars for her fortune. Her own magic was

weak and the side effects more interesting than damaging. So long as Kyra kept her secrets to herself in polite company, she gained more than she lost. The question that itched her curiosity, though, was *where* the magic came from. The Diante attributed it to their gods. The Lyron Kingdoms tried to ignore the concept altogether, and the few books that did discuss it called elemental attraction a *condition*. A fancy word for disease. This accurately described the effect magic had on most hosts' bodies, but it felt shallow.

The paradigm of disease little explained what was happening with Nile's growing power, triggered—according to Nile—by connecting with her twin. Kyra wished she'd been there to observe the event, but the recollections she received from the others made her question the paradigm.

If elemental attraction wasn't contagious—and everyone who had an opinion on the matter agreed that it wasn't—then how could any connection between Nile and Clay have influenced their magic? How could Nile's magic awaken when other Gifted were close? And if Kyra existed, with her weak magic and gentle side effects, then were there others like her? Those whose blood simmered with magic instead of boiling with it?

"Kyra!" Nile's hail interrupted Kyra's thoughts. The girl was striding toward her, her face tight. Catching sight of the movement, Catsper detached himself from his post at the rail and headed toward the inevitable meeting point.

The water caller's sculpted animal—a monkey just now—blew a raspberry at the marine.

The change of mood from the giggling Diante to hard-faced Nile and Catsper struck Kyra like a storm. Not that the pair's sentiments were new. Nile considered anything that fell short of unequivocal victory to be utter disaster, while

Catsper oozed enough paranoia to drown a storm. That their feelings were real didn't mean their predicted disaster actually existed.

Dana and Quinn, likely sensing a rat in the growing gathering, likewise set course for Nile and, by the time Kyra arrived, were already looking grave.

"The *Wave*'s lookout reports two sails off starboard," Nile told Dana, the very lack of irritation at his presence a marker of her concern. "A two-masted sloop and a larger frigate, fifty guns, perhaps."

"What do the Diante make of this?" Dana asked.

"Very little," says Nile. "Diante fleets run spot patrols as a matter of routine, and Bassic thinks he recognizes the specific ships."

"I taste no great worry." Kyra pressed her tongue to the roof of her mouth. "Present company excluded. Might I ask why are we not beating to quarters until the ships' identities are confirmed? Isn't that what ships do when something is amiss?"

"Because sending the crew to man their guns on a ship without guns get complicated," said Catsper.

Pointedly ignoring Catsper, Quinn put a hand on Kyra's shoulder. "An approach of two smaller ships you believe you recognize is not typically cause for alarm," he explained softly. "The Diante are neutral and have no reason to expect an attack. If not for the Bevnians' unusual tactics, we would feel much the same."

"Do you believe it's the Bevnians?" Kyra whispered, a chill spreading from her face into her core. Melted eyes. Screams. Blood staining the deck. Kyra gripped her wrist. If Catsper hadn't caught her when he had, hadn't shoved her down the ladder...

"We don't know who it is," said Nile, her eyes focusing on

something over Kyra's shoulder. Bassic and *Stardust's* captain Yulin, the latter bathing in coppery terror despite a jovial grin.

"Is all well?" Bassic inquired with calm confidence, the small, sour drop of concern concealed beneath a steady voice and straight back.

"We are not under attack, if that is what concerns Her Highness," the lanky Yulin interjected before Nile could reply. The man's voice had a high, nasally tinge further setting him aside from his baritoned naval companion. "No reason for fear. The Diante empire has not been attacked in over a decade. If you allow me to show you the ship, you will find some fine history living in its planks. Perhaps some wine might go well with the chilly weather as well?"

Nile faced Bassic. "The Diante may not have been attacked for a decade, but my ship was assaulted three weeks past."

"Not in Diante waters!" Yulin injected again, his hands wringing. "We are very careful with the *Stardust*. With our reputation of safety and tradition of being the height of entertainment, there truly is no cause for concern. The last international conflict, in fact—"

"We have fully identified the two approaching vessels as Diante, sir," Bassic said, cutting off Yulin to address Dana—a maneuver that interestingly triggered a symmetrical irritation in Nile and Dana both. "The ships are yet to make their signals, but there is some distance yet. Nonetheless, I will sail the *Wave* forward to assess the situation."

Nile touched the Diante's arm. "Stay outside their firing envelope until you are confident of their identity. Please."

A wave of dismay washed over Bassic, making Kyra wonder how two people with the same goal and profession could communicate so poorly. "My ship is a man-of-war, Your Highness. It's our duty to enter an enemy's range." He sighed, turning back to Dana. "Perhaps you should brief me on your recent engagement."

Dana cleared his throat and offered a sketch of the recent battle, his quiet Lyron words turning Bassic's face grave and Yulin's green. "We'd like to signal our ship, sir," Dana said finally, with a quick glance at Nile, who nodded. Another bad sign. If Nile was willing to bow out of the discussion... Kyra's mouth dried.

"Of course, though I truly expect the reality to be no more interesting than an unscheduled patrol." Bassic waved his hand. "The young gentlemen are at your disposal for signals, and the *Helix* is kindly reminded to hold position outside the Diante waters."

"Lord Vikon," Nile called, interrupting the midshipman's conversation with a pair of female Diante dancers.

Vikon frowned at being summoned but quickly made the most of the situation by puffing his chest in self-importance before taking leave of his admirers. Vikon's roving eyes prodded Kyra's backside and chest, making her soft yellow dress feel too thin.

Catsper took one step and somehow ended up behind her, his body a hard, protective support despite not touching her skin.

"Lord Vikon, assist with the signals if you please," said Nile. "Whatever the Diante lookout reports I'd like transcribed into Lyron signals and transmitted to the *Helix*."

Vikon blinked. "Have you a signals books along?"

"We have you along," Nile said dryly. "Have you not memorized the basics?"

Vikon jutted out his chin. "I've not wasted time doing things that need not be done. Memorizing signals is a midshipman's busy work. An officer always consults the—"

Dana broke away from the group with Vikon in midsentence, and headed for the *Stardust*'s middies to address the communication himself.

"What?" Vikon blinked in confusion. Then his eyes found Kyra and lit with interest. "No matter."

Behind Kyra, Catsper shifted his weight.

She stepped away from the marine, away from the whole circle of gloom. It was better to spend time with the Diante Gods touched, with their water animals and little bells and guileless laughter. Even if their sunny world was not real, Kyra wanted to pretend that it was for as long as the day allowed. Lying to herself, yes, but that was all she could do to keep from shaking.

When Kyra's gaze found Nile next, the princess was at the rail, her grip knuckle white while Captain Yulin's stewards desperately thrust sweet cakes and oysters under her nose.

"The *Wave* and *Crest* are on an intercept course," Nile said in acknowledgment of Kyra's approach. The young woman's gaze remained trained on the sea, as if she saw a whole world unfurling in the waves and foam. "The approaching ships have the weather gage, though. Even with that, they are closing faster than they should."

"Is there anything I can do?" asked Kyra.

"Not unless you can talk our way off this ship without appearing to distrust the Diante navy."

Kyra shook her head. Behind them, a quartet of violinists picked up an oddly jolly tune while the crew performed their duties with a precise, decorative flare, moving amid the shrouds in synchrony, as if following a drum only they heard.

"A breathtaking show of actors wearing seamen's uniforms," said Nile, following Kyra's gaze.

"How can you be sure they aren't both, actors and sailors?" asked Kyra.

"For starters"—Nile suddenly pushed away from the rail, heading for the ship's quarterdeck—"because the *Wave* just signaled and only Domenic seems of a mind to report it to the admiral."

Dana was, in fact, jumping off the shrouds. Landing on the deck with a grace to rival an acrobat, he strode to the fleet commander and touched his hat with one hand while keeping the other on the shoulder of a Diante middie who looked ready to bolt for the ocean to avoid the admiral's attention.

"The incoming ships are confirmed as the *Arrow* and *Thunder*, sir," Dana was telling Admiral Addus as Nile and Kyra approached. "Both are flying Diante colors but are still failing to answer the *Wave*'s challenge hoist. It's too dark to make out the details of the crew. Gun ports remain closed."

"Very good," Addus said, switching to Diante to address the middie in Dana's grip.

"He's ordering the *Wave* to hold position and fire a warning shot across our guest's bow," Nile translated for Domenic and Kyra. Her shoulders eased. "And to stay out of the ships' attack range."

A minute later, Kyra flinched as the report of a single gun echoed across the water. She listened for an answering shot, but none came.

Dana, still holding the spyglass he had somehow confiscated, trained it on the sea. "The ships are backing sail as ordered," he reported. "Full stop. The *Thunder* is lowering a cutter. Rowing toward the *Wave* now."

Nile's whole body tensed, sending Kyra's heart racing.

"Don't welcome that boat, sir," Nile said quietly to Addus.

The older man frowned, the only outward sign of the

mounting frustration Kyra tasted from him. "I value your counsel and experience, Nile," Addus said firmly, "but we must give some heed to common reason. Those are Diante ships. They have obeyed our signal to stop outside firing range—and thus outside hailing distance. You've requested my ships come no closer to our visitors, so the only means remaining for them to discuss the situation is by messenger boat."

'The signals—" Nile let her words die on the vine.

"Mr. Dana," Addus said, shifting his focus. "Allow me to thank you for—"

The deafening boom of an explosion echoed over the waves, cutting off the admiral's words. In the suddenly lit night, fire and smoke rose from the small boat beside the *Wave*'s hull and engulfed the man-of-war in a blood-red inferno.

CHAPTER 29

NILE

I stand frozen as the shards of a boat's hull rain into the sea. The *Wave* bucks under the assault, gulping water from the wound in her side. Above her deck, canvas catches fire, the sail burning quick and bright for all to see. The flame decimates the ship as if consuming dry forest grass, as if... as if a phantom wind is feeding the flames.

There is a heartbeat of silence aboard the *Stardust* before the screaming begins. Soul-crushingly frightened while the ocean itself roars in flames. Admiral Addus's voice rises over the din, ordering everyone except the crew belowdecks, demanding sail be set at once to get the unarmed *Stardust* away from here. It does little good, though, not on a civilian ship filled with more stewards and performers than sailors. Even the able seamen are cowering, though, their training having had little by way of handling an assault. The Gifted stand frozen.

Quinn and Domenic are picking up the admiral's commands, which Addus has the foresight to call in both Diante and Lyron. Even Lord Vikon, having suddenly found himself better trained than those around him, is assembling a work party. Catsper is giving up yelling orders and herds the civilians belowdeck by means of shoves and fists.

Standing tall on the quarterdeck, Admiral Addus turns to me. "Are suicide runs a common tool of naval warfare nowadays?"

I shake my head. The distant fire plays tricks with the light, and a trail of black smoke rises to the sky. "Before today, I saw it once in the last decade. But the Bevnians, they've changed—"

A second explosion rocks the world as the *Wave's* gunpowder stores explode. The massive cloud dwarfs the initial combustions to child's play, and an invisible shock wave, like hardened air, slams into the *Stardust* before the boom of the explosion reaches our ears. My ears ring, a pressure deep inside, deafening the world.

Then the ocean waves reach us as well. The clumsy barque bucks violently, the decks rising then falling two yards down from beneath our feet. My stomach lifts into my throat as I become airborne alongside the admiral. We crash down together, me onto my hands and knees, and him...

A scream escapes me as Admiral Addus cracks his head again a spar and crumples.

I rush toward him only to have Domenic's iron arm clamp around my waist, pulling me against him. "Leave him, Nile." Domenic's voice is quiet and firm. "The admiral is either alive or he isn't. We need to get the *Stardust* out of here. *Now.*"

I shove Domenic's arm away, hating him for being right. The deck is a mess of sobbing bodies, spilled food, and tangled lines. Captain Yulin huddles at the base of the mainmast, his left thumbnail between his teeth. "We are a civilian ship," he insists. "We are a civilian ship. No one shall harm a civilian ship. They won't. They can't."

"Can you signal the *Helix* to run?" I ask Domenic, who starts jogging toward the signal flags before I finish the sentence.

"Deck there!" a middie's young voice calls from the lookout platform. "Ten sails starboard. Twelve. More maybe."

My blood chills. The other ships of the Bevnian fleet must have kept their distance to avoid spooking us prematurely, as well as to keep their own hulls clear of the exploding skies. This isn't a chance encounter, a snatch of opportunity. This...is an invasion.

Why, though? Why fight a war on two fronts? Why attack now? Why, why, why?

I jerk myself back from theory to survival. The *Stardust* can't fight, can't stay here, and can't outrun the approaching host.

But I can.

"Nile," Domenic shouts from the mainmast. "Don't do it! Too dangerous."

I wonder how he's read my mind, and a part of me wants to smile even as the rest of me disregards the warning. There isn't a choice, not really. With my wind, we may or may not outrun the enemy. Without it, we are going up in flames like the *Wave* just did.

"Man the sails and helm the best you can," I shout back to Domenic over the sobs of well-dressed guests and wailing youngsters. Over the howling prayers of the steward I'd last seen serving sweet sticky dumplings, presently covering his head with his serving tray. Catsper and now Vikon are doing a tolerable job of getting the civilians belowdecks, but it will be up to Domenic and Quinn to knead the Stardust's crew into a working military apparatus. They'll have to just to keep up with the gale I'm about to unleash. My eyes find the sails, rigged fore and aft instead of the square of the man-of-war. Less maneuverable, but easier to manage with a smaller crew.

The magic in my blood bubbles happily, excited for the coming freedom. It has been here before, it knows what's coming next. I tighten the reins on it. Over my shoulder, the enemy fleet is closing in, the lanterns on the ships' masts clear beacons. No one is trying to hide now. They are trying to frighten us into striking our colors. Into surrender.

"The *Crest* struck her colors!" Quinn's voice announces from somewhere.

That's it. There is no one but me standing between the coming enemy fleet and our survival. The night wind touches my face, and the magic bucks against my restraint. *Out, out, out,* it begs.

"We have to strike," Domenic calls. "Everyone, get below."

No. I free my magic in an explosion of air that is as spectacular at the Bevnians' had been. The *Stardust* lurches as the preternatural gale hits her sails, the ship's bow rising into the air. *More, more, more.* The magic inside me echoes my own thoughts. More wind. More power. More speed to get this bloody floating bucket away from the Bevnians' snapping jaws.

My magic whips the wind, my lungs stretching and burning. It's all I can do to keep from choking as I pull in one tether of control, shaping the wind's direction to maximize the sails' set. The current of air attacks the sheets with the force of an angry storm, and I'm knocked back against the mainmast.

"Nile!' Domenic shouts as the *Stardust* lurches under the rush of the storm. "Enough."

The ship strains but flies. The bow knocks against the ocean, sending up fountains of salty spray that stings eyes. I want to turn my head to see the distance we are making, but my head cannot compete with the storm. No matter. The farther and faster we get away, the better. We need to ride my wind until it fails.

The snap registers as an abstract sound in my mind until I see a corner of the foresail separate from its tether, the line broken. The sheet flogs itself in the wind, the ship lurching in protest at the sudden change. Three seamen throw themselves at the helm, trying to keep the wheel from spinning wildly, while another screams as the gale rips a line from his hands.

"The mast!" Quinn roars, racing toward me. "Nile, stop! Some of the rigging here, it's... Storms, it was decorative. Can't bear the strain."

Decorative. The word echoes in my head while another line breaks with a crack and another sail flails. My eyes widen, Quinn's meaning finally penetrating. Snaps of hemp and timber echo like pistol shots through the deck. A rogue stretch of torn rope whips about, striking a man in the rigging. He hollers as his body is tossed into the dark sea. The deadly rope continues its sway, like a venomous snake striking at prey.

A man. I've just killed a man.

Storms. A panic washes over me, and I clamp down on my magic.

Except the magic is having none of it, hollering in fury and freedom, the wind as strong as ever. Stronger. Unlike anything I've felt before. The foremast bends beneath the strain, arching like the bow that it is not.

Stop, I demand of the magic, bracing my lungs for the ripping pain that will surely come. The pain does come, but the magic stays free. The sail inside me that I use to direct the wind strains as hard as the *Stardust*'s rigging. I try to slow the storm again, imagining myself a sail, a rope, a mighty giant taming a beast. Anything I can think of. My heart pounds, my breaths coming quick and sharp. My body shudders as I use every bit of willpower to haul a dam into place.

Another snap. This one more felt than heard. For a horrific moment, I think a mainsail slit along its seams, but it isn't. It's worse. That snap was inside *me*, the sound of my own magic breaking free of its leash.

I fall to the deck, gasping for breaths that feels like inhaling from a whirlwind. With no more need to heed my will, my magic summons its element with unchecked force and greater chaos. Terror races through my veins. The magic won't stop. The wind won't stop. The ship spins, gaining momentum with each rotation. The foremast cracks and falls into the sea, the sail dragging along the water.

I'm not just going to destroy the ship, I'm going to capsize us and kill every soul aboard. Just like I killed the man trying to rein in the sail.

"Nile." Catsper's face rises before me. My memory stirs as he grips my gaze. "I've a promise to keep," the marine says quietly. "I'm sorry."

With the speed of an adder, Catsper's elbow connects with my temple, and the world dims.

CHAPTER 30

NILE

J wake to a kick in the ribs. The night's darkness has given way to a waking dawn, and the infant rays of sunlight brush my eyes as I blink. I'm lying against the base of the mainmast. The coppery smell of blood fills my nose, and my left temple screams with each heartbeat. Teams of blond men and women are moving across the ruins of *Stardust*'s once-pristine deck, stepping over broken rigging and shards of wood, trudging over the mess I made of the ship when I lost control.

Me. Me and my magic.

I destroyed us.

The Bevnians sweeping over our deck look like sculpted ghosts, their muscles shifting beneath billowing shirts. Their skin is nearly as light as their hair and utterly smooth except for an occasional scar. No tan. No freckles. Not even a birthmark. The women are all taller than me, and even the smallest of the men rivals Domenic's size. Beside the smaller, darker-skinned Diante, the Bevnians look like a different species altogether. Predators.

The boot that just kicked me now nudges the bruise. "Live one," a male voice calls in Tirik.

I grunt and shy away from the pain.

"That one? She doesn't look promising," a Bevnian woman calls back. She has a crooked nose and holds a journal in her hand, making notes as she surveys everything. I decide to call her Clerk. "Hold fast until I check, Andres. It's easier to cull them now than later."

The man beside me, Andres, growls but stays where he is. Clerk strides over to the water-caller girl whom Kyra had befriended. The water caller is bleeding badly from small wounds and screams in terror. Clerk makes a note in her journal, picks up the wounded girl, and tosses her unceremoniously into the rolling sea. A Diante steward with a crushed leg, mercifully unconscious, is thrown overboard a moment later.

My chest clenches. My body is fully awake now, and fully terrified. On the foc'sle, those prisoners deemed healthy enough to be useful are being bound and organized into kneeling rows. Domenic is there, chin high and proud despite his painfully bound arms. Catsper and Kyra are there too, the latter shaking as fiercely as Catsper holds still. After a moment, I spot a tense Quinn and wide-eyed Vikon as well. Alive, alert, healthy enough to be holding themselves upright. The dizzying relief washing over me dissolves with the next heartbeat. Bound. Prisoners. My fault. A tingling sort of numbness grips my throat, my features settling into a mask of nothing.

Clerk's boots are moving again, stopping beside a young man I'd last seen using air currents to juggle colorful balls. Now he stands on his knees, praying to gods that never bothered to protect him from me.

"Magic?" Clerk demands of the boy in accented Diante.

"That one's mine," Andres calls, his voice dripping with impatience. "Check the girl if you must, and let's get moving."

Clerk kicks the boy's thigh. "Magic?"

"Air," the youth whispers. "Is that good or bad?"

"Prove it."

The youth swallows, and a small wind prances through the deck.

Clerk glared at Andres. "You trying to pull one over Lester?"

"My ship needs wind to move. Lester would be little pleased if we lagged behind."

"Make do with what you are given, or Lester will find another who can." Clerk sticks her broken nose into her journal and scribbles something before calling to another Bevnian to take the Diante air caller away. "Where is that girl, Andres?"

I push myself up onto my hands and knees, feigning health and strength I don't have. Weakness will get me thrown overboard. Andres nods approvingly at my newfound consciousness, and the two Bevnians circle me as if examining a new piece of rigging.

"Fully intact?" Clerk asks Andres.

Andres kicks my thigh with the toe of his boot. "Get up," he orders, repeating the command first in Diante, then Lyron.

I quickly force myself to my feet. The deck sways beneath me, but I bend my knees and ride the dizziness well enough to hide it. In the dawn-lit morning, mockingly calm with lapping waves crowned with white foam, I see three frigates holding position beside the dying *Stardust*. One of them used to be the Diante's *Crest*, though now it flies Tirik colors. Small islands of fire in the distance remain as the only tribute to the sunk *Wave*. I swallow. At least the *Helix*'s hull is not amid the captured ships.

Clerk and Andres finish their inspection with coordinated grunts. "Good enough," Clerk declares, and raises her pen over her journal. Her pale eyes flash to me. Pink with specks of black. "Magic?"

I lick my lips. The tingling inside me where my magic used to simmer is now nothing but terror. The mere thought of wind calling makes bile rise up my throat, and I must swallow before I can whisper the answer. "None."

A rope pulls my hands tightly behind my back, and I'm forced to my knees beside the others on deck. A pair of Bevnians with knives move through the lines of prisoners, cutting away clothing until we are all in our small clothes and shivering. Cold air nips my bare skin as my own coat and shirt are stripped away. A moment later, my hair falls victim to a Bevnian blade, which snips my long locks at the base of my skull.

The sun moves two hours across the horizon before the Bevnians finish their sorting. Those too weak, too injured or too young are tossed overboard to drown. Those identified as Gifted are rowed out to the *Crest*. The rest of us—including Kyra, who decided against confession—are left as we are. Shivering, kneeling, bound, naked. Soft whimpers and sobs sound around to my left and right. I'm too far from my friends to communicate, provided any of them still wish to speak with me. That thought alone should crush me, but instead, I feel as empty as the emotionless mask I wear. Hollow. As if I watch all this from afar. Even the sight of Admiral Addus, captured but alive, fails to rouse warmth.

My muscles are cramping by the time a Bevnian man in his

fifties strides onto the raised poop deck and looks down at the lot of us. Two younger warriors, a man and a woman, flank the older man. All three move with an aura of power, though the two younger ones stay a step behind their leader. The pair's arms are bare to the shoulder, black tattoos winding up snowy forearms and biceps in a pattern identical to that on the wide leather bands encircling their wrists.

There is something odd about the pair, something that turns my stomach and makes me vomit onto the deck. The horrid smell joins dozens of similar ones, ranging from blood to piss.

The older man flicks his hand at his younger companions. "Clean them up. No need to bring their vermin with us."

Both warriors turn to the sea, which rises in an obedient stream and hurtles at us full force. A wind and a water caller. Powerful ones. Questions echo in my head, trying and failing to stir my curiosity. How has a water caller survived this long if he keeps pace with the others? How in the name of all storms did he consent to tattoos? I can't bring myself to truly care for the answer. Not now. And certainly not when a hard freezing spray scatters my thoughts and I gag as water pours over my unprotected face. The cleansing continues for a full minute before a cold wind takes its place, and my whole body shakes like a foal's.

On the poop deck above, the older man raises his hand for attention. His thin hair is slicked away from his square face and his intense, slightly bulging eyes spawn crow's feet at their corners. "My name is Lester," he declares in a deep, booming voice that appears to come from all directions at once. A voice amplified by the wind. Just as the too-quickly spreading fire had been. "I am an admiral of the *New* Republic of Tirik navy. Which, as my Lyron friends can tell you, is, and will remain, undefeated."

I draw a sharp breath, finally staring at the face of the *something* that changed four months ago, when the beaten-down Tirik ships suddenly started sinking ours. The Tirik had allied with the Bevnians, and the Bevnians brought magic to the fight.

"Who is in command here?" Lester asks.

Admiral Addus rises to his feet, a difficult process for an older man with a limp and bound hands. Holding his half-naked body as if he were clad dressed in full admiralty regalia, Addus strides forward and bows to our captor. "You are in charge, sir," the admiral says in much better Tirik than the Bevnian's poor attempt at Diante. "But the people kneeling before you are mine. If you have instructions for them, I would be honored to convey them on your behalf."

My chest squeezes.

Lester beckons the admiral to ascend the poop deck. Though of an age, Lester is in better physical condition, his muscles as corded as any seaman's. Once the admiral stands beside him, Lester examines the man. Bare to his soaking small clothes and a bit saggy, Admiral Addus still manages to look the dignified leader, and the kneeling Diantes' chins rise proudly.

Lester nods to Clerk, standing behind Admiral Addus.

The woman steps forward calmly. The next moment, a knife flashes, and Admiral Addus's body crumples to the deck, blood burbling from his slit throat.

The screaming starts a heartbeat later as the prisoners realize what's happened. I am too hollow and empty to find my voice. I hear the unmistakable crack of a whip, and the screams of horror turn to howls of pain, our captors restoring quiet with brutal efficiency.

Lester wipes his hands on the thigh of his britches to clean off Admiral Addus's blood. He smiles. "As I've said, my name is

Lester. You lot should think of me as God. It will help you get on." He pauses, surveys us, and nods to Clerk, who descends with a bucket and brush to paint numbers on our backs. Lester smiles again and continues. "Some of you might believe you are prisoners. Let me snuff that rumor at once. You are not prisoners. You are slaves to a race that transcends yours. A race that is stronger and smarter, bigger and healthier, able to harness the magic that cripples your sad bodies. A chosen people. A race that now ascends to claim its rule above you. How comfortable your transition to your new world will be is entirely in your hands. The rules are simple: Do as you are told, speak only in Tirik—and never without permission. Now then"—he claps his hands—"who here knows how to cook?"

Silence reigns.

Lester sighs. "I little care whether the lot of you eat or starve. If you wish to eat tomorrow, however, someone better start volunteering his neighbor's skills."

Storms. After an eternity of silence, three men stand and bow. They are shaking, unable to even keep their heads lifted for the terror.

Lester nods to them. "Very good. I was worried about your hearing." He snaps his fingers, and two of his warriors appear before him. "Take them to the galley," he orders in Tirik before translating the order for the Diantes' benefit. As the three cooks start to shuffle after the Bevnian soldiers, Lester raises his voice once again. "Don't forget your meat. You need ingredients, do you not?"

With a dawning horror, I and everyone else finally realize what the man means, as his warrior directs the cooks to pick up Admiral Addus's body and take it below. I look away, clinging to my memory of Admiral Addus's kind eyes and wise, fatherly words. Admiral Addus, who was alive and proud just moments ago. A yawning chasm of darkness stretches so wide inside me that one more shove and I fear I will fall into it forever.

Lester turns to his own people. "Get the livestock transported to your ships, gentlemen. I want us sailing out before dusk. The same goes for supplies as well. We will be sinking this piece of rubbish."

CHAPTER 31

NILE

*D*omenic's eyes are on me, piercing my skin from the other side of the deck. I can feel them burning into my bare shoulders but cannot summon the strength to return the gaze. Could we have outrun the Bevnians if I hadn't destroyed the *Stardust*'s rigging? Would this captivity be easier for Domenic and the others to bear if they'd done all they could to save the ship, instead of my having ripped the choice from them? Is their agony my fault?

A set of burnt-orange slop trousers and shirt—likely from the captured ships' uniform stores—hits me in the face. My arms are released long enough to dress, then bound again. Rough hands shove me like a sack of grain into a boat, making my shins scream at the impact, but the pain is distant, as if it's happening to someone else.

I can't bear to twist back, to face Domenic, to see the empty space where Kyra had knelt before the Bevnians rowed her away. I'd asked for her to help with the Diante, and this is where following me has gotten her. My own magic is quiet for once, as if the wild run had burned it from my veins. My stomach turns at the memory, and I twist in time to vomit over the side of the boat.

Straightening up, I find us already moving and hold my breath to see which of two ships accepting prisoners I'm headed to, the Lester's newly taken *Crest* or Andres's much smaller *Arrow*, which had dispatched the suicide boat to the *Wave*. Thus far, all the identified Gifted have gone to Lester, as had Quinn, while Andres unhappily receives the boatloads of the remaining souls. Domenic is still aboard the *Stardust*, but Catsper and Kyra were taken to the *Arrow* hours ago, and I release my breath as my boat turns in the same direction.

Around me, the weeping wails of the Diante civilians are overwhelming. It's all I can do to keep from whimpering myself. I've never been captured before. Even on the *Aurora*, where I was mishandled like any common seaman, the choice had been mine—the choice to be at sea, the choice to keep my identity hidden, the choice to fight.

There is no choice now. I don't get to decide where I'm going, what I get to see, when I am permitted to relieve myself.

The boat comes to a halt with the familiar command of "Oars," and I cling to that branch of stability. Whoever these people are, whatever their relationship with magic, they are still only human. And fallible. Somehow.

The *Arrow* is small for a frigate, about one hundred thirty feet long and just over thirty feet wide. Snow-white Bevnians in sleeveless shirts reign over crews of... I stop and stare until one of the Bevnians shoves me along The hollow-eyed crewmen are *Tirik*. The Bevnians' supposed allies. These specific Tirik, dressed in the same burnt-orange uniforms that cover me and the Diante prisoners, are anything but the Bevnians' equals, though. These Tirik, men and women alike who move like landsmen, not trained sailors, regard our procession with a mix of hate and pity. Convicts, perhaps? Undesirables made to toil for their betters?

Andres watches us as well, his jaw tight.

"Another batch of landsmen? What in the gods' wrath am I to do with these runts, sir?" A man who I presume is Captain Andres's first officer growls as we pass.

"Break them to bridle, and they'll work well enough." Andres presses his lips together. "Admiral Lester generously gave us twenty-five percent beyond our allotment to compensate for the likely attrition. Make do, Saarik."

I strain to hear the rest of the conversation, but the guards order us to descend down the hatch, and my attention shifts to navigating the ladder with my hands bound. I'm finally shoved into a hold, a thin viewport near the overhead providing the only light. The smell is thick, some from the airless nature of the hold, some the unmistakable stench of lost urine and over a dozen ripe bodies. Damn. I count to thirty after the door locks in place before speaking up. "Hello?" I say in Diante. "Who is here?"

No response.

"Someone answer." My words take on a note of command and, for good measure, I repeat them in Tirik and Lyron. "Answer me. Someone. Who are you?"

"Would you shut up, girl? People are trying to sleep." The voice is female and hollow. And Tirik. Bodies shift with displeased grunts as a woman with frizzled hair crawls toward me. She is only in her twenties but the stooped shoulder and hollow face make her look old and frail. There is something not quite sane about her gaze, which darts about the hold without ever stopping on any one point for more than a heartbeat. She stops before me, her hands fiddling with the rope binding my wrists.

The knots come loose, and a whimper I can't swallow quickly enough escapes my lips. The rough hemp has cut into my skin, making both rope and flesh slick with blood. "Thank you," I start to say, but she's already moved on to untying the next captive.

"What's your name?" I call after the Tirik woman.

She turns back and looks at me as if just realizing I'm there. "Polman. It doesn't matter. Your name doesn't matter either, so don't bother sharing."

My eyes dart about to the other people in the hold in hopes of finding someone with better faculties, but everyone else is Diante and as new as me. Polman it is, then, crazed gaze and all. "Polman," I say with a soft voice, the kind used to calm spooked animals. "How long have you been here?"

The woman turns her arm over and stares at her forearm. It takes me a moment to see the lines of thin scars that line it in neat rows. Each mark is about half an inch long and not quite straight. Polman runs her fingers over the scars. "Five months, one week." She presses a nail of her free hand into flesh until blood flows freely and another small mark decorates the skin. "Four days." Bringing her mouth to the bubbling blood, she sucks at the wound as if trying to swallow a mouthful.

Bile rises in my throat, and I turn my head for a moment. No wonder the woman is isolated in the hold. I return to Polman's words. Five months—that's several months after the earthquake. After we—I—denied the Tirik access to the supplies in the Siaman. The crippling blow had quieted the People's Republic of Tirik for several months, and then...then the war escalated exponentially. The surprising Tirik victories, the unprecedented suicide attack.

Polman's attention wanders, and I call back out to her before she scampers off completely. "Where is Lester taking us, do you know?"

"There is no *us*." Polman growls at me. "I am going to stay here. I'm useful. Andres himself has said so, he said, *Polman is useful*. Only those who the Bevnians find useful are granted the privilege of serving them directly. The others go to the village."

I shift position, and my bruised temple thumps in pain. "Lester spoke of the *New* Tirik Republic," I say once I find my voice again. "What happened to the People's Republic? What were the terms of the alliance?"

"Alliance?" Polman laughs, then interlaces her fingers and bends them in and out. In and out. "The earthquake destroyed us," she whispers. "There was nothing. There is nothing. Then the Bevnians came. They took us in. Like stray dogs. There is no alliance."

Storms.

"The Bevnians are superior." Polman's words trip on themselves, and she dissolves into muttering. "We must all fulfill our potential in our own tier. An ordered world. A clean and powerful world."

My head pounds. The People's Republic of Tirik has been dead and conquered for months, with no one in Lyron knowing. None returning alive from battle to tell. "The Bevnians boarded my ship and took everyone prisoner," I say, hoping to get something more out of Polman before she loses her hold on sanity. Or I lose the hold on mine. "They took my friends prisoner. Do you know what they want with us?"

"Lester is growing his fleet. Extra people go to the village. Your friends might be here. Might be elsewhere. Might be dead. Are your friends useful? Andres was upset. He needs more useful people to build up his ship, and he got you."

The door opens, cutting off what passes for conversation between Polman and me. A man appears, the dim lantern in his hands giving his milk-white skin a sickly yellow haze.

Polman crawls toward him, her hands trailing along his thighs. "Hello there, Saarik," she purrs. "Have you come for me at last?"

Saarik kicks Polman out of his way and counts the prisoners while Polman whimpers. "Nineteen plus the dimwit," Saarik calls back behind him. "Here is fine."

"It looks tight, sir," a younger man replies. He sounds a bit like Andres, but softer, not as jaded.

"There's only so much quarantine space to pen them," Saarik barks, shoving another prisoner inside before slamming the door shut.

Relief floods me so hard that I press my palm into the deck to keep steady. "Domenic."

Domenic's back is quarterdeck straight, neither the lack of uniform nor the fatigue lining his eyes dispelling his aura of authority. The prisoners who'd cursed me shuffle to give Domenic as much berth as the small space allows. He squints, still adjusting to the gloom. "Nile?" The word escapes his lips and hangs between us. "Goddess. Are you hurt?"

"No." I shuffle forward and reach for his bindings. Domenic holds still as the knots protest, the hemp biting into bleeding skin. I did this. To him, to me, to everyone. Domenic had told me not to. Asked me not to. "I'm... Domenic—"

Twisting around, Domenic encircles me with his arms, pulling my battered body tightly against his chest. The *thump thump thump* of his heart echoes against my cheek, the warmth of his body embracing my skin. I only realize I'm crying when the tears cascading down my trembling face overflow onto Domenic's raw wrists.

CHAPTER 32

KYRA

*K*yra landed on hardwood, which was an improvement after being manhandled between ships, the prisoners' agony and fear gagging her. The taste was still there, shoving itself down Kyra's throat, but duller now, as if the emotions of the past hours had scalded her taste buds. At least hardwood was more stable than a rowboat. The thought of water made Kyra shake again. So much water and nothing to drink, so close and so unattainable.

The Bevnians had kept her kneeling half-naked on the deck for most of the night before shoving her into clothes and a boat. Hours of cramping muscles and fear and men's eyes. And now, still bound, she was here, wherever *here* was. Kyra had shut her eyes tightly after her first glimpse of the small hold, the world of darkness preferable to reality.

Something—something that was very likely a rat— brushed

over Kyra's calf, and she screamed.

A hand clamped over her mouth.

"And open your bloody eyes," a voice said into Kyra's ear, its familiarity making tears stream down her face. She somehow hadn't cried yet, but now, hearing Catsper, feeling his hand slip from covering her mouth to a calm pressure on her lower back, she shattered into pieces.

Catsper's voice hardened. "I said, open your eyes."

Kyra obeyed, blinking to adjust to the gloom. They were in a space three paces wide and four long, the only light coming from a small slit near the overhead and a single lantern. The shapes of two dozen others, all *Stardust*'s Diante, huddled in what little space they could claim. She could make out the faces of those close to her, but nothing more.

Drawing a shaking breath, Kyra focused on Catsper's chest, unable to meet his gaze. Although he held his emotions as tightly as ever, Kyra could do the math. He was solid, strong, brave; she was the weakness he found deplorable. "How long have you been here?" Her voice was hoarse.

"Three hours or so." Cool calm with a trace of annoyance. "Long enough to get myself out of the bindings. Tying everyone up was a fruitless exercise, by the way. No one is doing much moving with or without ropes."

Kyra swallowed. "Were you expecting an armed uprising?"

"Wouldn't have been the worst idea."

She chuckled. Actually chuckled before reality hit again, and so did tears. "Will you let *me* out of my bindings? Or are you waiting for me to plead?"

Catsper leaned forward on one knee, bringing his lips to Kyra's ear. "I'm waiting for you to let yourself out of your bindings."

Kyra glared at him and pulled against the knots until her

shoulders screamed. The hemp only bit deeper into her skin. It hurt, and Kyra hissed as blood beaded on skin.

None of the two dozen Diante men so much as bothered to glance her way. They just sat, breathing the thick air, which felt as though it might end altogether. At least Kyra had been on deck before, out in the open. The hemp scraped her again, and Kyra lowered her trembling wrists. If it took a trained Spade almost three hours to free himself, her pulling would be futile. This whole—

Catsper grasped her shoulders. Not painfully, exactly, but hard enough to draw her full attention. "Stop being a victim."

"Stop being an ass."

"If you can burn me, you can burn the ropes, Kyra."

Kyra blinked. Yes. Yes, she could do that. A small, controlled flame at the rope's core, just enough to weaken the strands. She should have thought of it herself, but after the effort to ban herself from reaching for fire aboard the ship, she'd overlooked that route entirely.

Tapping into the weak magic pulsing in her blood, Kyra focused the heat to a single point at the rope's core until the crackle of fiber told her the rope caught alight inside.

"Easy," Catsper said, his voice steady as he shielded Kyra's efforts from view. Not that anyone in the hold cared. The two dozen Diante huddled into themselves and prayed.

The rope snapped, flooding Kyra's shoulders with whimpering relief. She rubbed first her wrists, then the tops of her arms, with aching hands.

Catsper's gaze surveyed Kyra's every moment with disconcerting intensity. "Are you injured?"

"I hurt."

"That's not what I asked."

Kyra shifted herself to a more comfortable position. Her

tears were drying, and her annoyance with the marine was shoving her despair aside. "I'm not dying, which appears to be your only definition of a problem." She blew out a breath and rubbed her temples. She was a prisoner, stuffed into a hold of a ship run by insane cannibals. Her muscles screamed, her wrists bled, and there was a raw patch on her left hand where the flame had bit her skin. Her mouth was as dry as her stomach was empty. If the Spade wished to pretend none of that was worth consideration, then he was welcome to suffer in self-important silence. This didn't mean that the rest of the people in the hold had to follow the same Spardic absurdity.

Brushing her hands through what remained of her lush, dark hair, Kyra surveyed the room. Fear and pain hung thick in the air, but that was hardly insightful. What she needed was to talk to these people. Bond.

"Where are you going?" Catsper's hand clamped around her arm as she started toward the sobbing youth a couple of paces away.

Kyra little bothered wasting strength on trying to pull loose from his grip. "To get everyone calmed and see what they know. Unless you'd like to order everyone to stop whimpering and just cooperate? Maybe they can do some push-ups while they're at it."

Catsper's fingers released her. "Push-ups never harmed anyone yet," he said, sitting back against the bulkhead, which was as much of a *good luck* as Kyra was going to get.

Kyra made it three steps before an unfamiliar voice behind the door shouted an order in Tirik.

The prisoners exchanged confused glances.

The order sounded again, and, just in case, Kyra backed away from the door. It swung open a moment later to admit two Bevnian officers into the cell. Both men wore loose black pants and sleeveless vests despite the chilly air. A red-and-black insignia matching the New Republic flag the *Arrow* flew decorated the men's left breasts. The larger of the two carried a coiled whip at his belt. The brew of anger and disgust simmering from him blanketed both the prisoners and, if Kyra was correct, the man's own younger companion.

The younger man, who looked similar enough to Captain Andres to name them brothers, grasped a prisoner's shoulders and rotated the man to face the bulkhead. Repeating the Tirik command, which seemed to mean *face the wall,* he similarly manhandled a second prisoner. Firm motions, but not cruel ones. Not until a third prisoner, a proud young Diante whom Kyra had last seen guarding the *Stardust*'s water caller from accidental injury, stepped back before he could be grabbed.

The older Bevnian officer had his whip free quicker than Kyra could find voice to scream.

"Saarik." The younger man's palm rose in a calming gesture, buying the would-be mutineer time to comply before the confrontation escalated.

Kyra's eyes darted to Catsper. *See that? Don't get stupid.*

The marine's gaze narrowed on hers.

Please.

Catsper sighed and rotated crisply to the bulkhead when the order sounded again, the other prisoners following suit. Another command and more manhandling—efficient if not brutal—translated the new instruction to mean *line up and follow.* At least there seemed to be a plan, whatever it was.

On deck, Kyra found the other prisoners already sitting in ordered rows. There had to be over a hundred of them, but the three Lyron amid the sea of Diante called attention at once. Lord Vikon sat in the corner, staring dully at a bowl of mush his line had been given. At the other end of the group... Kyra's gaze met Nile's, and her chest tightened as the princess bent her head low in an unmistakeable gesture: *I'm sorry.*

Sorry? Nile was sorry for trying to save the ship? For failing to do the impossible? Kyra shook her head, even though she knew it would do no good. Not yet.

With Kyra's group settled alongside the others, the Bevnians distributed bowls of something lumpy but fortunately meatless. Kyra's stomach rumbled, and she made herself swallow, trying to neither taste nor think about what she was eating. The younger Bevnian officer, whom the others called Piranha, nodded his approval to her.

Over the next few hours, the Bevnians initiated an apparent regimen of evaluation and training. Andres, Saarik, and Piranha issued orders in Tirik, then demonstrated the required responses. Prisoners too slow to understand or too unenthusiastic to obey were encouraged with Saarik's whip, while a unit of armed sentinels wearing bandoliers of prefilled gunpowder cartridges patrolled the deck, their muskets as straight as any marine's. Around them, over a hundred Tirik prisoners, dressed in worn versions of Kyra's orange trousers and shirts, watched the initiation with a curious mix of hate, empathy, and satisfaction.

Kyra followed along with the crowd, kneeling to scrub decks, climb up the rigging, and haul a rope when she was told. Nile, Dana, and some of the Diante hands who'd been sailors instead of stewards on the *Stardust* were quickly pulled off for more advanced work. Catsper, unsurprisingly, managed to get himself assigned to dangerous work aloft, which earned the marine displeased glowers from Dana and Nile both while making Kyra's throat tighten with each gravity-defying leap.

Finally assigned to laundry duty, Kyra had almost convinced herself that the *Arrow* was a typical—if harsh—naval ship, when two prisoners who'd failed to make themselves useful were hauled onto the quarterdeck. Kyra recognized the first as the sobbing youth from her hold, now frightened into a stupor. The second, whom Kyra hadn't met, howled over his crushed left leg, which had fallen victim to a loose gun carriage earlier.

There was no ceremony. Andres and Saarik conferred quietly for a moment, then ordered the two killed.

No, not killed. Butchered.

Bile rose up Kyra's throat and she darted to vomit over the rail as a Bevnian cook efficiently cleaved and eviscerated the bodies, dumping the entrails overboard before chopping the meat into neat chunks. When Kyra returned to the two troughs set up middeck as her laundry station, a pair of Bevnian Gifted were summoning wind and water to clean the deck while the Bevnian sentinels made a show of drawing powder cartridges from their bandoleers and loading their muskets. Not that any of the remaining prisoners needed a reminder to behave.

After the midday murders, the day became a haze. Catsper, Nile, Domenic, and Vikon appeared and disappeared from Kyra's field of vision, all busy with one task or another. As she watched Catsper lope through the rigging, disappearing to a small speck eighty feet above deck, Kyra's throat closed. The ship swayed with the waves, the masts teetering over open ocean with each wallow. Not that falling onto deck would be much better than slipping into the sea.

The Bevnians allowed only Tirik to be spoken on deck, which effectively gagged the Lyron and Diante prisoners. At one point, mugs of water and weevily ship's biscuits were distributed, the Bevnians patrolling to ensure that everyone ate and swallowed their portion. By the time Piranha herded Kyra's group back to its hold, Kyra had energy for nothing but collapse.

The next day began with the same routine, though there was less movement between different tasks as the prisoners' strengths and weaknesses were better assessed. Some of the daily routine, such as scrubbing decks with a book-sized stone, Kyra recognized from the *Helix*. The standards appeared less stringent here, the Bevnians demanding speed over detail.

Kyra remained washing laundry, the screaming of her arms and back drowned only by the fear of what awaited her if she stopped. By the third day, however, even the fear failed her. Kyra's back cramped, the skin on her hands cracked and bled, and, thanks to Saarik's displeasure as her slowing pace, a welt seared the tender flesh between Kyra's shoulder blades. By nightfall, Kyra was shaking violently as she collapsed to the deck of the holding pen, her body a heap of exhaustion and pain.

"Sit up." Catsper's voice. A foot nudging her ribs.

Kyra shut her eyes tighter, buried her head deeper into her arms.

Catsper nudged her ribs again. In his world, this was likely the equivalent of a friendly embrace, but they weren't *in* his world. They weren't in any world Kyra knew. "Sit up," said Catsper. "Curling into a ball doesn't help. I've tried it."

Kyra's head lifted.

Gripping her shoulders, Catsper hauled her up like a rag doll. His eyes, green and demanding, found hers. "In case you failed to notice, our captors have you valued somewhere between a milking goat and a tolerably good work mule. There is no rescue coming. So make your choice: stay strong and healthy and alive, or feel sorry for yourself and die."

Kyra gulped, probing Catsper's eyes and words for the path of least resistance. She had no strength for anything more. Not even to sit upright. Catsper seemed not to feel such a handicap, not after hours defying death in the rigging, not now when there was nothing to distract from the cramping pain. He stood with legs braced shoulder-width apart, his rough orange uniform shaped by shifting muscles beneath, his green eyes alert like a cat's.

Catsper was everything Kyra was not.

"What do you want from me?" she whispered finally.

Catsper's hand cupped her chin, his head dipping down until his face was so close that Kyra felt his warm breath brushing the ridge of her nose. "Survive," Catsper said softly. "I want you to survive."

She searched his face, so tense and reined in that a muscle ticked on the left corner of his jaw. Power and energy condensed inside a man's body. A wall between her and the other prisoners.

"Why do you care?" asked Kyra.

"Because I do." Catsper pulled away from her quickly, his voice brisk, his attention suddenly on his own hands. "Tonight, you will stretch. Tomorrow, you start training before you injure yourself by tripping over your own feet."

"Training?" Kyra stepped away, pressing her back into the bulkhead behind her. Without Catsper's support, standing was cold and difficult. But what he was proposing, even the thought of it... She'd laugh if she wasn't on the verge of tears. "With...with you?"

"There are few others to choose from," Catsper said evenly. He sighed, running a hand through short-cropped hair. That was new. "It will be nothing like what I put Nile and Dana through. We'll build up your body, not break it down. If it means anything, I give you my word."

Kyra drew a breath. Unable to say yes. Unwilling to say no either.

Catsper crouched, balancing easily on the balls of his feet. "Can you bear it?" he asked quietly, as if having heard the words Kyra hadn't uttered. "Me gripping your wrists, my body very much in your space, all happening here in a room with no escape? Your muscles will hurt—in part from the daily strain, in part from what I ask. Confinement coupled with pain is a hard combination. For...anyone."

Kyra swallowed, her hands shifting to straighten her dress over her knees, only to remember she now wore burnt-orange trousers that scratched her skin. "I...don't want to learn to fight. There are enough people injuring each other in the world without my adding to it."

Catsper cocked his head to the side. "All right, no attacks. Self-defense?"

"No." The word came out harder than Kyra intended, but she couldn't help it, not with her blood rushing through her suddenly too-warm skin. "Just... Make me stronger. More flexible. Better balanced." She bit her lip. "But don't make me learn to hurt people. I don't want to be good at that."

The marine nodded gravely, then uncurled to his feet, amusement returning to dance in his eyes as he once again stood taller than Kyra. "All body work and no fighting? There is a word for that in the Spade training camps you know."

"Exercise?"

"Punishment."

Kyra chuckled.

Extending his hand, Catsper cautiously brushed his knuckles down Kyra's cheek. "Stretch today. Train tomorrow. And the day after that"—a tang of mischief peeked through his voice—"the day after that, we figure out how to communicate with Dana and Nile. If I know the princess, she'll have a harebrained idea on how to get out of this mess by then."

CHAPTER 33

NILE

"Y ou want to attack the *Helix*?" Domenic runs his hand over a fraying rope. With Andres leaning on the wind and water Gifted to propel the *Arrow*, there is more than usual stress on the rigging—which in turn keeps Domenic and me busy with repairs between the morning gun drills and afternoon sail practice. The small knives we've been issued for the task little qualify as weapons, but I feel better for having one in my boot. Domenic reaches past me to grab a fresh line, his fingers grazing my shoulder for a brief moment. I wonder whether he knows how I treasure these touches, reminders of a different world and a tentative, rekindling friendship. Domenic lowers his voice. "Did Saarik bounce your head off something too hard, or was it two weeks of work that made you go daft?"

Two weeks. After a few days of going through the motions,

my whole being concerned with avoiding whips and scars, I can finally think straight. Which seems to be making Domenic nervous. I blow into my cupped hands to warm them. The day is gloomy, with rough seas, gray skies, and a constant drizzle that allows nothing to dry. With over half the *Arrow*'s complement untrained landsmen, the ship handles so poorly that I marvel at us failing to capsize altogether whenever a serious wave bounces off the hull. It's little wonder Lester cut Andres loose from the fleet days ago with orders to get his ship in order or else sail the Arrow back to the Republic and hand her off to a captain who can turn her useful. Between the rough seas and a crew that can't understand—much less follow—most commands, we've not moved very far.

I squat next to Domenic to examine a thick line vital for controlling the mainsail. It, at least, is in good shape. "Andres needs a better crew, and he wants a better ship," I say quietly. The prisoners are allowed to converse only in Tirik, which Domenic speaks none of. I watch Piranha, the smaller of our Bevnian captors, who nonetheless makes Domenic look normal size, pace the deck. When the Bevnian is at the farthest part of his lap, I speak as quickly as I can. "*Helix* is the perfect lure, if we can find her. And with a bit of sabotage here and there, we can ensure the *Arrow* loses the engagement. Fails with those flesh-melting balls they keep below. We signal Zolan, and he'll figure it out."

Domenic's lips press together, the unvoiced request for details hanging in the air.

Details that I don't want to give him. Not when he might use them to sabotage my plan for my own safety. Not when knowing can get him hurt should things go wrong.

My jaw tightens, and I raise my face to the wind, the magic in my blood prickling. Not a healing friend eager to play, no, not anymore. What brews inside me now is a rabid predator, ready to kill the moment it breaks its chain. The crack of a breaking mast echoes in my memory, the rip of rope, the screams of dying seamen. I swear the magic basks in the memory, delighted at its former strength and freedom.

I'm at the rail in a moment, vomiting over the side. My heart flutters, my body shaking in dry heaves. Not a convulsion; I've had only one of those the past two weeks, but a dawning new reality. I can *never* touch that chain, never let the murderous magic escape. Even it if kills me. Until it kills me.

Domenic gives me the courtesy of feigning blindness, though there is a worried edge to his gaze. And silence, which I return in kind.

My magic... That's another topic best kept to myself for fear of what Domenic would do if he knew the truth.

Piranha turns back toward us, and Domenic waits out the rotation, his hands deftly making repairs until it's safe to speak again. "Even if the *Helix* is still here *and* Andres somehow decides to seek her out *and* finds her, we still can't coordinate this type of engagement without having someone on the quarterdeck privy to the Bevnians' orders and intent. Either that, or learn how to read minds." He shifts, putting himself between me and the cold wind. "Plus, I've a feeling Andres wants to fly this afternoon. One of those wind callers was up on deck earlier."

I curse. We are already a good distance from the *Helix*'s last known point, and the magic-harnessed wind and sea would put us too far for Andres to consider returning, no matter how juicy the potential prize.

Domenic shuts his mouth abruptly as Piranha enters hearing range. "Rope bad," Domenic says to me in his horrid Tirik. "Need fix."

I nod absently, my mind swarming in reflex to Domenic's news. If Andres wants to fly today... *Storms and hail.* We have to do something. Quickly. Scenarios, like games of wooden ships, play themselves in my mind, forming and dissolving too quickly for conscious thought. Domenic is right. We need insight into the Bevnians' plans to put our own into action. We need the quarterdeck.

My heart thumps in harmony with the Bevnian's approaching steps, and I've only a heartbeat to spare when an idea settles. "Tell Piranha you think this line is bad too," I whisper quickly, tapping the thick main line I'd been studying.

Domenic's incredulous stare pierces into me, but I've no time to explain.

"Please," is all I can whisper before I must scurry away, pretending I don't feel the crew's annoyed sneers. The captured Diante feed their dignity by reminding themselves that, unlike me, they at least are male; the Tirik prisoners dislike my Lyron origins as a matter of course, and the Bevnians believe me little more than livestock. "Bad rope." Domenic says dutifully a few paces away from me, a few paces behind me, bringing a perfectly healthy two-inch-thick rope to Piranha's attention.

The younger man frowns at the object. Unlike the Tirik and Diante prisoners, Piranha seems perfectly at ease with the harsh weather, wearing the sleeveless shirt the Bevnians are fond of. "The main line is fine," Piranha says after a moment, growling softly when Domenic presses the fiction. "Don't touch it. Just...go away."

Domenic bows in surrender and retreats, the tops of his ears pink from his unseamanlike declaration.

Sending a mental thank-you to him, I turn my attention to Kyra. Finding a moment to speak with the girl is more difficult, and the best I can do is a quick brush-by when our divisions are sent down to the hold for dinner. Whether she understands my whispered request or not remains to be seen.

The weather worsens by the afternoon, the newly impressed Diante civilians having the hardest time of it. In the past two weeks, they've learned the basics of Tirik commands, but the cold and the swaying ship are reducing them to miserable beasts willing to move only if staying huddled proves more painful.

"Can we blanket them, sir?" Piranha asks Saarik, the young man's eyes on a shivering sailor.

Saarik smacks the back of Piranha's head. "Have you never so much as trained a dog, boy? What damn message are you sending if you reward laziness with blankets?" Saarik turns his face in disgust as Kyra stumbles past, hanging on each rope she passes to keep herself steady until she finally reaches the rail and vomits, much as I had done earlier. Saarik rubs his face. "Though I say we cull the lot and restock. This shit isn't even worth taking back to the village."

Saarik's gaze cuts to me, standing too close to his coveted quarterdeck. I rush off before he can make something of the infraction. Domenic is right: if we are to know what's happening, much less have a chance of influencing it, we need a foothold in the middle of the officer cadre itself.

Half an hour later, Domenic's gut feeling about Andres's flight plans proves true as the Gifted Bevnians, healthy, beautiful, and tattooed, emerge on deck. The young woman in front, a gorgeous water caller with a delicate nose and full, pale lips, beams at the ocean, apparently unconcerned for the lurching ship.

The magic in my blood thumps in recognition of its brethren, sending a rash of fear along my skin. Fear and, perhaps, envy. Where are the tolls magic takes on the Bevnian

Gifteds' bodies? How do Bevnian water callers not bleed out, their wind callers not convulse? Do Bevnian metal callers keep their minds too?

My understanding morphs as a fourth Bevnian, a young man I've not seen before, trails behind the Gifted trio. As proud and large as the others of his kind, he moves with the clear precautions of a water caller's precarious existence. Slow, careful, watching his every step for fear of tripping, while a pair of sentinels clear a path around him. Clearly, not *all* Bevnian Gifted are free from side effects.

My breath catches. A cure. The bastards must have found a cure to turn some of their Gifted immune to magic's ill effects. Yet, of the four Gifted on deck, only three have received it.

Andres's lips press together, his gaze unhappily on the young man even as he speaks to Saarik. "Presuming Trice isn't here out of sheer recklessness, I take it Nora is about to ascend to the gods?"

"I have a day or two until then," the woman at the front of the Gifted trio responds in the commander's place, either unaware or unconcerned about the breach of etiquette. She waves her arm toward the water caller. "Don't worry yourself, Andres, Trice is ready."

Piranha lowers his gaze. "You'll be missed," he tells Nora.

"I'll be honored," she replies coolly.

"Stations, Mr. Saarik," Andres barks, ending the exchange. He calls out the heading to the helmsman while Nora and her two wind-calling companions take their places at midship.

"All hands prepare to wear ship!" Saarik calls into his speaking trumpet at Andres's nod.

My stomach clenches, the curiosity over the Bevnian Gifted yielding to more immediate dangers. I spread my legs wide, my hands braced on the rope I'm to haul, my gaze on the choppy seas and cresting waves. Exam time. For my plans, my schemes. *Storms.* Sabotage is not an exact science.

Around me, the crew starts into motion. Hollow-eyed Tirik plod to their stations, shoulders hunched against cold, insult, and lash. The Diante, who understand the routine commands by now, move with greater enthusiasm than their Tirik counterparts, but lose in clumsiness what they make up for in speed. The sight is uninspiring, and, despite their ignorance of my plan, tension crackles between the Bevnian officers. Handling a ship in agitated weather—be it natural or Gifted-stirred—takes skill, seamanship, and a synergy of both officers and crew. The *Arrow* must not just move quickly after all, she must move in the right direction and neither break nor capsize in the process.

Andres squares his shoulder. "Elements. Mark."

I hold my breath.

The Gifted trio turn their faces to the skies. The wind and sea gather with a collective sigh, growing and angering into a rising gale. The Diante begin to pray, quieting their moaning chant only when a rope's end enforces the silence. Andres lets the *Arrow* fall a few points off to larboard, and our sails fill with a glorious *pop*, the ship lurching into flight like a spurred stallion.

"Steady!" Andres barks. "Hold helm. Wear ship! Get us flying straight and hard, Mr. Saarik."

My oversized shirt billows and flaps as the ship turns into the wind, harnessing its flow for best direction and speed. Salty spray stings my eyes as the ship finds its course, accelerates, races. The bow rises, sails strain, the ropes—

Snap.

Even knowing what's coming, I flinch at the horrid sound of the main line separating in two. Right at the spot I'd asked Kyra to scorch at the core when I brushed past her on the way to dinner.

The crew screams, ducking as the broken rope whips around and the suddenly free section of canvas flutters in the hard wind. The *Arrow* turns about, unsteady and bucking in the rough seas.

Andres's eyes widen. "Elements, halt," he bellows even as Saarik calls for a new main line to be rigged, the rogue sail lowered, for ropes to be let out and hauled in as required to balance the ship.

They are good orders. Right orders. But they are unusual, filled with new words and difficult phrases in a language that half the crew barely understands. Even Domenic, whose seamanship the Bevnians have come to rely on, can do little to help. Keeping my face schooled, I marvel in gleeful horror at how quickly the *Arrow*'s bewildered crew—more concerned with doing *something* than doing the *right* thing—grasps the wrong lines, hauls too hard or not hard enough. At how quickly the *Arrow* starts to spin on her axis, threatening true damage to the rudder.

At how quickly the ship becomes the chaotic world I need her to be.

Because the key to persuading a superior to accept an offered solution is to ensure the right problem.

Filling my lungs, I slide a bit closer to Andres and add my voice to his—translating the captain's orders with clear, loud efficiency. The captain blinks at me. Once, twice.

I shut my mouth and cower, my shoulders curling in subservience. *No threat here, Andres. Nothing but a means to rein in your crew.* My heart pounds, my breath still while the captain assesses me, the ship, the crew. The Diante, though no more skilled than they were minutes ago, are at least throwing their backs into the correct tasks now, the slipped control of his ship creeping back into Andres's grasp.

"Looks like you've earned yourself a new duty, girl," Andres barks finally, sending a wave of triumph though my racing blood. "Stay at my side until I release you."

"Aye, sir," I whisper, my head still bowed as I ascend the quarterdeck, ignoring Domenic's gaze.

CHAPTER 34

KYRA

*T*he only person Kyra hated more than Nile, as she watched Piranha whipped within an inch of his life, was herself. Kyra hadn't known why Nile asked her to weaken the thick rope that looked like any other, hadn't guessed that Nile maneuvered the young Bevnian to vouch for that very line hours earlier. But Kyra hadn't asked either.

And now Andres and Saarik exacted their vengeance, not on the two women who sabotaged the rigging, but on the man who'd fallen victim to their trap.

Even Piranha himself felt he deserved the punishment—or *had* felt it when it started. He'd shored up enough dignity to conceal his fear, had hung on to that inner strength for a great deal longer than Kyra thought possible. That was when the only sound aboard had been the crack of leather and distant, rolling thunder. But that had been many lashes ago. Dignity was long gone now, Piranha's silence yielding to desperate, wounded screams that weakened with each new blow until his voice was a sad, hoarse whimper. Crimson ran from snow-white skin, a soft steam rising from the wounds as hot blood met cold air.

"Brother—" Piranha whispered, unable to do more than lift his head from the deck by the time Saarik was finished.

Andres's jaw tightened. "I have no brother." He spat before turning to Saarik, who still panted from the effort of shredding Piranha. "Dump him with the livestock, Saarik. If he can think no better than a mutt, there is little reason to keep him from their company. And get my deck clean." That last was accompanied by a snap of his fingers at Nile, who obediently translated the command into Diante and Lyron before following Andres to the quarterdeck.

Nile, who'd paid for her new position on Andres's quarterdeck with Piranha's blood and Kyra's honor.

"You realize our survival requires *killing* the Bevnians, right?" Catsper said once they returned to their hold for the evening. However he'd worked through what must have happened, he seemed neither surprised nor appalled at the result. When Kyra remained silent, Catsper began his evening exercise routine, his shoulders rising from and lowering to the deck in the corner of the holding cell. Around them, the Diante found their own privacy, some curling up to sleep, others talking softly, their backs turned. The usual orchestra of sneezes, snorts, and farts filled the room. Catsper paused in midmotion, stressing his abdominals. "Nile infiltrated the quarterdeck without killing anyone. Given the high value of that position, I'd say it came quite cheaply."

Kyra's face twisted to him. "You call that cheaply?"

Catsper's eyes chilled. "Yes."

"You weren't the one responsible for shredding the flesh off the one Bevnian on this ship who has a moral compass, a hint of compassion and humanity."

"The others were too likely to take their pain out on the prisoners. To question too much." Catsper turned over and started on push-ups, as if they were discussing the damn weather. "Saarik hates Piranha and laid the blame on the young man happily. Do not dare blame Nile for taking action."

Kyra's hands curled, her blood simmering hotter with each of the marine's words. Around them, the Diante prisoners kept to themselves, murmuring too quickly and quietly for Kyra to understand. The familiar stench of bodies mixed with the coppery memory of Piranha's blood, some of which was still on Kyra's clothes from cleaning the deck. Catsper was right—it hadn't been Nile who'd ruined that rope. Kyra had done that. Set a decent man up to be tortured. Destroyed.

"Plus," Catsper paused in midmotion, holding his body on flexed arms, "Piranha is Andres's little brother. Tension between an enemy's top cadre is never a bad thing."

Kyra punched him. Slammed her fist right into the man's jaw. As hard and viciously as she could.

Catsper's head rocked with the blow, but he remained still, only his brow twitching in questioning demand.

Kyra cradled her bruised fist to her chest, her chest heaving as if she'd sprinted. She'd...hit him. Hard. Not in self-defense or desperation, but because she'd wanted to hurt the bastard. Wanted to hurt him still. *Stars.* Blood left Kyra's face, leaving it tingling and cold.

Catsper snorted, resuming his exercise. "What, no apology? No declarations of self-loathing? Am I more worthy of being struck than a man keeping hundreds enslaved?"

"You are a stars' damned bastard," Kyra whispered. Her knuckles pulsed. "You and Nile both."

Catsper was on his feet faster than Kyra could draw breath. His nostrils flared, his hair—sliced short with a Bevnian knife—rose like a mane around his shadow-sculpted face. The Diante, who'd already left a corner of the cell to the two Lyron prisoners —pushed themselves farther into the bulkheads. As far away as they could get. Catsper was angry. Furious. The taste of it filled Kyra's mouth, where she usually sensed nothing from the marine at all. "Maybe it's time you stopped complaining about having to get your hands dirty." The words were a growl, barely human. "The imaginary world you live in, the one where everyone is good inside and we talk our problems away, it doesn't bloody exist. I knew as much by the time I was five. That you still don't makes you either an idiot or a coward. Take your damn pick and keep your fists to yourself until you decide whose side you are fighting on."

She rose to meet the marine's gaze, not flinching away, though even at full height, she barely came up past Catsper's shoulder. The Diante averted their eyes from her. Whatever the argument between the two Lyrons, the Diante men said without speaking, they wished no part of it. Especially not on her side.

An unkind smile touched Catsper's face as he too marked the distanced Diante. "I don't think your *friends* have any intention of coming to your aid. I think they'd sit on their asses even if I splattered you against the wall in retribution for the blow. Should we try, or has the reality of people and wars finally sunk in?"

Kyra swallowed, knuckles tingling as she rubbed the bruised flesh. Her mind hummed, her whole body hot and cold and numb. Catsper was right. There was a cost for everything, action and inaction. Piranha paid it today, but others had been paying it for a longer time still. Even leaving Kyra's home village had had a cost—for, with her gone, Kyra's brother would have certainly found a new target for his desires. There was always a cost. And Kyra was the only one not paying it.

"Kyra?" Something had changed in Catsper's voice, caution replacing threat.

She retreated, the hand that struck the marine reforming into a fist. She understood. Why Catsper had knelt on cold stone that first night, why he sought every danger, every punishment. The raking need to balance the scales of whatever cosmic force decided to charge one being for the sin of another.

Catsper stepped toward her. Slowly.

With a spin, Kyra slammed her curled fist into the bulkhead. The sound came before the pain, but that followed quickly enough, the split skin already bleeding as the bones sang. Tears stung her eyes, crept and rolled down her cheeks. Kyra pulled back her fist and struck again.

Catsper captured the blow midstrike, his other arm wrapping around Kyra's body.

Kyra braced herself for the growling, for a slam into a bulkhead or deck. She welcomed it.

Catsper pulled her into himself instead, his muscled body encircling hers. Warmth seeped through the thin layers of shirts between them, the arm he had around her back. Releasing Kyra's wrist, Catsper slid his calloused palm to cup the side of Kyra's head. "Have you lost your mind?"

Kyra blinked, her pulse racing her thoughts. She put her hands on his chest, trying and failing to shove herself away. "Let me go."

Catsper ignored the demand, staring down at her, his gaze hard. "There was no other way, Kyra. The Bevnians' insistence on everyone speaking Tirik is strategy, not vanity. They know the risk of channeling their orders through a prisoner, of trusting her to yell things from the quarterdeck they might not fully understand. And the only way for that to have happened was to show a greater risk lay in *not* allowing it." He swallowed. "So you don't get to do this, to claim ultimate responsibility for events so much greater than you."

"And you do?" Kyra countered.

To Catsper's credit, he didn't try to deny it. "It's different." His lips pressed together, the muscles shifting beneath orange cloth. For a heartbeat, Catsper said nothing more, his gaze looking into some other world before returning to Kyra. Even then, he said nothing, though a crack somewhere inside him leaked that familiar salty tang that once called Kyra to the top of a stony ridge.

Kyra touched his elbow.

Catsper nodded. Not to Kyra but to himself, as if making a decision.

"I was in charge of a training unit." Catsper's words came quiet, slow. "I'd been too vocal in my opinions, especially when it came to training youngsters, too good at stretching orders to do as I like. The assignment to the *Aurora*, a distant, irrelevant ship with an idiot of a captain and nothing to do but herd a unit of wayward boys, was intended as a punishment. A message to teach me to keep my opinions to myself. After the Battle of Siaman, Spardic Command believed me reformed and had a new assignment for me. I...I went around them. Again. Committed to a detail more in line with my preferences."

"You stayed to guard Nile's back, you mean," Kyra whispered carefully.

The marine nodded, a fine shudder running through him, his gaze distant and hollow. Whatever he was seeing now, it wasn't this prison, or this day, but something that tore him more deeply than the Bevnians.

"Command couldn't touch me for political reasons,"

Catsper whispered, powerful shoulders curling in, flooding Kyra's senses with salt. "So they went after my trainees instead. After the boys. Sent them to the front lines. I received the nineteenth death notice the day we met."

"So you left the Spades." Kyra kept her voice even, not daring to show a grain of compassion lest she make things worse. "Resigned your commission."

A ripple of fury. "There is no *resigning* from the Spades. The division commander was supposed to have killed me when I threw my epaulettes at his feet."

Kyra pulled her wrist gently out of his grasp and laid her palm against his cheek. Her skin tingled where his stubble prickled against it. "I'm glad he didn't."

Catsper's eyes met hers, a penetrating green despite the gloom. His free hand rose, the fingers brushing over Kyra's knuckles and coming away damp with blood. With each breath, the rise of his chest pressed into her body, steady if a bit quick. A leashed power, so close to the surface. Catsper swallowed. "You are wrong," he said, releasing his hold on her. Pushing her away. "I'm not who you imagine me to be."

The sudden inches of space between them were freezing cold. Kyra raised her chin. "Don't assume to know my mind."

"No?" Catsper's arm uncurled from his side, bracing on the bulkhead beside Kyra's head. "You think I've not done to others half the things the Bevnians do to this crew?" he purred. "Do you imagine I've not killed? Not made people bleed and cower? The beatings the Bevnian bastards deliver to their underlings, do you think I've not delivered to *friends*?" He stepped closer, invading her space. "The next time you feel like punishing yourself for condescending to join the war, let me know how to help."

Kyra took a step to the side, cleanly moving around and away, her heart still pounding in her ears.

"There is a reason Spades aren't permitted to resign," Catsper added to her back. "We aren't fit for civilized company."

CHAPTER 35

NILE

"**Y**ou took the quarterdeck." Domenic's voice is a soft rumble against my ear. A tight, strained congratulations, just like the arms he has around me in this cold, miserable morning. Not a lover's embrace—we aren't lovers, can't be lovers, shouldn't be lovers—but a practical cocoon of privacy and warmth in a dark hole filled with squirming, caught, farting prisoners all waking to another day of misery. The thin stream of light leaking from a horizontal slit near the overhead paints a stark line on the deck. Polman crouches beside the light, twisting her hand back and forth as if having a conversation with the rays playing off her skin. The others huddle against bulkheads and each other.

I squeeze Domenic's arm in what would be an apology if I was sorry. But my remorse is only for his hurt pride, not my actions. "I didn't tell you the whole of it because you didn't need to know," I whisper finally. "It was safer for you not to— especially if the episode ended differently. Plus, I needed to keep you from being *too* helpful in correcting the disaster, lest Saarik and Andres started to wonder whether you hadn't been anticipating it."

"And?" Domenic prompts. The man knows me better than I should ever have let him.

I bite my lip. "I think you are too good a seaman to let a ship slip further into danger than it has to, much less knowingly sabotage a main line."

Domenic's cheek rests atop my head, his muscles tense. "You didn't tell me because you don't trust me." His chest tightens as he exhales. "I'm arrogant, not blind."

My chest aches to find the right words to make things all right, even when I know the impossibility of it. "I trust you with my life," I say too quickly.

"Which is a remarkably narrow scope in the sea of all decisions you make," he says dryly. His arms tighten around me. "I understand why."

"Listen up, mutts!" Saarik's voice sounds from behind the door a moment before it opens.

Domenic and I spring apart, the loss of his warmth and presence painful enough to make me conceal a wince.

Stepping inside, Saarik wrinkles his nose, surveying the cowering prisoners with a mix of approval and disdain. "Quarantine is over. You will now be allowed to mess and sling hammocks with the other livestock. One word or foot out of line, and you'll be right back here with a few stripes to keep you company. Now, move."

DOMENIC STAYS CLOSE TO ME, watching warily as we follow

along with the others up one ladder to the main gun deck and are issued hammocks and form messes. After two weeks sleeping on hardwood in a dark, rat-infested prison, the change to a hammock and eating at tables—swung to hang between guns during meal times—sounds luxurious.

"Ash. Dana."

Catsper's call guides us to where he, Kyra, and Vikon are already claiming a territory. Pushing between disoriented prisoners swarming the gun deck, we make our way to the sternmost table that neither requires nor attracts additional company. The men and women of the Tirik crew, who had enjoyed the gun deck to themselves until finding it crowded with a hundred more souls, glower. Some do, anyway—the others are too vacant to care.

"Why the new accommodations?" Vikon muses, glancing around to ensure no Bevnian overseers are close enough to mark his language. They aren't—though I suspect their distance is part of its own calculation: stopping prisoners from speaking to each other over meals is not feasible, so the Bevnians must either spend their days punishing everyone or feign strategic ignorance. They are wisely choosing the latter.

"I imagine Andres is settling in for a long cruise," Domenic says, his gaze weighing each table with an experienced eye, as if he sees more than I do amid the crew. "His ultimate goal is efficiency, not mindless torment." He taps two fingers against the tabletop. "Plus, with a turn toward winter, fevers will be rising enough to make separating sick and healthy vital."

Vikon nods. I've not spoken to the boy directly since leaving the *Stardust*, and against all odds, he seems to be holding up better than I imagined. He's been assigned to duty aloft, often stationed in the lookout platform given his keen eyesight and at least the ability to differentiate a sail from a rock—most of the time.

"Did anyone see what happened to Quinn?" Kyra asks softly. "Is he... Did he..."

"He was alive the last time I saw him." I tighten my jaw. Many friends who were alive the last time I saw them might not be so any longer, depending on how far into Lyron the Bevnians had penetrated. Depending also on whether, between the *Thorn's* reports and other news, the Lyron kingdoms have worked out by now that our enemy has changed and the rules of the war with it. "He was taken to Lester's ship. Possibly marked to go to a place called the village that seems to be a holding camp for prisoners."

Beneath the table, Domenic's knee brushes against mine. I press my lips together and knock a ship's biscuit on the table, evicting a host of five weevils who scuttle across the hanging table.

"If you are done playing with your food, Ash, might you condescend to tell the rest of us your plan?" Catsper swallows a spoonful of lumpy stew. The slimy mush has a slightly rancid taste and is best swallowed quickly with plenty of water to wash it down. "I presume there is one?"

I stare at the scurrying weevils, searching out the lesser one. We might be free to use the Lyron tongue for a few minutes, but...

"We aren't in Felielle, and I'm not the same man who started the cruise." Vikon leans back on his bench in nonchalance only to hunch over again a moment later to contain his warmth. The Bevnians better start issuing coats and blankets to prisoners or risk being without a crew shortly. The boy presses his lips together and meets each of our eyes in turn. Even Kyra's, though the latter recoils. "You've little reason to believe me, but little choice too," says Vikon. "This table is all we have."

We. I didn't know the young lord even had that word in his vocabulary. From the way Kyra tenses, I don't think she did either.

"We need Andres to seek out the *Helix*," I say, explaining the plan I hinted to Domenic earlier. "I hate putting another ship in danger, but if we are to play with anyone, Zolan is the ideal dance partner. Smart, capable, quick on his feet, and far enough from the mainland that we don't risk greater disaster by guiding the cat right into the mousehole."

"Zolan is long gone," Vikon says.

"I doubt Zolan actually left," I say, Domenic confirming my speculation with a nod. "But he is smart enough to keep his distance."

"Will Andres risk attacking anyone with this crew?" Catsper muses. "I'd be drilling morning to night, not seeking out an engagement if I were him."

"Andres is under pressure. The tension is so thick on the quarterdeck, you can cut it." I let out a long breath. "The *Helix* is an ideal prize. Most of the *Arrow*'s crew is Diante and Tirik, so by targeting a Lyron ship, Andres avoids pesky worries about forcing prisoners to fire on their own countrymen. Also, in going after the *Helix*, Andres would need worry neither about reinforcements nor about Lester coming in to snatch the prize." Seeing Domenic's questioning brow, I clarify. "From what I heard yesterday, Lester has his fleet on the move. Wherever Lester's fleet is, it's not here."

Catsper nods, his green eyes thoughtful. "Beside the minor matter of sabotaging twenty-four guns to keep flesh-melting explosives away from the *Helix*, have you an idea how we sell this tasty *Helix* morsel to Andres? Unless he is asking you for strategy advice in addition to translation now?"

I give Catsper a vulgar gesture, but it's Vikon, of all people, who speaks next.

"I can help with the latter." Vikon straightens, brushing biscuit crumbs off his orange shirt. "Put my smarts and looks to good use."

Domenic rubs his face. "I don't think Andres is seeking a young man to take to his bed."

Vikon's face turns burgundy. "I don't expect commoners to think, but might you at least listen?" the boy snaps, sounding like his old self before regaining control of himself. "The Diante might have no women amongst them, but the Tirik do, and I speak the language nearly as well as Nile."

A corner of my mouth tugs. "You would describe your *Helix*-based heroics to the Tirik women while ensuring the Bevnians hear the ship's details?" I let my hint of a smile dissolve. "This isn't without danger, Vikon. Once the Bevnians overhear enough to be interested, they'll press you for details. And they may not be gentle about it."

The middie shrugs. "I'll tell them to talk to Dana. He is the damn first officer. Let him deal with the details."

At least some things never change, Domenic and I say in exchanged looks just as the ship's bell signals the end of the meal. I hurry to the quarterdeck to see what need Andres might have of me, slowing when I hear him speaking with Saarik.

"...Biron. Lester should have little problem there."

Saarik nods. "We can still join Lester for the second pass. He'll circle back to the village to relieve himself of livestock."

"I hope so." Andres purses his lips before shaking himself and signaling to the bosun. A moment later, the familiar tone of a bosun's pipe summons the entire ship's company to assemble.

My stomach clenches, neither the news of Lester's plans to attack Biron nor this sudden call to deck sitting well with me. The last time Andres gathered the crew at an odd time, it was to watch Piranha being flayed alive. Nothing is off-limits so far as the Bevnians are concerned.

The sight greeting me on deck is unusually solemn, however. Standing on the raised poop deck, Andres calls for silence while the ship's Bevnians form two lines of pure white. With everyone thus assembled, the bosun's pipe sounds again, and the *Arrow*'s Gifted come up from the companionway ladder.

Two walking, the third—Nora, the water caller who'd stood so proudly yesterday—carried in another's arms. Nora's eyes are closed, her skin dusky gray, like the gathering clouds. Trice carefully follows behind, fear and excitement waffling off him like perfume. And bringing up the rear is Piranha. Ashen and shuffling, the young man carries a large wicker basket in his arms—the basket held well away from his body despite the obvious discomfort the position poses to his injured back.

"On your knees," Andres orders the crew while the lifeless water caller is laid out on deck. Once everyone obeys, Andres bows toward the woman's body. "We honor you, Nora, Princess of the Waves, as the ultimate warrior and holiest of souls. We pledge that all Bevnian children shall know your name and honor your family for the sacrifice you made for our people. Our devotion is with you as you ascend to the gods, who await to open the gates of paradise to you."

While I translate Andres's speech into Diante and Lyron, the Bevnians take turns bowing to Nora before covering her with a red-and-black New Republic flag. With a final salute, an honor guard slides her over the side, beautiful as a queen.

A few of the prisoners start to shift in preparation to return to their day, but the pipe calls, and all wisely settle. Andres turns to Trice.

"Today is a day of great honor, the day your life has led to. Do you, Trice, pledge your life to the New Tirik Empire and to the great Bevnian people?"

"I do," Trice says. His throat bobs though his voice remains strong. "I am ready to do my duty."

Andres signals to Piranha, who gingerly opens the basket and leaps back from it, hissing in pain from his injured back.

Eyes locked on the open container, Trice walks toward it, reaching out with a hand that suddenly trembles. His magic trembles too, I can feel it roar in a terror that rouses my own Gift. Whatever is in that basket, Trice's magic hates, fears it—and my own is learning to do the same.

The hushed silence of the deck magnifies every breath of wind and creak of deck. Trice's throat bobs, and he swallows once before plunging his hand into the basket's darkness.

When Trice's arm emerges, there is a glittering black-and-red snake wrapped around the wrist. The Bevnians shrink away, only Piranha darting forward to close the basket's lid. The snake on Trice opens its jaws, its fangs flashing as it slithers up the young man's forearm.

Clenching his jaw, Trice gives the snake an agitating shake. It hisses its displeasure, and the man flinches before managing to square his shoulders again and raise his chin. For a man who'd likely spent all his life kept away from danger for fear of bleeding, the physical sensation alone must be the height of terror. The snake, unimpressed with its host's bravery, winds its way leisurely up Trice's arm, its head now probing the sensitive crook of his elbow. Trice hits the snake, and fangs rise into the air and plunge hungrily into flesh, making Trice holler as loudly as Piranha had earlier.

Trice drops to his knees, screaming and panting, blood pouring from his mouth where he must have bitten his tongue. The deck is silent as the snake's venom works through Trice's system, the trickle of blood running from his mouth slowing. Stopping. The way a water caller's blood never does.

Trace blinks, his eyes slowly lighting with wonder. As if in a trance, Trice pulls a knife from his boot and kills the snake before pulling its fangs from his flesh, leaving a small, clean puncture wound.

"We honor you, Trice, Prince of the Waves," Andres intones as Trice finds his feet and rises and smiles powerfully at the world.

My own blood chills. The Bevnians have indeed found a cure for magic ill effects. A cure that kills the patient. I swallow. This has been the Bevnian's true weapon all along, martyrs trained to give up their lives.

Andres bows to Trice. "You are the ultimate warrior and holiest of souls. We pledge that all Bevnian children shall know your name and honor your family for the sacrifice you make for our people. Our devotion is with you, from today until you ascend to the gods, who await to open the gates of paradise to you."

As I finish translating, Piranha retreats with the basket, holding it far enough away to suggest more snakes are slithering within.

CHAPTER 36

KYRA

Sitting with Nile and the others at the mess table the day following Trice's ceremony, Kyra found herself without appetite. The *Arrow*'s celebration of Trice, its new martyr-to-be, had stretched into the evening, with Andres ordering the ship returned to discipline only once the setting sun started to bleed onto the waves. Groans and sighs had sounded from the Bevnian officers as the fiddles and pennywhistles were put away, and even some of the Tirik and Diante crew cast mournful glances at where the dancing was wrapping up on deck.

"Andres and Saarik believe Lester's forces are making a run on Biron," Nile said, tapping the table with her finger. "I hope that Admiral Brice is fortifying against attack, but how the bloody hell do you defend against these bastards?"

"Whoever conjured the notion committing to killing

yourself for a cause will lead to greatness in the afterlife is rotten to the soul." Kyra hadn't meant to speak aloud, but the words came anyway.

"You are mistaken." Catsper tucked in to the horrid food. "The point isn't to kill *yourself* for greatness, but to convince *others* to commit suicide for your cause. You don't see Andres or Saarik lining up to be bitten by venomous snakes."

"Andres and Saarik aren't Gifted, so I think they would get no benefit from the venom," said Nile quietly. "The snakes' venom seems to counteract the elemental attraction's ill effects while increasing the Gifted's power and control over the element."

"Until the venom leaves them dead." Dana shifted, giving Nile a piercing look.

Nile shrugged, sending an uncomfortable taste tingling Kyra's palate.

"I doubt the Bevnians who sailed their boat into the *Wave*'s hull were Gifted," Catsper countered. "Nor the ones who killed themselves in Port Mead. The point is, no one in the Lyron League or Diante Empire is prepared to face an enemy that uses suicide as a tactic. That gives the Bevnians a tactical advantage."

Kyra crossed her arms and leaned forward, closing the distance with the marine across the table. "We are talking about lives, not tactical advantages."

"You are talking about lives," said Catsper. "I'm talking about tactical advantages."

Kyra leaned back and smiled sweetly. "You know what I think?" she purred, the very essence of nonchalance. "I think these martyrs are utter cowards. Running away from life instead of facing its consequences."

The marine stiffened for a moment, then resumed shoveling what passed for food into his mouth.

"What do you say, Catsper?" Kyra waited until the man had no choice but to look up again. "Can cowardice be turned to tactical advantage?"

"I think that if we are to find a way to disable the Bevnian weapons, then I've work to do." Catsper rose, letting his spoon clatter against his bowl. "Excuse me."

The resounding silence veiled the table. Glancing between Kyra and the departing Catsper, Nile cleared her throat and turned smoothly to Vikon. "Have you had much success describing your *Helix*-based heroics yesterday? I saw you speaking with several women during the celebration."

Kyra leaned away, determined to draw as little of the young man's attention as she could.

"CAN you tell whether my efforts are working?" Stepping up beside Kyra's laundry trough after the meal, Vikon lowered his voice and fiddled with a spyglass as if adjusting its joints.

"What are you doing here?" Kyra lowered her head closer to the laundry water, scrubbing an orange shirt with more force than required. The waves of excitement and fear washing over Vikon were so strong, it was a wonder the rest of the crew wasn't turning to stare.

"Can you tell whether I've piqued the Bevnians' interest?" asked Vikon.

Kyra bit her lip. The faster Vikon left, the better, but with Catsper—whose mere presence inspired Vikon to be elsewhere —still making himself scarce in the ship's bowels, Kyra was on her own. Her eyes slid to the hatch. There was no sign of the marine, and she feared Saarik would note the absence soon. "Yes," she told Vikon quickly. "I think they're curious."

"I think Saarik will ask me about it soon," Vikon pressed.

"I think you've been here too long," Kyra whispered back. "We don't need attention."

Vikon wrapped his hand around the edge of the laundry trough and swallowed, hunching his shoulders. "Tell the Bevnians you need help to bring the laundry down. They have little need of me just now. They'll let me go with you."

Excitement and fear. It was a wonder how emotions could taste so plain yet tell Kyra so little.

Kyra shook her head. "No."

Vikon slumped further. "Please," he whispered, a note of desperation now entering his voice. "When Saarik decides to question me... He might hurt me for the information, and I'm not like the others. I...I'm frightened, and I don't know who else to speak with. Please."

That explained the fear. For all his nineteen years, Vikon had been little more than a spoiled child before this cruise, and this task, one he volunteered for, was likely the first time the boy faced danger.

Kyra sighed.

"I don't think I can do this." Vikon's voice dropped further, a small whisper above the burbling waves.

Kyra's fingers clutched wet cloth. If Vikon backed out, or worse—turned the details of the plot over to their overseers to save his hide—the blood running across the *Arrow*'s decks might be that of her friends. Much as Kyra disliked Vikon, he was doing something Nile needed—and if Kyra could help keep him from straying, it seemed the height of selfishness not to. Catsper was right, they all needed to fight. And this, talking, working through fear, was one skill Kyra had over the others.

"All right." Drawing a fortifying breath, Kyra took a few steps toward one of the Bevnian overseers. "Can he help me bring up laundry?" she asked, summoning the best of her learned Tirik.

The man considered the request and nodded briskly.

Catching Vikon's gaze, Kyra motioned to the gangway ladder and led the boy into the privacy of the belowdeck gloom.

Vikon's shoulders sagged with relief, though the excitement and fear remained steady at the forefront as he followed Kyra down the ladder and waited while she retrieved a lantern. "Just one bloody moment of peace." The last, said softly beneath the boy's breath, was likely as close to a thank-you as Kyra was going to get.

Still, Vikon needed to talk, and she needed to listen. It would certainly be a more preferable use of her talents than sabotaging the ship's rigging. Holding the lantern to light their way, Kyra proceeded to the next ladder.

"I had an ulterior motive." She made her voice light, trying to put Vikon at ease. Even when people were ready to talk, words could be difficult to find. Harder still to utter. "Andres said we'll be permitted blankets, but the stock must be washed free of rat droppings first. It would take me all watch to bring the fabric to the deck alone."

A ripple of disgust. Vikon hesitated, as if weighing his anxiety against the unpleasantness of work.

Kyra supposed that expecting anything different from him fell too far out of the realm of reality.

"It's been a long few weeks," Vikon finally said into Kyra's back, his footsteps following her toward the next hatchway, which would lead them to the final lower hold. "Though it must have been nice for you four, getting cozy with each other while I rotted alone."

"It was paradise," Kyra said dryly, stepping onto the shifting ladder. The lantern in her hand swung precariously as she descended. "The Bevnians brought us fresh fruit while we lounged in Andres's cabin and watched the sea." Her feet found solid deck, and she sighed, making her voice soft. "What was it like for you? I cannot imagine enduring those days alone."

Vikon jumped down smoothly, a small growl escaping his throat as he landed beside Kyra. Vikon's hand grabbed her shoulder, his nostrils flaring as he spat his words. "Do not *ever* presume to make a fool of me, wench."

Kyra stepped back and crossed her arms, though her heart gave an uncertain stutter and quickened into a trot. "First," she said with a cool, loud voice that would do Catsper proud, "do not ever lay hands on me. Second, if you find my company objectionable, Lord Vikon, you are free to find employment elsewhere. Third," Kyra paused, taking a careful sniff of the boy's horrid breath. Yes, that was a faint tinge of alcohol she smelled. Wherever the idiot had procured the liquid courage, it was certainly inside him now. "We've little time before we must return to deck. I think we should talk about you."

Instead of backing away, Vikon took a step closer, the musk of old cloth, mold, and rat dung thick around them. "You are right," he whispered, pushing Kyra backward until her back struck hardwood. "We don't have much time."

Jerking away, Kyra opened her mouth to scream, only to have Vikon slam his palm over her face.

"We'll have to make it quick," he hissed into Kyra's ear, sandwiching her between his body and the ship's hull. "You can remember me in your dreams, however. I'll let you keep the memories."

Kyra's body went still, an icy cold jamming her joints and muscles and lungs. Vikon hardened against her, and Kyra's paralysis exploded into flailing, her legs beating the ship's hull and the man's shins, unable to budge either.

Vikon jerked Kyra away from the hull and slammed her back into it, sending the lantern tumbling from her grasp. "Don't make me hurt you," Vikon rasped into her face. "Don't turn the best minutes of your life into a nightmare."

"You are dead," a low, murderous voice said from the darkness deep to Kyra's left, making Vikon jump away from her. Steps sounded, the rage suddenly coating Kyra's tongue, so potently bitter that it drowned out Vikon's vileness. Another step and the man breached the pool of light cast by the fallen lantern, his features—Catsper's features—sculpted with violence. The marine's green eyes seemed to glow in the lantern light, his shadow large and very, very still.

"Kyra," the marine said, fear gripping the syllables. His hands, still dirty from whatever he'd been digging through, opened and closed at his side. "Are you injured?"

"No," she whispered.

Relief. Knee-buckling, bone-deep relief echoed from Catsper, flooding the cargo hold for a full heartbeat before the marine's anger shoved away all else. Deadly. Violent. Murderous. All aimed at whoever, whatever, had planned to hurt her.

"It wasn't what you think," Vikon croaked, his hands now raised as if to ward off a misunderstanding. "The wench wanted some—"

A new storm of fury encircled Catsper, and the marine was between Vikon and Kyra before the younger man could swallow his words.

Vikon froze. A coyote who suddenly discovered himself on the turf of a protective wolf. Fear rushed from him, the delayed reality finally penetrating.

"Don't kill him," Kyra whispered, her already racing heart pounding faster. Because she knew Catsper would. Over her.

Catsper would kill a man just to ensure the bastard never laid a hand on her again. *Stars.* Kyra's magic pulsed, her breaths so quick that her head swam. "Catsper—"

"Get comfortable, Lord Vikon," Catsper said, advancing on the man who'd dared to hurt her. "I will rip out your tongue first, and then I shall stuff your balls in its place."

CHAPTER 37

NILE

The screams echoing from below are my first indication that something is wrong. The Bevnians rushing toward the companionway ladder are the second.

Catsper.

He'd gone down to scout the flesh-melting projectiles, discover a means of sabotaging the bloody things before we found the *Helix*. If he's caught or, worse yet, if he set one off... *Storms and hail.* My hand closes around Domenic's forearm, my mouth dry.

"School your face," Domenic murmurs, though his muscles coil beneath my grip. As much emotion as he's willing to show.

Releasing Domenic, I start toward the companionway ladder, my heart racing, my chest tight around my ribs. My idea. My plan. My fault.

A Bevnian sentinel stops me with a bared sword aimed at

my heart. A musket is slung over the man's shoulder, along with two pistols tucked into his belt and a bandoleer of prefilled powder cartridges. All I have is a small knife to cut rope. Domenic grasps my shoulder, pulling me back toward the rail. The prisoners around us are retreating too, most raising their hands in preemptive surrender. A dozen more well-armed sentinels pour out onto the deck, corralling all the prisoners together while a bosun's pipe calls all hands to deck.

That's when tendrils of dark smoke filter from below, and my heart stops beating altogether. Fire. There is a fire in the bowels of the ship.

"Where are Kyra and Vikon?" Domenic murmurs into my ear, his face an emotionless mask.

I twist about, surveying the crowded deck. Faces stare back, frightened and indifferent, hollow and determined. None are Lyron. *Kyra. Storms.* What the bloody hell happened?

Outside the ship, water rises in an unnatural stream and attacks the hull and portholes, the Gifted braiding water and wind to put out flame. The combination is infinitely more efficient than the hand pumps that are usually rigged, and the Bevnians seem more furious than panicked over the inferno. Furious enough for murder.

"Easy," Domenic's low voice warns. "Keep controlled."

He'd know. He's spent years standing beside a tyrant, keeping his face indifferent as stone while he struggled to mitigate Rima's atrocities.

The sentinels clear a space around the quarterdeck, where punishment is usually meted out—the same center stage that was last used to turn Trice into a living dead man. On the poop above, another squad of sentinels forms a line, their muskets loaded and pointing down at us. Andres is there already, surveying the gathering. He snaps his fingers to summon me just as Saarik appears from below, the three Gifted behind him.

Between my bone-deep longing to do *something*, the too-tight proximity of three powerful Gifted, and the chain I've kept on my own Gift since the *Stardust*, my magic flares with a force so violent that I stagger. A furious, wild beast that wants *out out out* of the prison my body traps it in. My breath quickens, blood rushing through my veins so quickly, it makes me dizzy. My muscles tense and buzz deep inside, solid tissue and magical energy straining against each other. A hunger to call the wind to me is a jagged void in the pit of my chest. My Gift doesn't just want freedom, it wants to hunt.

A hand presses into the small of my back, and Domenic's warm body steps up silently behind me. A pillar of muscle and stone who has known for a while now just how dangerous I am. Who knew it before I did. Warned me. He doesn't tell me to go to Andres. He says nothing at all.

Swallowing, I raise my chin and step forward, taking my station at the captain's side—so very close to Trice—even as my magic bubbles and roars. Pressure building behind my eyes and the pounding in my head echoes like a Diante gong. *Bom. Bom. Bom.* I shake my head to clear it, but the movement is a mistake that makes the pounding worse.

Below, seaman after seaman stumble to the deck, some curious, some frightened, some too hollow-eyed to care. None of them are Catsper, Vikon, or Kyra.

"Silence," Andres calls, though thanks to the sentinels, the noise is already limited to whimpers and prayers whispered under breaths. Andres nods to the chief sentinel, and three figures with bags over their heads are pushed into the open space beneath the poop, and suddenly, my pounding head no longer matters.

Even with the heads covered, Catsper's lithe, panther-like body is as obvious as Kyra's fragile form. By process of elimination, the prisoner being dragged between two Bevnians must be Vikon. The Bevnians following in their wake are soaked in blood that is too fresh and copious to be all theirs.

"Is the fire contained?" Andres demands.

"Aye," Trice replies, climbing to stand behind Andres with the other Gifted.

On the deck below, Saarik has his prisoners on their knees, unbound but held at sword point.

"Report," Andres calls to his first officer.

Saarik pulls the bags off. Catsper's face is blank as if nothing of particular significance is taking place, but both Kyra and Vikon are appropriately terrified.

"Two bucks started a fight over a filly and knocked a lantern over in the process. More specifically, this one," Saarik kicks Catsper's back, "attacked this one," he kicks Vikon, "over this one." The final kick lands on Kyra, toppling her over.

Catsper lunges at Saarik, taking out two of the Bevnian sentinels before four others swarm in to grab the marine's arms. The lot have Catsper facedown on deck in a heartbeat, and I flinch as Saarik unhooks the whip on his belt and cracks the braided leather over Catsper's back. Once. Twice. A dozen. New blood wets Catsper's shirt as Saarik tries and fails to make the marine scream.

"Saarik." Andres's voice is deep and displeased. "Either put down the lot and be done with it, or get on with a demonstration worth remembering."

Saarik grinds his jaw but steps back, letting Catsper right himself as far as his knees. The marine's face is tight with pain, but his chin rises defiantly. He shoots a murderous glare at Saarik. No...not at Saarik, at Vikon.

Storms. So there truly was a fight. I find Domenic with my gaze, see the same bewilderment and horror that courses through my own veins. We missed it. Both of us. Were so focused on the Bevnians that we missed disaster brewing beneath our very noses.

Andres's heavy hand slaps the back of my head, the dull ringing as effective as cold water to jerk my attention to him. "If you've forgotten how to use your tongue, I'll be happy to remove it for you. I said, tell the Diante dimwits that the two bucks were fighting over a filly. And now everyone is about to witness the consequences of that nonsense."

My voice catches as I translate, my mind grappling for words and weapons. Nothing beyond a tiny work knife. But even if Domenic and I had swords, pistols, muskets—the two of us could no more take the ship than we could fly.

I could kill them all, the magic in my blood purrs relevantly, sending my heart thundering. Despite the cold wind, sweat beads on my temple.

Andres puts his hands on his hips and glowers down at the bloodied prisoners. "Keelhaul all three." Andres turns his gaze on the crew. "Have the cook make those who fail to survive into stew for the slaves in place of their usual feed. A dozen lashes to anyone who refuses to dine."

Vikon, who fully understood Saarik's words even before my translation, throws himself at Saarik's feet. Keelhauling isn't just a likely death sentence, it's torture. Vikon's eyes are wide, a puddle of urine joining the blood dripping from him. "Please!" Vikon's voice rises. "I wasn't fighting over the wench, sir, I was defending the ship." Vikon points a finger at Kyra. "She attempted to set the *Arrow* aflame. With magic. Wanted to burn us all to a crisp when I found her. It's her. It was all her."

Saarik steps away from Vikon in disgust but turns a questioning face up to Andres.

Vikon's hands tremble as he pulls off his bloody shirt, now more rags than clothes. "Look," he gasps, pointing to charred skin along his breast and flank. "She did this. A fire caller. She wants to burn down the ship."

Saarik silences Vikon with a kick and turns on Kyra. "Is that true?" Saarik demands through me, regarding the girl like a coyote toying with a choice mouse. "A fire caller amidst our livestock?"

"N-No," Kyra stammers, her whole body trembling.

Beside me, Andres's face sparkles with excitement. Has been sparkling ever since the possibility of a Gifted appeared before his very nose. The captain's tongue caresses his lips. "Check her."

Saarik raises his hand to silence Vikon, whose mouth is already open, and snaps an order to Piranha. The young Bevnian flinches but disappears to do Saarik's bidding. Silence reigns over the deck, each minute of Piranha's absence stretching for an eternity. My headache returns, pulsing as the magic struggles for murderous freedom.

Then Piranha places a familiar wicker basket before Kyra, and nausea drowns out my pain.

"Pick a snake," Andres calls out to Kyra. "Don't be afraid, girl. If you are Gifted as the buck claims, the venom will tether your magic. Make you stronger and healthier. And if you aren't... The death from the venom is kinder than what Saarik has in store. A win for you either way."

Saarik's heavy boot nudges the basket toward Kyra.

She leans away.

"Rope," Saarik orders, holding out his hand while a Bevnian trots up with a coiled line. He holds the object before Kyra's face. "Do you know what keelhauling is?" he asks, his voice hypnotic even through my emotionless translation. "We loop a line beneath the ship's hull and tie you to it. Then, we drag you along the bottom of the ship all the way from one end to the other. If we pull quickly, the barnacles—these are sharp growths on the hull—will shred your flesh. If we pull slowly, allowing your body to sink low enough to avoid the sharp edges, you'll drown before it's done. Either way, what water and sharp edges spare, the rocking ship will make up for by knocking your head as the seas roll." Saarik pauses as Kyra sobs, a smile growing on his face. "Can you picture it?"

"Stop playing with your food, Saarik," Piranha snaps suddenly.

Saarik's face heats, but it's Andres who motions two sentinels to force Piranha to his knees and hold him there.

Saarik leans closer to Kyra. "Well?"

My breath stalls.

Kyra says nothing.

"A demonstration," Saarik growls, jerking his chin at Catsper. "Seize him up, and keelhaul the bastard."

"Don't!" Kyra shouts, only to have Saarik knock her to the deck with the back of his hand.

Two Bevnian sentinels level their muskets as a third approaches the kneeling marine. I wait for an explosion of limbs and fury, but Catsper holds still, allowing the Bevnian sentinels to wrap a rope around his waist. The marine's eyes are hard and unrelenting as they lock with Saarik's. No sound, no word, no surrender.

No fight either. Catsper is smart enough to know when resistance is futile.

My small work knife slides into my hand, and I know without looking that Domenic is doing the same. For all the good it will do. My breath comes quickly, the rising magic surging so hard that the wind comes despite my efforts. A leak of magic forcing itself around all my shields. Air stretches my lungs, the searing pain dropping me to my knees.

"If you pass out," Andres tells me under his breath, "I will throw you overboard."

I barely hear him. *Storms.* My eyes sting in foreknowledge of what's coming. For a heartbeat, I'm on another ship at once, the masts cracking, the ropes whipping innocent people overboard. I did this. I brought us here. Any time now, Catsper will be just as dead at my hands as at Saarik's. Him and everyone else.

Domenic's gaze sears into me, confused and expectant. I called on my wind to knock his hat off his head; surely I'd tap it to save a friend's life. Domenic doesn't know it's different now. I'm different. The truth finally pierces my heart like a driven nail. I must fight with every ounce of strength—not by wielding the winds to protect Catsper's life, but by bringing everything to bear *against* those winds, by forfeiting one friend's life to keep the others from being torn to shreds.

Just as Vikon proved himself a danger greater than the slavers, I am a greater threat still. As vile an abomination as that flesh-melting powder. As the Bevnians.

The sentinel finishes securing the rope around Catsper, whose blond hair ruffles in the wind, like it's often done in training or when the marine climbed the shrouds.

"Ready!" the sentinel calls, and there is no one to stop to him from pushing the marine toward the rail. Not me, whimpering on my knees. Not Domenic, whose attempt to shove forward is met with a pointed musket. Not Catsper, who opens his body to the sea below.

CHAPTER 38

NILE

*K*yra moves.

Not toward Catsper, who is about to tip over the rail, or even toward Saarik—but toward the closest sentinel. The man, twice Kyra's size, blinks in confusion as the small, ferocious girl clamps her body onto his thigh. Kyra's thin hand reaches up, her fingers splaying open against the sentinel's flesh. Lightning resolve flashes in her eyes—and then the bandoleer of gunpowder packets strapped to the sentinel's chest explodes with a resounding boom. Blood and entrails are still raining down on the deck when Kyra knocks a second sentry into Saarik and sets off the second bandoleer powder charges with the same brutal efficiency.

This time, the explosion roars back at Kyra herself. She staggers, her eyes wide, and crumples to the deck while Saarik's body crackles and flames.

"Kyra!" Catsper's bellow thunders across the ship. "Kyra!" Grabbing the rope attached to his waist, Catsper loops it around the neck of the sentinel closest to him. They fall together, the entangled guard choking and thrashing as Catsper snatches the man's knife and saws himself free. Not a proud warrior facing death, but a feral predator.

Catsper's blade just severs the rope when a second sentinel leaps atop him and flattens the marine onto his back. A few paces away, the others scatter back from the spreading flame.

Trapping the sentinel's hand and foot, Catsper bucks his hips. The pair flips over, and now it's Catsper who sits astride his assailant. A flick of the blade, and Bevnian blood spurts on the deck. Catsper is up and moving toward Kyra before the Bevnian finishes twitching.

"Trice! Douse that flame!" Andres roars to the trembling water caller behind him. After a lifetime of protecting his hide, the Gifted stands frozen in the face of combat.

"Charge!" Domenic shouts to the prisoners, slugging the first Bevnian he can reach by way of demonstration. The sentinels on the poop discharge their muskets, felling several of the prisoners before rushing into the brewing fray, swords bared and white hair streaking in the wind.

I force myself to my feet. My lungs scream, and the wind coming toward me grows with each heartbeat. Narrowing my eyes to my target, I take one step. Another, my bare foot splattering the warm urine Trice spilled on deck. And then I reach around the water caller's neck and place my blade against his jugular. "You are *my* water caller now," I purr into the man's ear.

The stream of water attempting to douse Kyra's flames dwindles to a trickle, leaving bits of black smoke rising into the air.

Andres turns, the question on his face dissolving when he sees me holding Trice. To his credit, Andres merely crosses his arms and looks me in the eye. "A poor choice of hostage, girl. Trice doesn't fear death, for it runs in his veins already."

I swallow, forcing my voice to work. "Not planning to kill him." My knife twists up, the tip swinging to slice through the Gifted's lip. For a man who's lived this long only through meticulous avoidance of any injury, the unexpected pain and taste of his own blood is enough to set him howling. "Rock the ship, Trice," I order.

Andres's jaw hardens, a frozen ice statue silhouetting the screams of pain and triumph filling the mid decks below. My knife presses into Trice's lip again, and the pungent stench of fresh urine rises up between us. Andres crinkles his nose in disgust.

"Rock the ship, Trice," I say again.

This time, waves rise to bang the hull with loud, echoing thumps.

"More!" I demand, my incision shallow but terrifying long. And slow.

The ship lurches like a skittish jackrabbit.

"You are going to capsize the whole damn frigate, girl," Andres growls.

"Order the boats lowered," I tell Andres. "Take all the Bevnians and cast loose. Either that or go down with this ship."

Another cut, another wave striking the *Arrow*.

"You'll drown too," Andres counters. "You'll kill hundreds of people. Murder them."

I force a smile to my face. "Like you said about Trice, we've nothing to lose." My wind slips the leash further, and a gust of wind twists the sails. I grin as if it was Trice's magic, not mine, that made the ship tilt. "I fear you've little time to decide,

Andres. Trice is losing his courage with each heartbeat. Who knows what horrors he'll be sending our way soon." I pause, swallow, and drop the game. When I speak next, my voice is sincere. Respectful. One officer to another, one last time. "We all live or we all die, Andres. Give the order and do right by your people. You can come back to kill me another day."

Murder shimmers in Andres's eyes, but he turns toward the melee below and bellows for the Bevnians to stand down. The command requires repeating before it's heeded, but after a few moments, weapons are lowered. Not altogether happily, by either side.

It's my turn now, and I gather a lungful of breath as I turn to the newly freed prisoners, whose blood still boils with a potent brew of exhilaration and revenge. "Stop! The Bevnians have surrendered!" My words rumble across the deck, slowing some swinging fists, some kicks of downed men. "We are not murderers! Stop!"

A large Tirik man holding a kneeling Bevnian's throat releases him, passing the word to others until the violence settles like a slowly dying flame. Not all at once, not without final spiteful blows, but it settles.

A wave of dizziness washes over me. I grip Trice more tightly to keep myself upright while the ship's boats swing into the ocean and the remnants of Kyra's fire are doused with buckets and pumps. The girl herself still lies on the deck, her chest rising and falling with gasps. Unconscious but alive. My attention returns to Andres, my voice dropping. "Captain, please be so good as to have your officers descend quickly. I imagine if any decide to linger, their experience will be less than pleasant. The three Gifted will be staying with us." Under very tight guard.

"The next time I see you," Andres tells me softly, his snow-blond hair streaking as he brushes by me, his head raised to tower over the world, "I will make sure you never sleep soundly again—until you sleep forever."

"Of course. Until then..." I smile, showing my teeth, "One trade, if we could. I would consider it a personal favor if you take Lord Vikon off my hands and leave me Piranha instead."

The heap that is Vikon raises its head. "Nile!" he shouts as the Bevnians haul him along. His wide eyes lock on mine with a genuine disbelief. "You can't. We are family. You and I, we are family."

I stay upright only long enough for the Bevnian boats to shove off into the choppy seas, then shove Trice into the arms of the closest seaman. The man says something I can't hear. Not with the wind still coming for me, my magic leaking and pounding. Andres's two boats make swift distance. I put their chances of drifting to land or ship at about one in ten—and if the ship they happen to come upon is Lester's, I imagine there might be more than Andres who chooses to jump overboard with the boat's anchor tied about his neck. Either way, the Bevnians' fate is in their own hands now.

Our fate is in mine.

I see only my own feet, focus on nothing but the one last thing I must do. My hands grip the rail separating the raised poop deck from the main deck below. A small jump, and my legs clear the beam, protesting as my knees take the impact. Around me, people argue and swarm, Diante and Tirik prisoners still high on the rush of battle. None of them are sure of what to do now. I leave the lot to Domenic's care. He will keep the ship safe.

I need to make sure Domenic still *has* a ship a bell's time from now.

The lid of the wicker basket is heavier than I expect, the

whispering from inside loud as a gathering storm. My chest squeezes as I behold the slithering mass of lithe bodies and forked tongues, the flesh-piercing fangs with venom powerful enough to rein in my magic. To keep me from destroying this ship we just reclaimed.

Trice's screams echo in my head, and I brace myself for the pain. One last breath and reach inside, extending my hand toward our hissing salvation.

"Nile!" The top of the basket slams closed, a muscled arm shoving me away to land hard against the deck. Domenic's face hovers above mine, his blue eyes dripping with terror. "What are you thinking?"

I struggle to rise, not caring how many people are watching. Listening. "I can't control the wind," I say softly at first, then louder, the truth spilling and mixing with tears I hadn't known were there. "I can't *control* it, Domenic. The *Stardust*—"

Domenic's hands wrap my shoulders. "This isn't the *Stardust*," he whispers.

I cringe as a spurt of magic escapes me, heralding a gush of piercing wind. "It's worse." My voice catches. "There is no working this out. You think I've not considered my options—"

"I *know* you've not considered your options." Domenic's hands tighten on my flesh, his fingers digging in hard enough to bruise. "Because none of your options have included me."

I shake my head. "That venom will give me a month in which we might find the *Helix* and get this ship to safety. I'm the one who handed us into the Bevnians' clutches. Let me set it right."

"Let *us* set it right together," Domenic counters. "Trust me, Nile." He releases one grip to cup my face with his calloused palm. His voice gentles, a low, soothing sound that ripples through my core. "I'll handle the ship through a storm. And you and I, we've weathered your magic before. Trained with it. You don't frighten me. Let me help. Work with you."

"And if..." I swallow. "What if you are wrong? Over two hundred people—"

"I'm not wrong." Domenic's jaw tightens. "But if I am, I will do what must be done to protect the ship. All right?"

My head is as heavy as an anchor to lift and lower through a nod, my heart racing so quickly, the world swims before my eyes.

Domenic leans close and brushes a kiss against my forehead. Warm and confident. "Five minutes. Can you hold out that long?"

I nod again but can't force myself to release his wrist, which I don't remember having taken hold off.

"It's all right," he says quietly, holding my hand while his body swings out and opens to the ship. A captain assessing the situation. When he speaks next, Domenic's voice is so filled with command that all the crew stops to listen, broken grammar and all. "Attention, all hands. Sails in. Secure ship. Prepare for weather. Gifted." His face turns to Trice and the two wind callers. "Prepare to counter the winds, or I swear there will be hell to pay."

Silence. Glances. Then movement. Tentative at first, then more organized as the seamen pull themselves together and repeat Domenic's orders among themselves. My breath still, the wind blowing my hair. There is nothing that makes the *Arrow* a crew. No trust, no friendship, not even a common language. Nothing but the primal need to survive the battling terror of the unknown, all hinging on following the orders of a man they met weeks ago.

Domenic gives my hand a reassuring squeeze and unfurls to his full height, his calm presence filling the quarterdeck. My heart thumps. This is why the Felielle Admiralty gave Domenic the *Raptor*. Not because of gender or patronage or tradition—but because Domenic is *good*. The kind of captain the best of admirals should want in their fleet. The kind I want on my side as well. Domenic's voice sounds again, loud without shouting. "Piranha. Where is the closest land with safe anchorage?"

Piranha frowns, either at the question or at Domenic's broken Tirik, but speaks grudgingly. "One day due east. A small island. Nothing there."

Domenic nods. "And is your back well enough to help navigate this ship?"

Piranha's gaze shifts from me to the snakes, then to the strengthening wind that's already beating the canvas.

"Mr. Piranha," Domenic says coolly, and the young Bevnian flinches. "You may join the crew as an officer or a prisoner. The choice is yours."

Storms and hail. Domenic is walking a tightrope, the chasm on each side deep and deadly. Yet he holds his head high, his face calm and confident as he stares down each set of eyes that rise up in challenge.

Piranha clears his throat, the crew shifting on their feet.

"Aye aye, sir," Piranha murmurs, then repeats louder. "Sails in. Secure ship. And prepare for weather."

Relief washes over me, but Domenic lets nothing but a small nod show as he leaves the sailors to their business to crouch before me. Strong hands wrap over my forearms, and blue eyes fill the whole of my world. Warmth from Domenic's body heats the air between us, and the familiar scent of salt and brine drifts into my lungs.

"On the count of ten." Domenic's voice is hypnotically soft. "Concentrate on nothing, *nothing*, but keeping that fierce magic of yours calling a steady, hard gale. You've granted the *Arrow* a fighting chance when you removed Andres. Now let me carry the burden for a few minutes." A corner of his mouth twitches. "Let's see if you can do something more impressive than skidding my hat across the deck."

And so I do.

CHAPTER 39

KYRA

*T*he world lurched, as if forces mightier than mortals battled each other over a tasty morsel.

Kyra whimpered, her body still screaming from that explosion of powder cartridges that threw her to the deck. Pain crackled along the skin on her left breast and shoulder, mixing with a different sort of pounding that echoed in her skull. She shut her eyelids tighter. Beyond them, there was a rain of blood and entrails, of sudden flame that bit skin hard enough to make her howl. There was wind too. That was new.

Then, she wasn't on a deck anymore. No, Kyra was in the air, someone's arms solidly beneath her as the wind rushed by them, whipping hair and skin. Kyra's face pressed against a soggy shirt, the copper of blood filling her nose.

Kyra recoiled from the smell, her eyes flying open. Nile stood beside Domenic, her magic rallying up a gale, though the wind was already slowing. Bodies littered the swaying deck, Saarik's lifeless gaze stared at Kyra, oblivious of his half-decimated, half-charred chest. She screamed.

"I help her," a Diante voice said above her. "My late grandmother taught me."

"Touch her, and I'll reunite you with your grandmother," Catsper replied with eerie calm. He shifted Kyra in his grip, bringing his green eyes to lock with hers before Kyra could scream again. "Look at me," Catsper ordered, bending against the wind. "Look at me and nowhere else."

She did, gripping the marine's neck when he maneuvered them down the companionway ladder and shouldered his way toward Andres's great cabin just as the ship lurched violently. Absorbing the punishing motions, Catsper kicked the door open with his foot.

"If you *ever* pull that again, I will kill you myself," Catsper growled, setting Kyra down on Andres's cot. "Understand?" Fear. Yes, that was coppery fear Kyra tasted from Catsper as the man crouched beside her and brushed her hair free of her face.

The touch lit a flame along Kyra's skin, the sensation swift and powerful enough to shove all else from its path: pain, fear, thought.

She swallowed and lifted her fingers toward Catsper's. Too slow. She was too slow, and Catsper's hand was already gone from her cheek by the time her own reached the destination.

"I see you condescended to join the fighting," Catsper said. "And found a damn bloody way to go about it." At Kyra's eye level with barely two feet between them, Catsper filled the entirety of her vision. His brow creased, tense despite his controlled voice. The hand that brushed Kyra's skin moments ago now was braced on the mattress.

"I thought one of us should." Kyra let a corner of her mouth twitch up. "Since you wanted a break."

Catsper flinched.

Kyra's chest tightened around her ribs like a band. The man who danced with death and had taken a lashing with hardly a grunt *flinched.* Reaching her hand toward Catsper, Kyra covered his knuckles with her palm. "I... I didn't mean—"

"You meant exactly what you said." Catsper's jaw tensed, the muscles flexing along his face. His head lowered, and Kyra held her breath, waiting for the command to mind her own problems. For him to pull away from her touch. Instead, he stayed stone-still, like the statue he was on the ridge in Port Mead where she'd first found him. A breath of silence chilled the room. Another. Finally, Catsper rolled back his shoulders. "There was someone worth fighting for just now."

Kyra pushed herself up on her elbow, her free hand shooting forward to grip the man's chin. "You are someone worth fighting for," Kyra said, her voice hard. Catsper's face still hostage in her grip, she studied his eyes. Green with tiny speckles of yellow, as if a feline of the species truly was in his ancestry. On his right, a thin scar lined the angle of his jaw. One of so many that no one ever saw. Kyra's pulse quickened, her whole body heating as she pushed herself toward him.

Catsper stilled, only the rise and fall of his shoulder betraying his breaths.

Kyra's own lungs halted, air trapped in them as her lips gently brushed Catsper's.

The marine's eyes widened, his coiled muscles frozen in place while a trickle of need escaped those shields, tingling on Kyra's tongue. The intensity of Catsper's gaze burned into Kyra's soul, his eyes drinking in the flickers of her fingers, the blinking of lashes. The need grew, burrowing down through

Kyra's core until she didn't know where Catsper's desire ended and hers started. And yet the man still refused to move, his muscles locked in iron check.

"You won't hurt me," Kyra whispered to him.

Catsper's fingers rose to brush the singed inside of Kyra's left shoulder. "I already have." He rocked back on his heels and uncoiled himself upright. "You are covered in blood." He stepped back toward the other end of the cabin. "There—I saw a casket of drinking water. I'll fetch it."

"Wait." Kyra pushed herself to sit. Stand. Step toward him. The last was a mistake, as the ship tilted beneath her and what little balance Kyra had dissolved into mist. Catsper caught her before she could fall, that lethal, predatory movement returning now that he paid it no attention. Their gazes met, and he swallowed, his throat bobbing.

Kyra knew she was pretty in a way that appealed to men, that it took no effort at all to attract a man's touch. Whether she wanted it or not. But she didn't recall a time when *she* longed to brush her hand along a man's skin, to connect on a plane deeper than words. Until now. Until him. *Stars,* but that tiny brush of lips lit up more nerves deep in her body than whole nights of sport ever had.

Except, for the first time ever, the man before Kyra refused to press the opportunity. To take more than she offered. To dare accept even that. Catsper's hands, both bracing her hips to steady her, sang with tension. His breathing quickened, and he shifted his eyes to the overhead, exhaling with forced slowness.

Kyra's fingers closed around the collar of Catsper's shirt. "Take it off," she whispered.

His breathing stilled, his hands releasing her carefully to hover at the garment's hem. "Are you—"

"Yes."

Catsper gripped the bottom of his shirt, muscles shifting with the motion.

"How far did Piranha say that island is?" Nile's voice reached in from the pass-through, and Kyra's heart splattered into her stomach.

Catsper's hands slipped back to support Kyra's elbow just as the door to the great cabin opened to admit the princess and Dana, both looking the worse for wear.

"A day with good winds." Dana held the door open for Nile before following the girl inside. "There is little there, apparently, but safe anchorage and dry land, but it will suit."

Face as unperturbed as always, Catsper nudged Kyra toward the cot. The marine sat too, his own body bladed subtly between her and the others. Sitting shoulder to shoulder with him, Kyra felt the rapid beat of Catsper's heart echo through her skin, racing her own galloping pulse.

Stars damn ships and close quarters.

"Good, you are here," Dana said, nodding to Catsper and Kyra in turn while he pulled up two chairs. "Are you two whole?"

"Is the ship?" asked Catsper.

"For now." Nile dropped into a chair. Behind her, Dana reached for Nile's shoulder, pulled back before the hand connected, then changed course again to splay his fingers between her shoulder blades after all. Nile dropped her head into her hands. "But we need to get to land before I make it otherwise."

"Don't give yourself too much credit." Dana sat beside her. "The crew might sink itself before that happens."

"Are we going—" Kyra's words faltered. Home. She was going to ask whether they were going home. But their home wasn't hers. And their war?... Beside her, Catsper shifted his weight, moving slightly away. Giving her space. His bloody shirt stuck to his back, the wounds still oozing through the fabric.

"We must head to the closest land first, ensure that the *Arrow* and her crew—and me—are all fit for sea." Nile's voice was heavy with fatigue. Fatigue, but not surrender. Not now, not when the Bevnians had stripped her naked, not when she had sacrificed her dignity to protect her ship. "Then...Andres and Saarik thought Lester was targeting Biron, so we must assume the Ardent Ocean waters are fully hostile. Even if the route was safer, a crew of Tirik and Diante prisoners would never agree to sail to Lyron. Continuing on to the Diante Empire is our best choice. We go to finish what we set out to do: negotiate a full military alliance and give Lyron a chance against these bastards."

Kyra sucked in a breath. Not an end to a mission, but still the start. After everything, it was still only a start.

"With Diante support, we may even be able to free some of the Tirik prisoners to rouse opposition to the Bevnian stronghold," the princess added thoughtfully. "Storms, maybe we can find this village and drag Quinn back to work." A small smile touched Nile's lips, then dissolved. Reaching out, she brushed her fingers against Kyra's. "I do remember the promise to take you to Milan." She turned to Dana, her eyes not demanding but questioning. "The archipelago is closer to us than the Empire's heartland."

The man nodded. "It would be a good trial. I wish to be comfortable with Nile's wind and the crew's abilities before we spend any more time in open ocean, but yes, after that, we could stop in Milan."

Catsper tilted his head, a brow rising. "Remind me which one of you is in charge today? I lost track."

"Domenic is the *Arrow*'s captain," Nile said, her voice solid.

"The operations of the ship and crew are fully his responsibility."

"And Nile?" Catsper asked. "Is she the first officer now?"

"She is the mage," Domenic said, spreading his shoulders. "The Bevnians are bastards, not idiots. We can't afford to sweep the Gifted out of sight because convulsions can be inconvenient. So Nile and I will work to integrate her skills into the ship's life. And if—when—we recruit Diante ships to join us, she will act as a Lyron admiral would."

Kyra's breath caught. Mage. Squadron. Vision. War. Kyra's friends were already regrouping, organizing, turning from a castaway gaggle of survivors into a navy.

"Will you be my lieutenant of the marines?" Dana asked of Catsper.

There was nothing in Catsper's immediate nod that would ever tip off Dana and Nile to the coppery pain and fear that rippled through the marine as he accepted the assignment. Nothing to hint at the complex man Kyra had learned to see behind the confident facade. Catsper's friends took him at face value, as he wanted them to. Just as they believed that his wounds bothered him as little as he let on.

Behind Catsper, Kyra's palm rose to rest gently on his back. Finding her magic, Kyra called the heat toward her, gathering it like a spiderweb from the surface while a soft chill remained to sooth the wounds. Catsper tensed as the coolness spread, but Kyra kept her attention on the others. On Dana. For while the men and woman before her knew how to wage war, they little knew how to heal its wounds. How to come through it with their souls intact. And she didn't either. But she could learn. Wanted to learn. Because while the people around her fought, someone needed to make sure they lived too. "Requesting permission to join the ship's company, Captain Dana."

To Dana's credit, he only inclined his head in question. "In what capacity?"

"Ship's counselor." Kyra raised her chin. "Unless you wish to weather the nightmares of seamen who've just endured slavery, someone else will need to."

"Naval ships don't carry *counselors*," Catsper growled, managing to make the word sound vulgar.

"Until today, they didn't carry mages either," said Dana, turning to Kyra with thoughtful eyes. Nile opened her mouth to say something, then closed it, giving Dana the room to decide his crew for himself. After a moment, the man extended his hand. "Welcome to the *Arrow*'s officer gun room."

<End of SEA AND SAND: TIDES Book 3>

Did you enjoy SEA AND SAND? Reviews are an author's lifeblood. Please consider saying a few words about this book on Amazon.

Nile's adventure continues in TIDES Book 4. Coming 2018.

SIGN UP FOR NEWS AND RELEASE NOTIFICATIONS AT www.subscribepage.com/TIDES

ABOUT THE AUTHOR

Alex Lidell is the Amazon Breakout Novel Awards finalist author of THE CADET OF TILDOR (Penguin, 2013). She is an avid horseback rider, a (bad) hockey player, and an ice-cream addict. Born in Russia, Alex learned English in elementary school, where a thoughtful librarian placed a copy of Tamora Pierce's ALANNA in Alex's hands. In addition to becoming the first English book Alex read for fun, ALANNA started Alex's life long love for YA fantasy books. Alex lives in Washington, DC. Join Alex's newsletter for news, bonus content and sneak peeks: www.subscribepage.com/TIDES Find out more on Alex's website: www.alexlidell.com

SIGN UP FOR NEWS AND RELEASE NOTIFICATIONS

Connect with Alex!

www.alexlidell.com

alex@alexlidell.com

ALSO BY ALEX LIDELL

TIDES

FIRST COMMAND (Prequel Novella)

AIR AND ASH (TIDES Book I)

WAR AND WIND (TIDES Book II)

SEA AND SAND (TIDES Book III)

TIDES Book IV - coming 2018

SCOUT

TRACING SHADOWS - coming April 8, 2018

UNRAVELING DARKNESS - coming 2018

THE CADET OF TILDOR

SIGN UP FOR NEW RELEASE NOTIFICATIONS AT
www.subscribepage.com/TIDES

Reviews are an author's lifeblood. Please consider saying a few
words about this book on Amazon.

www.ingramcontent.com/pod-product-compliance
Lightning Source LLC
Chambersburg PA
CBHW031211120726
47905CB00002B/299